THE VIKING KING'S LOVE

A VIKING TIME TRAVEL ROMANCE - #1 OF THE TO LOVE A VIKING SERIES

KENNEDY THOMAS

QUEEN OF CROWS PUBLISHING

CONTENTS

.

CHAPTER ONE

A MODERN GIRL IN AN ANCIENT WORLD

I sis reached for the garden hoe, grimacing as the blisters on her palms came into contact with its wooden handle. She had never done such labor-intensive work. No one in her newly "founded" village had.

They were modern people, from the 21st century. No one had to toil for their food anymore. That was what grocery stores were for.

But there were no grocery stores in this new land. Or old land, which was more technically correct, but it felt like another planet to Isis. The cultures and customs seemed bizarre and wild. The hierarchy of these people wasn't based on wealth or success. Instead, it was based on what clan you were born into, since a clan's prestige was then decided by the brave acts and grand deeds they carried out.

Vikings. Isis had given them little thought before her kidnapping. She was half Black, half Hispanic. Of all the cultures she thought about, it sure as hell wasn't old dead Vikings. Except now they weren't dead or old, not to her, not anymore.

Isis thought about her family at home. She knew her mama was doing everything within her power to try to find her little girl, but she'd never find her. That thought took Isis' breath right out of her lungs. The American government had tossed them to the wolves, and sometimes, looking into the eyes of these wild men, that felt literal.

One hundred people were snagged straight from their lives and plopped hundreds of years back in time. *A social experiment,* that's what the smiling baboon had told them it was when they awoke in some sterile gray underground facility. But Isis had heard the whispers, and she suspected they were in it for more than that. For what exactly, she didn't know. "More like a deal with the devil, if you ask me," Isis mumbled under her breath as she tilled the soil.

One hundred people. And Isis just *had* to be caught as one of them. They wanted to see what the Vikings would do, they said, when faced with a woman of every shape, size, and race. As if they were all lab rats to be poked, prodded, and then watched within a cage.

Isis knew they had cameras. She knew they were watching. In fact, they promised they would be. Lifting up her middle finger, she shouted, "Take notes on this, scientist baboons!"

Baboons. It was an insult her eight-year-old niece loved to use. Isis had found it mildly amusing before, but now that she knew she'd never see that cute little diva ever again, she had found herself adopting it, seeking comfort from the childish word. It made her feel close to home somehow, reminding her that her heart was still with them, that she was still Isis Lozada, the funny American girl that liked staying up until the sun rose and scrolling social media until her thumb hurt, even if those things weren't very applicable to her anymore. They couldn't be, half of them didn't exist.

"Who are you shouting at?" asked Amanda Balan, the most basic pumpkin latte and *Uggs* girl to exist, and Isis' next-door neighbor, with her hands on her hips.

"The scientists that brought us here. Or the universe. Whoever wants to listen." Isis threw the till to the ground again. The food the scientists gave them wouldn't last forever. They had been clear. *If you don't grow your own food, you will die.*

Sometimes when her entire body ached and her blisters popped, she'd lie on her bed on the dirt ground, in the hut the scientists called her *"new* home". Death felt preferable.

"Well, I don't want to listen, so can you keep it down? I'm sure the universe would still hear you if you whispered." Amanda gave her fake ass laugh, the one that made Isis want to punch her in the face. "Thanks, neighbor!"

"I'll shout if I wanna shout. But you think my talking is shouting, so better get used to it." Isis rolled her eyes as she mumbled under her breath.

"Hello, neighbor." Another voice cut through Isis' mumblings, making her hold up a hand to block out the bright sunlight. It was Violet, another one of the hundred girls in Isis' new so-called "village". She lived in the hut across from Isis' and was one of the few that seemed genuinely nice. Violet's blonde hair was thrown up into a ponytail as sweat glistened on her ivory skin.

"Hey, Violet. You out working, too?" Isis smiled, relaxing in the friend camaraderie the two of them shared.

"Yeah. Beautiful day out to do it. And we need to make sure everything's ready for spring so we can plant. I *think* I have mine all tilled. Don't know if it's right or not, but one can only hope, right?" Violet let out a nervous chuckle.

"Yeah. We gotta stay positive. Put in the hard work, do our best. That's all we can do, right?" Isis encouraged as she threw the till down once more.

"Yep, my thoughts exactly. Do you need any help? That way you can be done faster."

"You don't need to be doing anything else?" Isis scratched her head through her makeshift bandana.

Violet shrugged. "There's always something else to be done, but I was thinking I can help out, and then we can cook dinner together?"

Isis laughed at her friend's expression, like a kid trying to negotiate for ice cream. "Sure, that sounds fun. Let's do it."

The two women chatted as they worked, making it easy to forget where they were and what happened to them.

But the universe refused to let them forget for long.

The sound of horses disrupted their conversation as masculine voices spoke in a foreign tongue.

CHAPTER TWO

AND SO THE VIKINGS CAME

Isis and Violet peeked around Isis' hut to see five Viking men sliding off of horses. Women slowly emerged from their houses, preparing themselves for whatever it was the men wanted. Much to Isis' surprise, nothing tragic had happened. The Viking men seemed to treat them with more respect than the modern-day men did. That came as a shock to Isis, who thought they were brutal savages that did whatever they wanted, especially when it came to women.

The feeling still stuck with her as the men looked around the village. She did not trust them. Perhaps they waited until the women let their guard down before they struck.

Violet looked at Isis, her full pink lips pursed into a frown. "What do you think they wanted?"

"I don't know, but I still don't trust them. I don't want any part of this if I can help it. There's a reason the government sent us here, and it can't be good." Isis returned Violet's whisper.

"What should we do?" Violet asked, biting her lip.

"Wait it out. The other girls have been swooning over these dudes, so let them have what they want. They want to shoot their shot with a Viking, let them be the bait. That's what I say." Isis scoffed, shaking her head.

Violet jiggled her legs nervously. "But what if they get hurt?"

Isis shrugged. "Not our problem. I'm not saying we avoid helping if we can, but what can we do if they act like idiots? We aren't responsible for them or their actions. If they want to fall all over these ancient dudes and drape themselves across them, what are we gonna do? Tear them off and risk our lives in the process? Nah. Stupid people gonna do stupid things. There ain't no saving them from themselves."

One of the Vikings marched over to a group of women, studying each of them. He turned back to his comrades, who waited by the horses, shaking his head. He then walked over to another group, eyeing them up and down. Some of the women shied away from his gaze, others stepped into it, proudly showing off their figures.

Isis shook her head, rolling her eyes. "Some people have no shame. If you wanna bump with 'em, fine. But try not to act like you a fluffy show-dog trying to win a blue ribbon in the meantime."

"It's hard to believe anyone would be so eager to...*you know*...with someone just because they are Vikings." Violet shuddered. "They can't even communicate with us. It'd be nothing more than sex, pure and simple."

"Hey, like I said, if that's what they want, good for them. Maybe it's not the smartest thing, since we don't know how these guys feel about women and sex. Maybe they get hurt, maybe they don't. You want to go about it? Fine by me. Just try to have a little self-respect and not act like you are on auction. Too many women have a lack of self-confidence and pride. We need to be treated how we deserve to be treated, which is like queens. So we shouldn't act like slutty maids, do you know what I mean?"

Violet nodded. "Yeah, I agree. I hadn't even thought about what the Vikings might do to them...scary."

Isis chuckled. "I doubt they've thought about it, either. Like I said, stupid people are going to do stupid things."

The Viking finally found a woman he seemed to admire. Her arms crossed her petite figure as she looked the Viking man up and down as well. The Viking turned back to his comrades once more, but this time he gave a slow nod. He began talking to the woman, a playful smile on his bearded face as he wrapped his arm around her. The girl raised an eyebrow at him, clearly not understanding a single thing he said.

Meanwhile, one of his friends back at the horses walked forward, something in his hand Isis couldn't quite make out. It was rather small and black, and when he arrived at the girl and the other Viking, he spoke to the man with his arm still wrapped around the girl. The Viking responded, pointing to her upper arm. The man with the object nodded, lifting the thing in his hand to her arm.

The girl cried out in pain before shouting, "He's tattooing me!"

Isis and Violet looked at each other with wide eyes. "Are they marking us?" Violet whispered, fear shaking her voice.

"Like pigs being sent to the slaughter." Isis grimaced as Violet began to tremble beside her. "Hey, it's going to be okay, Violet. We've got each other. We'll find a way out of this, I promise. We just gotta be strong and hold on. They aren't gonna get the best of us. We're two tough queens. They can't break us, right?" Isis nudged her friend, trying to cheer her up with a playful grin.

Violet released a nervous chuckle. "Yeah, yeah. We'll get through this. We've got to."

"That's right, we've got to. We're too brave and strong to let something as crazy as this beat us, right? We've got to make it home to tell this whacked-out story."

Chewing on her bottom lip, Violet shot Isis a concerned glance. "You really think we'll make it home someday?"

"Yeah, I do. Like I said, we've got to! They've got to hear about this. They'll never believe it. I mean, I barely believe it and we've been here for a week now." Isis exclaimed as they watched the girl getting tattooed with the Viking man, who selected her carefully holding her in place as the other man marked her.

"It does seem rather impossible to believe. I would have never thought this could ever happen. I mean, why does our government even have this kind of technology? What do they hope to achieve by sending us here?"

"I don't know. But you can be damn sure I'm gonna find out and stop them. You can bet I'm going to put a stop to whatever these punk-ass Vikings got in store for us."

CHAPTER THREE
THE MARKINGS

"So they are marking them with their names?" Violet asked, her nose scrunched up in disgust. "Claiming them as their own? Like we're their property?"

Isis slouched in her chair, feeling the satisfaction of being right. These men *weren't* to be trusted. "Yeah. Like I said, pigs to the slaughterhouse. Disgusting."

"More than disgusting, Isis. It's inhumane and abominable. And our own people sent us to this fate. Who's worse, the Vikings with their crappy culture or the twenty-first-century suits that know better, but don't care?" Violet scoffed, poking at the fire in her house, stirring it back to life.

Giving a wry laugh, Isis sank further into her seat, rubbing a hand over her face. "You don't have to tell me the government sucks. My life has reeked of that fact since before I was born. But yeah, I get your point. They *especially* are pieces of shit for this."

Violet nodded enthusiastically, sitting back in her chair with a sigh. "I can't believe Anna actually went and spied on the Viking town. She could have been killed."

"Yeah, but that's black girl power for you. She got us invaluable information. Guess we know the reason they want us now, huh?"

Anna had returned to report that there were barely any women in the Viking town, most of them old. She only saw a handful of children during her all-day camp out of the place, but there sure were plenty of young men.

Violet gave a slow shake of her head. "I still can't believe this. I feel like if they just asked, a lot of women would have volunteered for this. They shouldn't have *stolen* us as they did."

"I get you. I know one hundred women that would sign up to be shipped off to be married to a Viking. Lots of single women out there, desperate for a dude. They don't have to kidnap us. But I suppose if they want to keep their time-traveling gizmos a secret, they couldn't advertise for it."

Isis stood, grabbing a nearby chopped log and positioning it on the fire, feeding the flames.

"That's a good point," Violet admitted as she nodded. "Hadn't thought of that. But Isis, what are we going to do? I don't want to marry some Viking only because he thinks I'm pretty enough to suit him." Violet confessed, dropping her voice to a whisper.

Isis frowned at Violet, the two women sharing a look of sadness between them. "I don't know, Vi, but we just gotta stay strong. We may not understand everything just yet, but we'll get there. Together."

Violet nodded. "Together."

That night, Isis dreamed of being dragged through the streets, a sweaty Viking pulling her along by the leg. He laughed as other hairy men cheered on either side of the dirt street. "Look at my prize! She's fine stock, good for breeding many children!"

Isis woke up in a cold sweat, gasping for breath. She hoped that it was *all* a terrible nightmare, but the ache in her back told her she still slept on a thin mat on the floor.

There was no escape from this hell.

But some hours later, Isis had nearly forgotten her nightmare as she punched some dough she had managed

13

to make, sweat trickling down her temple. But as sounds trickled in through her flimsy wooden door to her hut, she was reminded of the terrible vision in the night. The images flashed through her head as she heard a man's voice and husky laughter accompanying it.

"Nope. I ain't going out there. They can pick their ladies and be gone. I ain't stopping for them." Isis muttered as she threw herself into kneading her bread again.

Several minutes later, the camp fell silent. Isis wiped her forehead, humming to herself an old song her grandmother used to listen to. The men were gone again, and Isis could breathe easy until their next return.

That's what she thought, anyway, until her wooden door banged open. A giant of a man that barely fit through her doorway stood there, grinning at her while his eyes gleamed with vicious amusement.

The dough fell from Isis' hands as she gaped at the man, her heart thudding inside her chest.

Was this the moment she received her mark?

CHAPTER FOUR

THE WHISPERS THAT STING

The big Viking man, with his wiry, unkempt beard and a smell of urine and sweat, looked Isis up and down, studying her figure. With a grunt, he shook his head before storming out of her home.

Relief filled her. She had not been chosen by that disgusting man. It stung a little, being found unsatisfactory by a brute, but Isis was too grand of a woman to let it faze her. With her door still wide open, she could see the man look several more women up and down before finally selecting one, marking her before leaving.

When the men left, all of her fellow women looked at her, eyeing her with raised eyebrows. After a few moments of confusion, Isis stared at all of them right back. "What? What are you staring at?!"

The girl that had just been chosen lifted up her chin, pride settling in her eyes. "I was one of the few left to be chosen."

Isis squinted at the young woman. "And? What's that gotta do with me?"

A small smirk slithered onto the other woman's face, but she turned, saying nothing. The other women followed her lead, the crowd dissipating. Isis scoffed and walked back into her abode, closing the door firmly shut behind her. Were these fools already defining who was better based on what dumb brutes thought of them? They didn't even know what the markings were for yet! They could be choosing who they wanted to be slaves for all they knew.

The thought sent a sharp chill down Isis' spine. She knew the Vikings were ruthless, but did they keep slaves? She couldn't remember. Her high school history teacher would be disappointed with her. But history was never her thing. Math was. Numbers were comforting. They were either right or wrong, there was no gray area.

But in this horrid land of Vikings, all Isis could see was gray.

Isis kept her head down and tended to her land. It was small, but surviving was no joke. She was a hard worker and a fast learner, but even so, adjusting to this new life was difficult. Her time was fully consumed by all of the chores she had to do to simply eat dinner and remain somewhat clean. She had no time for all of the drama that seemed to go on in their tiny village.

But the drama always seemed to have time for her.

Isis was walking to the well to fetch some water, walking adjacent to one of the homes of the other women, when she heard loud whispers coming from within. "He took one look at that fat cow and backed right out!" Laughter ensued.

"And she didn't get why we were all staring at her. Because she's one of the only ones not chosen yet! All of the other girls he was looking at after her were already marked, so he knew he couldn't pick them. When he finally found one that wasn't marked yet, he snatched her right up! But he *still* didn't want Isis. And no wonder, with how sweaty she is all the time working, and she doesn't even *try* to look nice for them or come out to see them or anything. And then she wonders what it has to do with her? Okay honey, you do you. But you gonna be left here, farming that small plot of land all on your own for the rest of your days while we off sitting in the laps of Vikings. Ha!"

These fools lived not far from Isis, just two houses down. But they still dared to gab about her with their window open. But Isis knew they didn't have the guts to say any of this to her face. No, they were just idiots that thought they wouldn't get caught.

Isis made the rest of her way to the well more loudly than need be. The voices quieted down at once as she passed, the women stopping when they heard a noise outside. Gasps erupted as they saw who it was, making Isis smirk as sweet silence reigned in that house. Sometimes quiet humiliation was the sweetest of vengeance. Raising a mirror to throw their own ugly ass faces at them was Isis' style of revenge.

But Isis tried to convince herself that the bitter sting in her chest from their words didn't hurt. Why would it? It's not like she hadn't been called worse before. She knew she was a bigger girl, they weren't telling her anything new. But even in her fat state, she could apparently haul ass and work better than they did. She may be fat, but at least she wasn't ugly like them.

Pretty is as pretty does.

CHAPTER FIVE

MAN OF MYSTERY

A nother morning, another day with much more to do. Isis was exhausted, but this was her new life now, for better or for worse. Isis grabbed the flimsy basket she had attempted to weave out of the tall grasses just outside the village, but the thing was terrible. It was barely functional, but Isis was determined to adapt. Her survival depended on it.

Isis shoved as many of her dirty, sweat-soaked clothes that she could fit into the awful basket, grabbing a bar of soap from the supplies given to her by the government that she had dedicated to washing her clothes with and set off towards the creek that ran near the village. Isis always did all of her washing downstream so that it didn't interfere with any water they fetched for drinking or cooking, but there was no guarantee the other women did the same. But Isis could only control herself, sadly enough. These women seemed to have no sense or wits about them.

Dawn had just risen on the horizon, sending golden light sparking across the darkened sky. The village was as silent as death as most of the women slept soundly, and would for quite a few more hours. But Isis' anxiety woke her every early morn, reminding her of all that she needed to do for the day if she needed to survive.

She wasn't sure how the other women planned to survive once the food stores from the government ran out. Looking out at the unkempt fields of almost every house she passed, weeds tall and proud as they dominated the land, it would seem they didn't have a plan. Either they weren't thinking ahead, or they were depending on these Viking men to care for them in some way or another.

Stupid to risk your life in such a way if you asked Isis. They couldn't even speak the same language, but these girls were expecting to be pampered and indulged by these brutes. Why would the Vikings do that? It made no sense.

Isis poured her anger out onto her clothes as she scrubbed them in the stream. Her muscles ached, but it felt refreshing to feel the coolness of the water on her palms as she let her frustration out through the chore.

A snapping of sticks made Isis' body tense. Isis only knew of a couple of women that might possibly be awake at this time. Most wouldn't be caught dead out here this early. Setting down her soaking clothes to survey her surroundings, Isis' heart raced as she imagined some wild animals sneaking up on her, intending to make her its breakfast...

But Isis saw nothing. No deer, no wolves, no rabbits, nothing so much as a gopher. Isis took in a steady breath, calming herself down. Perhaps her anxiety was just playing tricks on her again. She returned to her chore and kept working at it.

A deep sound behind her made Isis freeze once more, paralyzing her. While she had suspected a wild beast was attempting to sneak up behind her before, she had not imagined something so horrible could be trying to prey upon her. It was far worse than any of the creatures she had been imagining, and this horrid sound could only come from this terrible beast.

Talking. For what could be worse than a wolf? A Viking man.

She spun around, sending the sand from the creek flying about. A tall, broad-shouldered man with long black hair and a finely kept beard leaned against a massive tree not far from her. She didn't know what he said. It seemed to be in the same language she had heard all of the other Viking men speak. But her mind was a frenzied mess anyway, trying to figure out a way to escape.

The man put both of his hands up, as if in surrender, seeming to notice how fearful Isis was. He spoke again, his voice calm and steady. He slowly approached her, and Isis' heart hammered in her chest, preparing to bolt if need be. If he so much as lay a hand on her, she would run. She would fight. She would do whatever it took to survive.

And woe was the person who ever underestimated *her*.

CHAPTER SIX

FRIEND OR FOE?

The Viking walked some distance away, further up the creek. He swished his hands in the water, seeming to demonstrate something. Isis furrowed her eyebrows, not sure what he was trying to communicate. The scenario seemed strange to her mind. The fact that this Viking was not eyeing her like a piece of property to buy almost did not compute for her.

It was a sad day indeed when that was the standard to go by.

Upon seeing Isis' confusion, the man slowly edged towards her, still crouched. Isis' entire body tightened with tension, but she sensed this man was not here to mark anyone. What he *was* here for was a mystery, but Isis felt at least somewhat safer in this situation than with the men barging in and marking her like an animal at an auction. Or not marking her, for that matter.

The Viking sidled up next to her, gently taking her article of clothing from her hands. He bent down, lowering the shirt into what Isis knew was the frigid water, and began to scrub. It was in the same motion as he had done before, but it made much more sense now that the tunic was in his hands. It appeared that he found her form of washing to not be the best, and decided to demonstrate a better way.

And to Isis' amazement, it seemed to be a better way after all. The stain she had been working on vigorously with no success seemed to be washing out with this man's technique. The way he held his fingers allowed his wrist to do all the work instead of trying to muscle it out.

Although if something *did* need to be muscled out, she would wager he would have no problem with that, either. Now that he came closer, she could see the outline of the firm muscles of his arms, large and capable.

Isis felt her throat tighten as she observed him. Well-groomed, he even smelled pleasant. Like the trees and the sea, leather, and soap. Compared to the Vikings she had seen prior, who smelled of body odor, sweat, and alcohol, this man seemed like an angel compared to demons.

He handed it back to her before gesturing for her to try, at least that is what Isis thought his hand motions meant. She tried to mimic what she had seen him do, and thought she had done it well. Thankfully, the man seemed to agree, nodding his approval.

Looking her up and down, he placed a flat hand on his chest. "Bylur."

Isis thought about it for a moment, but before she could figure it out, the man did it again, saying the same word once more. Finally, understanding dawned upon her. He was introducing himself. Isis followed his lead, placing a hand upon her chest. "Isis."

A small smile found its way onto his lips. "Isis." He repeated, eyes twinkling.

Isis nodded before pointing a finger at him. "Bylur...?" she asked more than said, struggling to pronounce it.

"Bylur." He repeated once more, and Isis nodded, feeling more confident this time.

"Bylur." He smiled and nodded when she said it once more, this time far better.

Isis turned back to her clothing, continuing to scrub at it like he had shown her. She turned after a moment, to see if she might be able to communicate with him further in some way, but he had vanished. She took a few moments to look around, trying to determine where he had disappeared to, but could make out no signs of where he had gone.

It felt strange. Isis had been convinced she had despised these Vikings. She was even beginning to loathe them. And yet, one interaction with one single man had shifted things. She was still leery of all of them, to be sure, but the breaking of the ice had been a thrill. To figure out how to communicate, despite the language barrier, despite the major cultural differences and even time differences...it was more exhilarating than she had ever imagined.

Isis couldn't help but wonder if she would ever see the strange man again.

CHAPTER SEVEN

LAST GIRL LEFT

Isis continued on with her day after her strange encounter with the Viking man, completing many chores before most of the women, in their hastily put-together village, had even left their huts.

Violet, her only real friend here, found her watering her seedlings out behind her house.

"Isis, I am sorry I did not show up for dinner last night..." The blonde approached with a frown, her arms crossed in front of her, as if she was hugging herself.

Isis facepalmed, setting down her bucket as she turned to her friend. "Oh, Violet. I completely forgot we planned for you to come over. I fell asleep before I had even finished making dinner, so I didn't even notice. I'm so sorry. I was exhausted last night."

"You are exhausted every night, Isis...it's one of the reasons why I admire you so much. I worry about you sometimes."

Isis waved her off with a flick of her hand. "No need to worry, girl. I'm just getting done what has to be done. It's the responsible thing to do, for survival's sake."

"Yes, well, speaking of survival..." Violet paused, biting her lip.

Isis turned to fully face her friend, studying her closely. "What is it? You look upset."

"I am upset." Tears brimmed in the younger girl's eyes.

Stepping forward to pull Violet into an embrace, Isis wrapped her arms around her. "What is it? What's happened? Was one of these dumb bitches mean to you? I swear, if they don't get their heads screwed on straight, I'll smack it into place..."

"No, no, it wasn't them this time, though they can be awful." Violet paused to take in a shaky breath. "No, when you were out collecting wild berries last night, the men came again."

Isis pulled back, looking at her friend with wide eyes. "What?"

Violet gave a slow nod of her head as a sad smile appeared on her lips, her brows pinched. "It finally happened, Isis."

The blonde girl pulled up her sleeve, revealing a black tattoo sitting on her skin, red and swollen. "I've been marked."

Isis let out a slow breath. "I'm sorry, Violet. None of us deserve this. Well, maybe some of the others do, but you certainly don't...to be marked like we are property...I hate this."

"There's more, Isis. I wasn't the only one marked last night. It was a large group of men. Ten other girls were marked."

Isis raised both of her eyebrows. "Ten? Is there any even left? I mean, I know the unmarked ones' numbers were dwindling, but that seems like that would kill us all off."

With a pained expression, Violet gave a slow nod. "Yes, Isis. It would. In fact, there's only one unmarked woman left among us."

Isis felt all of the air leave her lungs as understanding hit her. "I'm the only one left, aren't I?"

Violet gave another slow nod. "Yes." The girl wiped her cheeks, trying to dry them of tears. "I tried to hide the best I could, but they searched the village, and for quite awhile, too. They were savages. Brutes. Nasty. I tried my best, but my best wasn't good enough. And the man who marked me..."

After a moment of waiting, Isis placed a gentle hand on her friend, knowing this must be difficult. It has been for her, and she hadn't even been marked. The thought of it made her sick. "Yes? What about him, Violet?"

"He was awful. He smelled terrible. His fists were wounded and bloody, but like with old, dried blood. Like he had beat someone, Isis. He grabbed me, bruised my arm." Violet rolled up her sleeve to reveal the purple and blue mark. "He seemed angry. He seemed to like it when I cried, Isis. It was terrible. And if what we suspect might be happening is true...what if I belong to him now?"

Isis wrapped her arms around her friend as Violet burst into tears once more. "I'll do everything within my power to make sure you don't end up in that position, Vi. No matter what it takes."

CHAPTER EIGHT

MARK OF REDEMPTION

Isis had seen the mysterious man in the woods several more times, all at a distance. Sometimes he saw her, sometimes he didn't. Isis believed he watched over, or at least observed their village for some reason. Perhaps he was a guard or something. But was he there to protect them or to make sure no one tried to run away?

Whenever he and Isis noticed one another, the Viking would bow his head in greeting, solemn but respectful. He never came across as grimy or grabby like some of the other men did. Instead, there was a sense of honor about him. Isis didn't trust many men, especially not any of the Vikings she had met, and while this one hadn't quite earned her trust yet, she would dare to turn her back to him, which was saying something. She had no fear of him, at least, which was better than nothing.

Isis continued to work hard. Her land was the only thing she currently had control over, so she clung to caring for it with fierce desperation. The truth was she was scared. She didn't know what was going to happen. What would the Vikings do? What would the *government* do? What would the other idiots in this village do? She didn't know, and she had no control over any of those things, even though her life depended on them. So she focused all of her energy on the only thing she could do anything about. There was no point in making herself sick over something she had no control over.

Another day went by, each feeling longer and harder than the last. Arising yet again at dawn, Isis yawned, preparing herself for another day of backbreaking work and ridicule for doing so from her fellow village women. Violet was still in an emotional state, as Isis often caught her staring at her tattoo in horror.

Every tattoo looked a little different, a different design belonging to each man. That's what Violet and Isis' theory was, anyway. Violet's had a war hammer going through a skull, surrounded by a blocky design with sharp corners. It was everything Violet wasn't, denoting violence, sharpness, anger. But from Violet's description, it suited the man who marked her perfectly.

There was frost on the ground as Isis left her hut, the golden rays of the sun barely cresting on the horizon. Isis shivered in the chill of the morning, the few period-appropriate outfits given to each of them by the government not suitable for a colder climate. They had some time before winter set upon them, but Isis felt dread for that coming time. They were not prepared. Not even she was, with all of her hard work.

Isis needed to wash her wooden dishes, but the idea of plunging her hands into the ice-cold stream water first thing this morning was not appealing. Instead, she decided to get moving, plucking any weeds out of her field and Violet's field while she was at it. She had promised to care for her friend, and she wasn't about to break that promise anytime soon.

Her shivering soon changed to sweating as she finished up her field and switched to Violet's. The sun was now fully in the sky, warming up the air at a steady pace. It had been a good choice to do this first thing, while it was still cool.

About fifteen minutes into her work on Violet's field, she heard the clearing of a throat behind her. Isis paused, turning around leerily. Her shoulders lost all of their tension at the sight of Bylur, the Viking man. She at least knew she was not about to be attacked in any way. At least she thought. He'd probably had already done it if that was his intention.

He dipped his head in a bow towards her, as he had been doing as of late. "Isis."

His deep voice saying her name sent chills down her spine, which Isis wrote off as her sweat cooling off from her lack of movement. She returned his bow of the head. "Bylur."

The shadow of a smile creeping up underneath his large beard surprised Isis. He said a phrase in his language but did not seem to expect her to understand. Crossing his arms, he observed her with a twinkle in his eyes. Isis shifted from foot to foot, unsure of what he expected of her.

All at once, it became clear as he brought something out of his fur coat and stepped forward.

It was the same device that the other men had used to tattoo the other women.

Isis looked at the thing with wide eyes, her feet frozen in place. Should she run? Fight? But there was nowhere to run to, no safe hiding place. She could fight, but she doubted she could win against him on her own, and even if she cried out, she didn't think any of her fellow women, except perhaps Violet, would come to her aid.

There was nothing to do but stand still and let it happen.

As he gingerly took her arm, pushing down the cloth to reveal the skin of her upper arm, Isis resisted the shaking that wanted to take over her body. The pain of the makeshift needle shot up her nerves as it pressed into her skin, and Isis didn't want to admit the truth.

She found relief in the pain. She had finally been marked. Her pride refused to confess it, but deep down she knew she had felt left out and unwanted by the refusal of all of the other Viking men. Why had she been the only one unmarked for so long? Yes, she was probably the biggest in the entire village, but did that truly mean she was so unappealing? Or was it her darker skin that scared them off? Either way, she would not apologize for how she looked. It angered her and hurt her all at once, but now that it was happening...she felt relief.

The man before her was not like the others. Perhaps she was foolish in thinking so. Perhaps it was just wishful thinking on her part since he had chosen her, but he acted far more...*noble* than the other Vikings. There was something majestic, even in the fluid way he walked and moved. And here he was, marking her arm to claim her.

Despite not fully knowing what the tattoo meant, the idea of it sent a thrill of excitement up Isis' spine. It was as if her body and emotions were betraying her logic, the logic that she would never belong to anyone, that this entire situation was wrong.

But when Bylur finished the tattoo and looked up, his blue eyes gazing into her brown ones, all of Isis' logic seemed null and void.

Maybe the tattoo meant something else. Perhaps he didn't intend to make her his slave. He certainly wasn't looking at her in that way. But in her heart...in her heart, something had become attached.

She belonged to him, whether she liked it or not.

Chapter Nine

DOUBT

As that same day progressed and the air grew warmer, Isis was forced to switch dresses from her long-sleeved that she wore in the chill of the early morning, to her short-sleeved dress that was best for the warm sunshine of the late afternoon. A churning of emotion swirled in her stomach at the idea of the other women seeing her tattoo, both good and bad emotions. She knew they would have something to say about it, they always did.

Bylur had smiled at her once his work upon her skin was complete, before he backed away, giving her a full bow, which she returned, before disappearing into the forest. He almost seemed one with the trees. Was that a real thing?

Isis had been right, yet again. As she drew water from the well, many women fluttered about, most of the village were now awake at this hour. The whispers began at once, she felt the staring sear into her. *"She finally got marked."* A huddle of women thought they were being quiet, but they were certainly *not* doing so, making Isis roll her eyes.

"Yeah, but by who? When? Every other marking has been public. They rode up, loud and proud, chose us in front of everyone. Why would hers be so different?" One scoffed. "Something is fishy about it, I'm telling you."

"What, you think she did it to herself?" Another woman gasped at the thought.

"Maybe, maybe not. I don't know. If she didn't, then the man was probably too ashamed to be seen marking her." The first one snickered.

Isis' stomach sank like lead. She almost felt like she was going to be sick. Was it true? They had a good point. Every other choosing had been very public and witnessed by almost everyone in the village. When Bylur was marking her, she felt it had been special for it to be so private. Like it was a special moment just between them, something they alone shared. But now that the other women pointed it out, Isis had to wonder at the reasoning behind it.

Was Bylur ashamed of her?

Isis hurried off with her bucket full of water in hand. Bitter tears pricked her eyes, but she refused to let them drop. As she poured water onto the little plants that were starting to sprout in her field, she took a moment to look at herself.

The clothes weren't tailored to fit her. None of them were. Hers was tight in all the wrong places, her big body restricted by the material. Her hair was frizzy and unruly without any products to properly take care of it. She was dirty and sweaty. Her fingernails were cracked and caked in dirt. No, she had not always been like this. But she had not always had to grow her own food, either, so there was that.

Observing what little of her own appearance she could see, she could totally understand why any man would hesitate to choose her. In fact, it was a miracle any did at all. She didn't blame him for being ashamed. She was ashamed of herself, no matter how hard she tried to be.

She had always struggled with hating her body, ever since she hit puberty and ballooned into a big girl. Hormones weren't fun, nor were they kind, at least not to her. She had worked hard to combat those feelings, but now they rose to new heights, and the emotions that were welling up within her threatened to tear her apart.

"Isis! Is it true what they are saying? Have you been marked?" Violet ran up behind her, her eyes wide with her question.

Isis turned to give a sad smile to her friend. "Yes, it is true." She shook her arm at Violet to demonstrate her point.

Violet's features pinched together with concern. "Is he horrible? What happened? Did he hurt you at all?"

Isis shook her head. "We had met several times before. He is strange...I don't know how to describe him. But he was far more gentle with me than yours was with you. His name is Bylur. He marked me this morning while I was weeding your field."

Violet's eyes widened in surprise. "You know his name? No one else can communicate with them. How do you know his name?"

Isis shrugged her shoulders. "He patted his chest and said his name. I did likewise. It seems like that is his name, not sure what else he could be trying to communicate."

"Wow, well...I hope that is a good sign. I truly hope he is kind. It inspires hope in me that any of them were not cruel in their marking." Violet turned slightly, a frown resting on her face.

Isis reached forward, patting her friend's arm. "Hey, remember what I promised. We're in this together, and I'm not going anywhere."

"Not if you can help it, I know. But what if you can't help it, Isis? What if they take us all away and separate us?" Violet turned back, tears shining in her blue eyes.

Isis pursed her lips at the thought. "Then I'll figure something out. We'll cross that bridge when it comes, okay? Until then, we stick together, no matter what."

Isis had no idea at the time just how much that promise would soon be tested.

CHAPTER TEN

AS THE WORLD CHANGES

The world Isis Lozada lived in was unstable and ever-changing. Not that she realized this when she awoke that morning, thinking that all would be the same as it had been since they arrived in this foreign era. But the truth of the matter was things would always be shifting and transforming for her now, and it had only just begun. The path she was forced down was a curving, winding road.

The day had started like any other. Isis awoke early at dawn, before anyone else. She worked hard in her fields. She then bathed in the stream and washed her clothes, bringing them out on a makeshift clothesline to dry. All of this was done by that time the other women had arisen and started their day with the sun high in the sky.

The clipping of hooves jolted Isis from her thoughts as she hung the last of her articles of clothing on the line. She froze in place, not sure what to do or think. Every last woman had been marked, so the only possible reason for the Vikings to return was that they had come to claim them, or whatever they wanted to do with them. They were about to discover just why they were marked and what it meant, a topic Violet and Isis had discussed at length for weeks now.

A murmuring of conversation rose up in the village square near the well. The women of their village obviously found something worth whispering about. Isis knew that she should go and see, in the very least to be prepared for whatever was about to happen, but she found her feet could not move.

After a few more moments, Violet peeked out from the other side of one of their huts, her blue eyes wide as her blonde hair made a curtain in front of her face. "You have to come and see this, Isis! He's some kind of royalty. He's wearing these fine furs and his horse is *huge.* The other Vikings are rallied around him, but he's obviously the leader. Isis! We're about to find out what all of this is about! You have to come!"

Isis felt her mouth grow dry. Some kind of royalty? Did Vikings *have* royalty? Isis didn't know. Yet again, she was kicking herself for not paying more attention to history. But how did she know it was going to suddenly become so relevant?

She felt herself go numb as her feet moved, each step feeling like she had bricks tied to her feet. Finally she made it to where Violet stood, her friend grabbing her hand and pulling her to where other girls stood gawking.

The horses were some of the finest beasts she'd ever seen, their muscles rippling and their shoulders tall. These were big horses, bigger than Isis would have thought. And the men who rode them, despite having their backs turned to Isis, clearly wore finery. Fluffy furs covered their shoulders, cloth hanging from it in the form of a sort of cape. They seemed far more prestigious than the other men that had come into town, even having some jewelry that seemed suspiciously familiar to the modern time.

Whoever these men were, they had come in contact with people from her time before. Perhaps they were even the ones who had arranged this entire terrible ordeal.

But one man stood out, even from across the village. Violet was right. For as finely dressed as all the men were,

44

this one wore the most lavish garb. The rust-colored pelt of a fox draped across his shoulders, his long black hair braided in places. His broad shoulders were pushed back in perfect posture on his horse, giving him an air of regality and confidence. This was clearly their leader.

A man sitting next to the leader cleared his throat. "Good morning, fair ladies from the future!" Gasps and murmurs rose around the village. The man was speaking *English.* "We understand this must have been a trying and confusing time for you, coming from a different time. Not to mention, a different land, without much explanation. But the simple answer is this: we Vikings made an ally out of some...interesting people from your time. They needed something from us, and asked what they could do in return. And so we told them, we needed wives."

CHAPTER ELEVEN

THE WIVES

Wives. They needed wives. It made sense, and it fit into the theory that Isis and Violet had. They had wondered if they would be slaves of sorts, but some would consider a forced marriage to be the very same concept.

"The designs that have been placed onto your skin are temporary markings to signify the start of your courtship with the man that gave it to you. We apologize for any confusion that happened. I am the only speaker of your language currently. Our Greatest King and Chieftain, who sits next to me, asked me to learn it with great haste. I was off with those that sent you, working with them so I could learn it. I have only returned, and I hope my speech is adequate." Isis turned to share a look with Violet, equal concern and curiosity expressed in each other's eyes.

The man waited a moment, looking over the women as if giving them a chance to speak. After a minute of heavy silence, the man next to him, the King, leaned towards him to whisper in his ear. The translator nodded, and the King sat straight once more.

Clearing his throat, the Translator piped up again. "Our Great King and Chieftain would like to express his thanks for your patience and understanding. He would also like to welcome you all to his lands, and share his hope that you all will have and make a happy home here."

More silence drifted through the village square. All of the women shared pensive looks, none daring to utter so much as a whisper to one another.

The men shared a look upon their horses before the King nodded, his long dark hair moving as he did. "Very well, if there are no questions or concerns or anything anyone would like to add..." He paused again, waiting for anyone to break the silence. He continued when no one did. "...then our King would like to formally claim his soon-to-be bride, so that they might return to his home village and prepare for their wedding. As I am sure all of those who have claimed you will be coming to do so in enough time. But as our King, he chose first and will marry first."

An excited cry broke from the group as a girl moved forward, pushing other women out of her way to approach the men, barely coming up to the shoulders of the mighty horses. "I was chosen first! So I am to be his wife?" The woman scrunched up her nose and tilted her head, clearly thinking she was cute.

Isis disagreed. She looked stupid.

The Translator furrowed his brows, turning to speak in low whispers to the King. The Chieftain pulled back, a confused expression on his face as he shook his head. He returned some words to the Translator, not quite as quiet as the other man had spoken.

The Translator turned to the woman, sitting up a little straighter. "Forgive me, madam. There seems to be a small misunderstanding. I have no doubt it was my fault since I have not fully grasped the language. But our King, and several others from his Band of Brothers, chose first, but it may not have seemed like the first for you. You see, the Marking is only given if one is sure that they want to marry the person they gave it to. Our Great King and Chieftain verified from afar that the person was indeed one he would want to marry. He was granted the luxury of time. He selected someone and everyone else was directed not to mark that person. So the first person marked was not necessarily the first person chosen, you see."

Isis turned to share a confused look with Violet. Her friend seemed frightened, her arms were crossed, and she had her back against the wall. Isis rushed to her, throwing an arm around her shoulder. Violet leaned in to whisper in Isis' ear. "We were right, but I wish we weren't." Isis nodded in response, giving Violet's arm a squeeze.

"Oh." The woman who had approached turned and slipped back into the crowd, shoulders deflated in disappointment.

The King and the Translator were speaking to one another again in low tones. No words were able to make it to her from where she stood at the edge of the village. The Translator finally nodded before they both sat back straight on their horses. "My Great King has told me the name of his chosen. Isis, please step forward."

CHAPTER TWELVE

PLEASE STEP FORWARD

Pure terror swept down Isis' spine, enveloping her in an icy chill. Her name?! Why did it have to be her name?! She didn't understand. She hadn't been chosen or marked until recently. She had been the *last* to be chosen, not the first.

Violet looked at her with wide eyes, her pupils small as they darted over Isis and the scene around them. All of the women of their village began to turn, eyes finding Isis' form and staying there. Another set of chills ran down Isis' back as she took in a deep breath, moving forward towards the center of the village where the men on the horses waited.

As she approached, they began to turn, following the stares of all the other women, which led to Isis. The translator seemed to have a curious expression on his face, and the third man on the opposite side of the Viking King looked bored, a blank expression of disinterest present on his features.

But the man in the middle. The Viking King, as she was finding out, turned. Their eyes met at once, and Isis nearly halted her progression forward. It was *him*. The man that had marked her, helped her, been kind to her. A fire erupted within Isis, one of desire and anger, resentment and pleasure. How could such mixed emotions live within her? She was overjoyed that the *King* had chosen her, and that she was not the last to be chosen after all. A sense of pride swelled up within her at that. But, at the same time, she was now in a position that she didn't want to be in. One she didn't *ask* to be placed in. She was going to be a *Viking King's wife?* And no one thought to *ask* if she wanted that kind of responsibility or to play that role?

More than that, she had suffered in the last few weeks. The old anger that had burned since she was first kidnapped still raged on brightly. The audacity of being taken from her home and brought her, only to be tossed into a marriage she didn't want. It didn't matter if he was kind or not. It didn't matter if he was better than some of the other men. She still had *rights*. And she wasn't about to let them go just because some man was soft to her.

She put the fire of her emotions into her gait, walking faster and with a little more intensity. Setting her shoulders back, she held her head high, refusing to be seen as subservient in any way. She was no slave. She was Isis Lozada, and she was a Queen before she ever stepped foot here. She didn't need some King to validate that.

The Translator tilted his head at her. "You are Isis?"

"I am," she said with a swift nod of her head.

"Excellent!" The Translator smiled, rubbing his hands together giddily. "If you'd like to join us, our King would like to bring you back to what will be your home. As I said, you have a wedding to prepare for."

"I don't recall being asked if I wanted to get married," Isis simply stated, and whispers erupted all around the village as her words echoed throughout the crowd.

The Translator frowned, deep grooves forming in his forehead. "Forgive me, Lady Isis, but what do you mean? Is that not what you came here for?"

"No," Isis responded, clenching her jaw tightly until her teeth ached.

The village was so silent, she could hear the swishing of one of the horse's tail.

Turning back to the King, the Translator switched languages and began to speak in low tones, presumably explaining the situation to King Bylur.

Bylur. Isis' heart twisted at his name that so freely popped into her mind. Feelings swirled inside her chest, complicating the situation all the more. But still, she had to express her validity as a *human being* with rights and her own free will. If she didn't stand up for it, who would?

Once the Translator had finished speaking, Bylur turned to her with wide blue eyes, shock evident within them. He hastily responded to the Translator, his voice hoarse with desperation.

The Translator simply nodded and turned back to Isis. "Our Great King wants to know how you came to be here with a bunch of women that agreed to become wives for us."

Anger rose up further in Isis' chest. She knew that the Translator was simply conveying the message as bluntly and directly as he could, but it felt clipped and harsh to her ears, even if Bylur's tone when *he* asked the question didn't seem that way at all. "That's the thing. I don't know where you are getting your information, but *none* of us came here by choice. We were brought here against our will. We didn't volunteer to be wives! We didn't volunteer to be here at all."

CHAPTER THIRTEEN

THE ONLY BRAVE ONE

Gasps erupted from around the village, and a hissing sound came from over Isis' shoulder. She soon felt a hand wrap around her arm, yanking her back. Amanda was there, her perfectly groomed hair sitting prettily around her shoulders. "What do you think you're doing? Are you *trying* to ruin a good thing for us?"

Isis couldn't believe her ears. "What do you mean *what am I doing?* I'm standing up for our human rights! We were *kidnapped,* Amanda, and now we are being forced to marry people. People we don't even know. What if they are abusers, hm? Have you ever even considered that? What if you get hurt and beat around?"

Amanda rolled her eyes. "Well, we all know that *I* wouldn't get beat around. *I* would make whatever man was lucky enough to have me very happy—"

"You're a sick bitch, you know that, right?" Isis' face twisted with disgust. "And your ego is so inflated it makes you blind to the real world."

A venomous look settled over Amanda's features. "You mind your own business, fat cow. And watch what you say to me or I'll send my 6 foot 5 god of a Viking over to whatever puny one decided to finally settle for you."

Isis couldn't help the chuckle that erupted out from her. "You haven't gotten the message, have you, Amanda? That puny one that 'settled' for me, as you say, is the *King*, and he had the choice of the whole damn crop, which includes you, and he *still* chose me."

As all the color drained from Amanda's face, a throat cleared behind them. Isis turned to see the Translator looking quite amused. "Apologies for interrupting your...*discussion*, ladies, but I couldn't help but overhear." Isis nearly chortled. They had been shouting. It would have been impossible for him *not* to hear. "I would agree with Lady Isis in that you best watch your tongue, uhh, forgive me, I cannot seem to remember your name. But the point stands. Lady Isis is currently set to become your *Queen* if things do not change. I highly suggest you not disrespect anything of the King's. He is highly protective and might take offense to your words."

Amanda looked as if she was almost ready to faint. Isis couldn't stop the smirk from spreading on her face at the sight.

"As for your...what did you say exactly? 6 foot 5 god of a Viking? Well..." The Translator paused to fetch a ledger from a bag that was strapped to the horse, flipping through its pages for a moment. "I see that your mark belongs to Gerwig from the House of Isebrand. I have known him since he was born. He is no god, he cannot even hold down three meads at Winterfest."

Isis' chest constricted with laughter she was trying so desperately hard to contain. It only worsened when Amanda turned on her heel and fled, disappearing into the crowd in a blur of shame. Isis met Violet's eyes from within the crowd, and the humor left her. Her friend was silently crying, tears rolling down her pale cheeks, her blonde hair nearly creating a curtain to hide her emotion.

"Lady Isis? Is everything all right?" The Translator asked, bringing Isis' attention back to him.

Isis took in a shaky breath as she turned back, observing Bylur's stern but concerned expression as he looked between the Translator and Isis. "No, actually. While I will always tell the truth and speak my mind, the main reason I tell you just how we have been forced into this situation is because of my friend. She says that the man that marked her wasn't kind, wasn't gentle. He hurt her and seemed to enjoy hurting her. She doesn't want to marry him, and I don't blame her."

The Translator frowned before reaching up to scratch his beard. "This is a very confusing matter. Your people were very clear that you knew all of this. Are you saying that they lied?"

Isis nodded. "They did. And I am not surprised. They took us by force, after all."

The frown only deepened upon the Translator's face. "This is an issue, Lady Isis. Some things cannot be reversed."

"*What?*" Isis exclaimed, feeling a sinking feeling take over her.

"There is magic in the Marks, Lady Isis. Once they have been completed, it is almost impossible to be undone. When we mark you, we swear an oath to be bound in marriage to you. We swear it to the gods. If we were to break that, we would be struck down."

Isis didn't believe in any of their gods, but still a feeling of horror took hold of her. Even if they wouldn't be struck down, they *believed* they would, and that was enough. "So you are saying that it's too late?"

The Translator gave a slow nod, his grim expression dark and haunting. "The marriages must be carried through with."

CHAPTER FOURTEEN

SEPARATION

"No, no. You can't do this. We shouldn't be forced—" Isis argued, her voice cracking with desperation.

"I did not say anything about *should,* Lady Isis. I agree with you. Any good man would agree with you, this *should not* be happening. But it is too late now. The magic has been sealed upon your arms. We cannot break the bonds that have been forged without risking angering the gods, not to mention the people that brought you here, although I suspect my King would gladly do so if he could." The Translator cut her off, shutting down her argument at once.

Isis' voice was quiet when she spoke again. "So where do we go from here?"

The Translator sat up a little straighter in his saddle, taking in a deep breath before slowly exhaling. "Well, you will join us on our journey back to our city. You will be treated kindly and with respect, given anything you need or want, and will serve as King Bylur's wife."

"All right." Isis nodded, feeling her stomach tighten with hopelessness. It was a lost cause then, there was no room for a debate. How could she say no?

Male voices began to converse in the Viking tongue. As they did, Isis looked over her shoulder at Violet once more, only to see her blonde friend crying even harder than before. Isis fully turned, walking through the crowd to reach her, embracing her tightly. The two cried together for a minute or so before Isis pulled away, having heard the male voices ceasing to talk.

"I'll make sure you are okay, I promise. I'll check into things. I guess...I guess I have a position of power somewhat now. I'll do my best to use it to protect you, okay, Violet? This isn't over. We're still best friends and we've got each other's back, don't we?" Isis cradled Violet's cheeks with both of her hands.

Violet nodded, tears still rolling down her face. "I believe you, Isis. Please just don't forget me—"

Isis pulled her friend into another tight hug as Violet began to cry again. "I could never forget about you, Vi. You're my friend, and I'm loyal to my friends."

After another few moments, Isis pulled back, giving Violet one final squeeze before heading back towards the men waiting on horseback. "What about my things?" She directed her question to the Translator.

"We'll have someone come and fetch them at a later date. You'll have everything you need until then in the city. If it is not already in your chambers when you arrive, you can ask for it and it will be brought to you," The Translator responded before gesturing to King Bylur and his horse. "Now, you will be riding with the King. He would prefer you sit in front of him."

Isis bit her lip, eyeing the horse. Although it was big and quite muscular, she still had her doubts. "Are you sure that horse can handle both the King and me? I'm not the smallest girl here..."

Muffled laughter erupted around the village, making the Translator frown at the women that still watched on. "Yes, Lady Isis. King Bylur's stallion is a warhorse. He carries the King and many sacks of equipment around on a regular basis. And our Great King also uses him to lug heavy grains of oats and the like around quite often, with him still in the saddle. You will be just fine, I assure you. Have no worries."

Bylur slid from his saddle before Isis could form a reply to the Translator. Bylur's long fur coat elegantly swept down with him. He stretched out his hand towards her, beckoning her closer. Isis took in a deep breath and approached before she lost her nerve.

Placing her hand in his, the contrast of the two struck Isis. His was much larger, to start, making hers seem small, even though she had never thought of herself having that small of hands before. Most women were much smaller than her. Smaller hands, smaller bones, smaller waists.

Secondly, her hand was so much darker than his. He was so white in comparison, even though Isis wasn't the darkest due to her mixed heritage being half Hispanic, making her skin deliciously dark compared to his. The colors complemented each other well, and she couldn't help but like the two colors sitting next to each other.

And lastly, although Isis had developed some calluses and blisters during these weeks working the fields and doing hard labor to survive, her hands were nothing compared to his. Years' worth of calluses lied upon his hands in layers, showing a long-time record of hard work. *I've never heard of a King that works as hard as his subjects*, Isis thought to herself.

Raising her eyes from their joined hands, she met Bylur's steel-blue eyes, a swirling of understanding passing between them. Isis held no fear of him.

Within moments, he assisted her in getting up on his remarkably tall horse, putting his hands on her waist in an effort to help hoist her up there. Isis tried not to think about the warmth of his hands through her clothing, or how it felt when he brought himself up behind her on the horse .

As they departed the village, Isis made sure to turn and wave to Violet.

It was strange, leaving the village behind. She certainly didn't consider it as home, and yet, it had kind of become that since her forcible removal from her world. It was the only thing she had known since then, and the familiar was friendly enough. And now she was leaving that, too...

But was the destination that lay ahead of her more welcoming and kinder than the last?

CHAPTER FIFTEEN

THE JOURNEY FORWARD

The landscape that they traveled through was nothing like Isis had ever seen before. Rolling hills with the greenest of grasses, wildflowers dancing in the wind. After about an hour of riding, Isis' stiff frame became weary. She was holding herself as straight as a board, and her back was starting to ache from the strain of it. She was ever-aware of the presence of the man behind her, casually holding the reins of the stallion on her lower thighs.

She was debating leaning back or simply relaxing, but she wasn't sure how to hold herself on the horse any other way. She had never ridden a horse before and it was far more daunting than she had ever thought—being up here was a lot higher up than she would have imagined.

It was right about at this moment when she smelled something different in the air, a slight saltiness as the breeze picked up. The thought distracted her from her aching body as she looked about for any difference but saw none. It was only a few short moments later when the source of the smell came into view.

The rolling hills abruptly ceased to exist, cutting off into a steep cliffside. Beyond that, all Isis could see was the cerulean sight of the ocean, stretching out until it met with the bright blue sky and disappeared on the horizon. When the wind settled for just a moment, her ears could strain to hear waves crashing upon the rocks somewhere far below. It was a beautiful sight.

The three horses and their riders walked parallel to the cliff, making Isis a bit nervous, but ensuring she had an endless view of the gorgeous ocean to her right. The beautiful scenery was nearly hypnotizing, and it was a few minutes before Isis even realized that she had unconsciously leaned back into Bylur at some point during her dreamy gaze out into the sea.

Isis nearly bolted forward when she realized, and the horse gave a nervous flick of his ears at her suddenly panicked state. It was impossible for Bylur not to notice, Isis knew.

So after Bylur removed a hand from the reins and patted the horse's side, speaking in soft soothing tones, Isis wasn't surprised. She wondered whom he was trying to calm down more, her or the horse.

After another moment, Bylur slid a hand about her waist, pulling her into him as she had been before. His words were spoken directly into her ear, as soft and calming as the ones he had spoken to the horse. Once he had finished, the Translator stepped in to convey his message. "Our Great King Bylur says to save your energy. We still have several more hours to go, and you cannot sit like that the entire way, you'll exhaust yourself. Relax. And try not to spook the horse."

Isis wanted to stick her tongue out at the Translator, who wore a smug smirk of knowing. She took in a deep breath and tried to relax, her muscles screaming at her to do as Bylur wanted. He hadn't removed his arm from around her waist, she noted, so she was already flush against him. *I had better get used to this anyway if I'm to be his wife.*

Focusing on the beautiful pure blue of the ocean, Isis took in a deep breath and relaxed, trying to calm herself. After a moment, Bylur said something else, releasing his arm from around her and patting her thigh as he picked up the reins once more. Isis looked over to the Translator for the translation of what Bylur had said, but the man didn't seem to be paying any attention. Instead, he had wandered off some distance away with the other rider, the two men conversing from appearances. The wind was strong enough that it carried away their voices so she could hear nothing, if she didn't see their mouths moving Isis wouldn't have even known.

Observing the two other men, she tried to see if they were doing anything suspicious. But as she watched, Bylur began to softly hum in her ears, his deep voice vibrating through her as she leaned against his chest. It made it hard to think. Who knew horseback riding could be so tiring?

The other two men seemed to be joking with one another, laughing and giving each other friendly shoves. Nothing seemed to be amiss, the two seemed comfortable, as did Bylur with the situation. Isis noticed the two men often looked around them, keeping tabs on the surrounding hills for any sign of trouble. They were guarding them while still giving her and Bylur some space. *How considerate.*

The steady patter of the horse's hooves against the soft grass calmed Isis. The wind felt good against her face, cooling her. Bylur's hummed song soothed her, lulling her into a dozing state. The occasional crash of the ocean waves joined in the symphony, and Isis didn't even realize she was falling asleep before sweet slumber claimed her.

CHAPTER SIXTEEN

THE TRANSLATOR

Dreamless sleep rolled through Isis' mind, a swirling storm of unconsciousness. As her brain roused awake, one thing came to her mind: *I hadn't slept this good since this horror show started.* Loud noises startled her, making her jostle up out of the comfortable position she had been resting in. To her horror, she discovered she had made herself right at home within Bylur's arms, her face snuggled right into the crook of his neck.

As she sat back up, another horse moved beside them in her peripheral vision. "Sleep well, Your Highness?"

Yet again, Isis was struck by the urge to stick her tongue out at the Translator. Instead, she knew her expression must be sheepish; she felt the tingling warmth of a blush on her cheeks. "Yes. How long was I asleep for?"

"Long enough that our city is within sight." The Translator gestured with a nod of his head in front of them, causing Isis to look forward.

Tall hills rose up on the sea cliffside, decorated with many wooden angular houses. They were distinctly...well, Viking. What Isis recognized as such, anyway. People mulled about all over, cows with long horns chewing grass in front of the buildings. It was a rather beautiful sight, in a strange way, anyway. Like observing a historical time long past, but actually in person. Up until then, it was easy to think they were just playing pretend, but *this* felt tangible and real, taking Isis' breath away.

"It's beautiful," Isis muttered under her breath.

The Translator chuckled beside her. "I agree."

Isis looked over at him with narrowed eyes. "Who *are* you anyway? How does a Viking learn the English spoken hundreds of years from now?"

Before the Translator could respond, King Bylur piped up behind her, and from his tone of voice, whatever he said seemed to be a question.

The Translator looked taken aback, what seemed to be mock offense shown on his face. "The King has just asked what I have done *now* to offend his soon-to-be wife. Can you believe that? He said *now* as if I have a habit of offending you." The Translator scoffed. He then turned to the King and responded in their language, and although Isis couldn't make out what he was saying, she sensed that he replied in a teasing and jestful manner. Not an ounce of fear in his voice, despite just being questioned by his King.

Behind her, King Bylur laughed deeply at the Translator's reply, the sound vibrating through his chest and into Isis' back. He returned the Translator's comment with another laughing reply of his own.

Isis turned to the Translator, an arched eyebrow in question. The man laughed at her expression. "The King has informed me that I must endeavor to answer your questions with as little sarcasm and annoyance caused to you as possible."

"Is that so?" Isis challenged, enjoying the casual banter between them.

The Translator nodded, a smirk hidden somewhat underneath his beard. "I am Frode Shattershield, cousin and adopted brother of King Bylur. As for your other questions, I have always been an avid learner and fascinated by other cultures and languages. Which has not always been accepted by my people, truth be told. When the strangers from the future, or "your people", came and presented us with an opportunity for an exchange, I spoke up and presented the issue that we would all have wives that did not speak our language and we did not speak theirs. What kind of marriage would that be? So, they offered to educate one of us to speak the language of our soon-to-be wives at least to start. Then whoever learned could help teach the others, as well as the women that came, the opposite language and help translate. It was a unanimous agreement that I would be that person. I spent many moons working with quite a few of your people, immersed in your language and working hard for it to flow naturally and be current with the phrases and words that you speak."

"Well, it's a pleasure to meet you, Frode. Can I ask, when you say many moons, does that mean simply months or...is it longer than that? How long have you been working with 'my people', as you call them?" Isis asked with furrowed brows, trying to speak in a simple manner so it was easier for Frode to understand and translate if need be.

Frode took in a deep breath, eyes looking into the distance as he tried to work out the time. "Yes, oh, it has been months, I believe, as your people would put it. It's been quite a long time. For us, we usually measure by moons or harvest. It's been at least two harvests that I have been learning this and working with the people. It seems strange that they did this to you, as they seemed quite pleasant to me. But now, I'm questioning everything if these are the type of people to force their women into marriages."

Isis blinked, horror overcoming her expression as she processed the information. "At least two harvests? Wouldn't that be at least two years in my people's time measurement? That means that they have been planning this for a very long time. Why would they do this? What did they want from you that they were willing to kidnap so many women and drag them into another time to give to you?"

Frode frowned, his brows knit together in an anxious expression. "I'm not sure I should be telling you any of that. I believe that is something that the King should tell you when he deems appropriate. Just know that we are all suspicious of them now, thanks to you. They weren't fully honest and because of that we now realize that they are possibly a threat. We will deal with them accordingly moving forward."

Isis simply nodded. Frode then switched languages, presumably to explain their conversation to the other two men. Some level of conversation rose up around her, but she stared ahead, observing her new home from a distance. After some time, when the talking had died down some, she felt King Bylur's hand reach down and give her knee a slight squeeze. It didn't feel as strange as she thought it would. Instead, it felt like a show of support and a promise.

Isis didn't know why, but she felt like she believed whatever promise he had just given her.

CHAPTER SEVENTEEN

A NEW PLACE TO CALL HOME

C hildren ran across the streets in simple brown linens, their feet bare as they skipped through the green grass. The day was warm and a cool breeze drifted in off the sea, whipping through the children's hair as they played. As Isis and their party moved in closer, the sound of the horses' hooves changed from muffled on the grass to more of a clopping sound as their path took them onto a dirt road. The children stopped their playing to look up and stare at Isis, their little eyes filled with awe.

Isis had never been a spectacle before, at least nothing compared to this. It felt strange, but she supposed it made sense since it could very well be that they had never seen someone with dark skin before. Tightness in her chest squeezed, she could only hope they didn't see her in the way many others had before in history. She hoped this wasn't a sign that she would be seen as something other than human, just like them.

The buildings were bigger than Isis had originally thought. Some of the angular roofs rose at least two stories high and were longer than she had realized from far away. A particular building caught her attention. It sat on a hill, in the center of the village, and was more colorful than all of the rest, with blue paint decorating the sides of the wooden logs that made up its walls. The rest of the buildings had no color, except for the moss that grew on some of them.

As they moved further into the village, people began to file out of their houses to look at the arriving party. They seem to study her as if they were trying to decide whether or not she was good enough. Isis noted a distinct lack of younger women, all of them were men or children, with several older women, graying and wrinkled.

Soon, they arrived at a simple house that looked like any other, after winding their way through the dirt streets for several minutes. Isis fidgeted in her seat, all of the stares from the Viking people making her nervous. Once again, King Bylur gave a soft pat to her knee, before sliding down off of the horse, taking the reins with him and leading it to a wooden post in front of the house. After securing the horse to it, he turned to see a younger woman exiting out of the front door of the house.

She was the first woman still in childbearing age that Isis had seen since they arrived. Her long brown hair was braided down her back, and her stomach was enlarged with child. She smiled widely at the King before running forward to embrace him. A cold, sickly feeling came over Isis as she observed the interaction. She wasn't sure if this culture permitted more than one wife, but if they did, Isis would think that the King would be the first one to have more than one. Just when she thought that this might not be as terrible as she had imagined, she now had to worry if she would become nothing more than a breeding wife for this King.

After a moment of cheerful chatter between the king and this woman, Frode turned to her, a soft smile on his face. "This is Shieldmaiden Agda. She is married to Arne Ivarsson, the other man that has accompanied us today. But most importantly to you, she is King Bylur's sister, and thus mine as well. You'll be staying with her and Arne until after your wedding feast with the King."

THE VIKING KING'S LOVE

Agda greeted her husband with a passionate kiss, before greeting Frode warmly, and then finally turning to Isis. The smile on her face was enough to make Isis at ease, the excitement and friendliness present within the other woman's eyes brought peace to Isis' mind.

She beckoned Isis down from the horse, assisting her with the maneuvering. She took Isis by the shoulders when she was firmly standing on the ground, eyeing her up and down as she continued to smile. After a moment she nodded in seeming satisfaction before patting Isis' shoulders and saying something in their foreign tongue.

Frode cleared his throat, a grin on his face. "Our sister welcomes you to our humble village. She is excited to have a new sister."

The woman continued to rattle on, while Frode interjected to translate every now and then. She expressed her excitement at the prospect of having a sister, as she did not have one until now, with Isis.

Isis turned to Frode inquisitively. "You have no wife? Or have you just not brought her from our village yet?"

Frode shook his head. "I did not choose a wife as the others did. I am concerned I'll be too busy helping Bylur with the translation of things in leading the new members of our

people to have a wife of my own. And the prospect was..."
Frode paused, frowning. "Well, in any case, I have decided I
am not ready to marry yet, even if others do not agree with
my decision."

Isis gave Frode a warm smile. "I sense that you are not
afraid to depart from what is expected of you. I respect that
and admire you for it."

"Thank you. That means more to me than you know."
Frode returned her smile with a genuine one of his own
before turning to the others and speaking in the other
language.

After a few more moments, Isis was brought inside and
shown to a humble corner of the house, a curtain hanging
from the ceiling providing the only separation and privacy
from the rest of the house. A small but sturdy wooden
bed filled one corner of the room, hand-woven blankets
covering it. A small chest lay at the end of the bed, and a
washbasin sat in the other corner. It was almost inhumane
compared to the life she knew before disaster struck, but it
really wasn't that bad compared to what she had become
accustomed to since arriving in this time of Vikings.

Frode leaned forward. "Don't worry, it's only temporary
until you move into Bylur's house, and seeing that he is the

King, his furnishings are far more extravagant. But you will be well taken care of with Agda, I assure you."

Isis nodded and opened her mouth to speak when King Bylur's deep voice filled the small room, silencing her. Isis looked between the different people, trying to gauge what was happening. When everyone but Bylur and Frode left the room, a small stirring of nervousness rose up within Isis.

Frode chuckled at her expression. "Don't look so worried, Lady Isis. He isn't going to bite."

Isis still felt nervous despite her new friend's reassurance. Vikings weren't exactly known, as far as she knew, for their kindness. When Isis thought of Vikings, she thought of war and violence, conquest, and battles. They were always shown with battle-axes and war paint. She didn't know if they were kind to their wives, but that was the point. *She just didn't know*. She didn't know their culture, she didn't know their ways, and she was scared to cross some cultural boundary she didn't know existed.

King Bylur spoke again and Frode nodded as he replied. He turned back to Isis, sighing at her still-fearful expression. "Well, he just asked for me to leave as well, but I assure you, my brother is one of the kindest and most honorable men I know. I'm aware that might not mean much to you, since

you don't know me or our ways, but...I must say it anyway."
Frode frowned, eyebrows pinched in concentration as if he
was trying to decide whether or not to speak his mind. "It
bothers me that you fear him. It forces me to question the
kind of culture you come from if the men lay a hand on
their women enough for you to be fearful of being alone
with him. In our culture, that kind of behavior is met with
terrible repercussions. Most of our women are not to be
trifled with, and men have reason to fear them should they
incur their wrath. I can see you have a ferocity of your own,
Lady Isis. I hope you can overcome this fear soon enough."

Frode turned and left the house before Isis could reply,
leaving the space heavy with thick silence. Isis turned to her
soon-to-be husband who seemed to be studying her.

Could he really be trusted?

Chapter Eighteen

A Moment With The King

Isis' body was tense with her nervousness as she and Bylur looked at each other. After a moment, Bylur stepped towards her, watching her carefully. Isis saw no threat in his gaze, not like she'd seen before in other men. But there was still fear and hesitancy within her, not due to anything that Bylur had done, but because of what others had done in the past.

Without removing his gaze from her, he raised a hand to her upper arm, a single finger tracing the tattoo he had marked onto her skin. A chill ran through Isis unbidden. Bylur paused his tracing of the tattoo as goosebumps broke out onto her skin, his finger remaining in a stationary place upon her arm. Tilting his head at her, his dark blue eyes roamed her face, his gaze growing in intensity at what he saw there.

It was fascinating how Isis could understand what he was trying to communicate with only looks and expressions shared between them. They did not know each other, and yet, words were unneeded.

Removing his hand from her arm, Bylur gestured to the tiny room Isis would now be calling home. He then looked at her expectantly, as if he had asked her a question. Isis realized he was inquiring whether or not she was okay with this, if the room would be adequate enough for now. It was kind of him, seeing as his sister and brother-in-law didn't have to welcome her into their home and sacrifice their own space and privacy for her. Many men would be offended if it *wasn't* adequate, and yet, he still asked.

Isis nodded assuredly, her tight curls bobbing along with her. Relief eased onto Bylur's features at her response. He then frowned, his eyes turning back to the tattoo on her arm. His hand reached up and tapped the mark, eyebrows furrowed in question once again.

What he was asking was loud and clear in his ocean eyes. *I just learned you didn't want this. Are you upset by it? By me? Do you want it gone?*

Isis took in a breath, trying to decide how to answer. It wasn't as simple as the last question. For one, it wasn't a yes or no question, not really. Her feelings were far more complicated than a one-word answer could express. She frowned, pursing her lips as she tried to find a way to communicate how she felt. It was difficult, and for the first time, she felt the strain of the language barrier between them.

She pointed at Bylur's chest before nodding yes, adding a small smile to it to further illustrate her answer. She then hesitated a moment, trying to decide to follow through with the second half of her answer. What if he took it the wrong way?

Bylur raised his eyebrows, leaning forward in anticipation. Isis slowly exhaled before pointing to the mark on her arm, frowning and shaking her head no. Bylur furrowed his eyebrows, his lips pinching downwards in a frown. For a moment, Isis felt terrified that he *had* taken it the wrong way and was offended or something. He crossed his arms before he looked off in thought, his brows still knitted together in concentration. He then looked back up at her and nodded, eyes filled with compassion.

Isis gifted him with a smile at the sight, dipping her head towards him in thanks. A smile twitched onto his otherwise stern features as well, before he raised his hand to run his thumb across the skin of her tattoo once more.

The smile didn't leave their faces as he pulled his hand away for a moment, only to raise it higher to Isis' cheek, stroking her skin with his thumb. Isis raised her eyebrows in surprise. She hadn't been expecting that. She knew that she should be discouraging him, swatting his hands away, enforcing the idea that she wasn't available as something to be traded in marriage. That she was a human with rights, and that she and *only she* could decide who or if she married. The rational part of her brain was screaming it. And yet, looking into Bylur's eyes, she saw no sign that he was looking at her as if she were *his*. His movements and the look in his eyes spoke of hope and a desire for her to be his, not a demand that she already was.

There was desperation in there, too. Vibrant and zealous desperation that was full of emotion. What it meant, Isis wasn't sure. A look could go only so far to communicate something. But whatever it was, Bylur seemed to *need* her to understand. It prickled her that she didn't.

Isis gave a small frown, tilting her head ever so slightly, not far enough to pull away from him, but enough to express her confusion.

Bylur blinked, stopping his gentle stroking on her cheek but not removing his hand. He frowned, looking down as if trying to figure out a puzzle. Presumably, he was desperate in trying to figure out how to tell her what he needed to.

He let out a sigh, lifting his hand up even higher to twirl one of her curls around his finger. He then dropped his hand and gave her one last smile before turning and leaving the room, his large shoulders barely fitting through the doorway.

CHAPTER NINETEEN

SHIELDMAIDEN AGDA

Isis followed Bylur out of the small house, and the King turned to Frode and began speaking in harsh tones, his voice low and dark. Isis sucked in a breath, trying to do her best not to take a physical step backward. The Translator gave a firm nod, his face grim, lips pressed together until they were thin.

Next to them, Agda looked over her shoulder at Isis. She hissed, cutting her brother off and speaking to him in a reproachful manner, looking between him and Isis. Bylur blinked before looking back at her, eyes widening as he took in her demeanor. He turned back to Frode and said something more, his tone changing entirely. This one was much calmer, almost soothing.

Frode nodded before looking towards Isis, his expression serious. "Our Great King Bylur wants you to know that his anger is not towards you, but your captors, as we have now learned they were. He was just giving me directions to deal with them and how we should move forward."

Relief spread through Isis like a comforting blanket laid over her. She nodded, letting out a breath. "Thank you, Frode." The Translator nodded before turning back to his king, seeming to possibly translate her response.

The men began to converse again, Bylur's tone occasionally getting heated before he would glance over and see Isis, diminishing the heated flames of his tone of voice at once at the sight of her. Her stomach twisted and turned at the feelings it stirred within her, that he was willing to protect her even from his own emotions.

After a few minutes, Agda huffed and then walked over to Isis, smiling brightly. Isis had always thought the Viking people would be emotionless and stoic. She was pleased to find she was misinformed on the matter.

Looping her arm through Isis', Agda began to drag her off, back into the house. She began to chatter in the unknown tongue, her voice warm and friendly. She must have known that, even though she couldn't understand her, the attempts at welcoming Isis and including her felt like a breath of fresh air. No one but Violet had been so kind to her, not even amongst her own people. And yet, here was this stranger from another time, another country, another world entirely, *or so it felt,* and...she was going above and beyond to make Isis at ease. It almost made Isis want to cry.

After a little while, Isis began to notice a pattern in the items Agda was showing her. Small handmade blankets. Whittled little objects that looked like toys to Isis. A big wooden box that could be a crib of some sort. She blinked at Agda before pointing to Agda's stomach before putting her hand on her own and rubbing it, a question mark clearly evident in her face. The woman before her smiled brightly before nodding.

Yes, I am with child. She could strangely almost hear her saying it, even though she had never heard Agda speak English. Isis smiled brightly, giving a small clap of her hands to show her excitement. Agda laughed before she began speaking again, moving about the house to show her a few more items.

A sudden understanding dawned upon Isis. *That little room is most likely their nursery. They are sacrificing not only their privacy but the room of their child for me. Why would they do such a thing for a stranger?* Isis looked back to the open doorway, through which she could still see Bylur and Frode talking. *But it wasn't for me, was it? It was for him. The wife of her brother. That kind of loyalty says something about him, doesn't it? That his sister would be willing to give up so much for him?*

Isis turned back to Agda, who was grinning at her like she caught her red-handed.

After a few more minutes, a knock sounded on the wooden frame of the door. "Lady Isis, Agda is to help prepare you for the feast tonight that is set to celebrate the betrothal between you and King Bylur. If you need anything, I will not be far. I will be dealing with some things regarding your...captors, but then I will be back to help translate between yourself and Shieldmaiden Agda. Then the feast will begin. Do you have any needs before I go?"

Isis took in a deep breath, processing the information. "I don't think so, Frode. Thank you for all your help. I don't know what I would do without you translating. I think this entire thing would be a lot scarier without you."

Frode smiled warmly, giving her a little bow. "Happy to be of service to my future queen. Besides, I like this job. I get to see Bylur squirm and be nervous around you. He's usually unperturbed by the entire world." A catlike grin grew upon the translator's face.

"Don't enjoy it too much or else he'll notice!" Isis laughed, and Frode joined her.

"I'll be sure not to do that, Lady Isis. I'm sure he'll inflict upon me terrible wrath if he were to notice." He then turned to Agda, the two conversing for a minute before he nodded, smiling brightly at them before leaving.

The door clicked shut as he left, basking the house in silence. Isis turned to Agda, who was smiling at her warmly. She wasn't scared of Agda at all, not with how pleasant the woman seemed to be, not to mention kind and welcoming. But it would take quite some getting used to having only one person speak your language, and that person being busy occasionally, leaving you with a language barrier centuries deep.

Agda's smile grew before she leapt into action, pulling dresses fit for the finest of Viking maidens out of a chest. She neatly arranged an interesting set of tools upon the only table in the house, before standing up and looking at Isis expectantly. Clearly, it was time to get ready for this grand feast...

Isis took in a deep breath. This was going to be interesting.

CHAPTER TWENTY

TO THE CELEBRATION

The experience of being groomed by a Viking woman was interesting. Especially for a black woman. For one, Agda seemed rather confused by her hair and how to care for it. It was difficult to explain without speaking, but Isis found a way. Agda seemed understanding and accepting of it all, even willing and eager to learn. But her kinky and curly hair was *not* going to be able to be braided like Agda's was. The shieldmaiden had one long, thick braid streaming down her back, and Isis' hair would never cooperate, even if it was as long as Agda's.

But soon they were able to work together to prepare. The two women accepted in an unspoken agreement that Isis would just have to stand out and be different. It was physically impossible for her to blend in, after all. Agda's bright smile and oohing and ahhing over her different features were enough support that Isis felt okay with standing out. She came to terms with it with help from Agda's kindness.

It wasn't long after that Frode came knocking at the door, which Agda answered. "Are we all ready? My, don't you look lovely, Lady Isis." The Viking's smile was genuine but without a trace of flirtation. If Isis had to guess, he was smarter than to even consider her anything beyond being his brother's wife.

"Thank you, Frode. Agda helped me immensely." Isis turned to smile at her new friend, who smiled back, clearly able to understand the compliment despite the language barrier.

The three set off, Frode leading them down the rocky path. The boots Agda had given her provided the practical effect of protecting her feet, more than the flimsy things the government had given her when they had dropped her off in Viking time. They seemed to be headed toward the large building Isis had noticed on their way in, the only building with any sort of painted color on it. As dusk settled over the village, it felt almost eerily silent. They passed not a soul on the way there.

Agda chatted as they went, her tone light and cheerful as she paused every now and then to let Frode translate. She talked mostly about her coming babe, and how she was thankful that Isis was entering the family. It made Isis smile and her cheeks warm, but her nerves still rattled with the silence of the atmosphere. What was tonight about again? Where was everyone?

Two torches blazed brightly on either side of the door to the large building, their flames flickering about so wildly they looked almost angry. Isis pressed her lips into a thin line as they approached, turning to Frode with a frown. "Where is everyone? Why is it so quiet?"

Frode nodded to the building they headed towards. "They are already all within. Tonight is a great celebration! All are invited and even expected to be there. It would be offensive not to attend, and none would dare turn up their nose at the Great King Bylur. Even so, they all respect him too much to be scared of him in such a way."

Isis felt somewhat relieved at the knowledge. It made the ghost town of a village a little less eerie. "What's expected of me tonight, though?"

"Hmm. An interesting question. I suppose it might be best for me to allow someone that has been in your place to put it into words." Frode turned to Agda, speaking quickly with his foreign tongue. The other woman patted Isis' shoulder, directing her words to Isis, her gaze warm but a feisty fire was held within. Frode nodded before translating for Isis. "She says that tonight's purpose is to celebrate your union with Bylur, but also to announce it, build it in stone. It is a loud statement that you will be his wife and that the people must accept it. In order for that to happen, you must be shown off as..." Frode paused, narrowing his eyes as he looked to the sky. "My apologies, I was just trying to find the right words in your language. Perhaps...*attached* would work well here. Tonight is about showing clearly that you and King Bylur are now attached, together, and not going to part."

Isis crossed her arms, nerves prickling her skin again. "And how am I supposed to do that? What am I supposed to do?"

Before Frode could reply, Agda cut in, asking a question. Frode quickly answered, and she smirked, patting Isis' arm. Perhaps she had asked for the translation to the question. Her grin only grew as she looked at Isis, making her nervous, to which Agda seemed to pay no mind. Agda said something to Isis, her tone sly and playful.

Frode chuckled. "She says you are not to worry about that. Bylur will handle it fully." A blush tinged the man's cheeks above his beard, making Isis raise her eyebrows. "That no one doubt that you are Bylur's woman by the end of the night.

Isis had the firm feeling that tonight was not one she would ever be able to forget.

CHAPTER TWENTY-ONE

OF FEASTING AND CELEBRATING

The silence that hung heavy in the air broke as soon as Frode opened the door shattered as a ruckus of laughter and loud talking, the clattering of dishes, and the occasional pounding of something. As the door revealed the large room within, Isis finally understood just what Agda and Frode had meant by a celebration.

The room was massive, taking up the entire building with its lofty heights and wide hall. Though Isis could tell it was a giant room, it was also packed to the brim with people, all of them looking quite happy. Each person seemed to have a tankard in their hand and were talking merrily with one another as they drank.

Frode ushered Isis in, Agda at her side as they slipped into the masses, shutting the door behind them. What appeared to be teenagers and a few middle-aged folks carted around trays of food, laughing and joking with each person they stopped by, seeming to have just as much fun serving the party as everyone else who was attending. Frode led the two women into the center of the crowd, towards a long stretched-out table that filled the center of the room. It was possibly the longest table Isis had ever seen, made to fit dozens upon dozens of individuals.

As they arrived at the table's edge, Isis spied King Bylur sitting on the opposite side of the table at its head, laughing and joking with a cluster of people around him. It was at this moment that the room seemed to quiet, and Isis took a sharp intake of breath as she realized people were staring at her, finally noticing her presence in the room. Some gazes were warm and inviting, others were piercing and suspicious. But most were simply curious and interested as if she were a rare sight to observe.

Which, she supposed, she was. Here she was, standing as a Black-Hispanic woman in the middle of a bunch of pale-faced Vikings. It was startling and slightly disconcerting. Yet again, the question of *why* this was happening to *her*, of all people, swirled around in her mind.

A loud, booming voice startled Isis out of her thoughts as she nervously looked around the room, bringing her attention back to the head of the table. Bylur had stood, reaching his arms out wide. She had never heard him speak so loudly, and it was evident that the man *chose* to be quiet. He clearly had every capability to project his voice and command a room.

Chills ran down Isis' spine as his eyes landed upon her, his warm brown gaze caressing her from across the room.

Frode leaned toward her, whispering in her direction. "Our Great King Bylur welcomes you as his honored guest to tonight's festivities." Isis nodded her understanding, her breathing coming in quick bursts. She *hated* being the center of attention like this, especially when some of that attention was scrutiny.

Bylur spoke again, with a voice breathless with wonder, and eyes dancing with light. His hands moved to reach towards her as his eyes never left her face. His fingers gestured for her to come to him, and Isis broke her gaze with the king to look towards Frode and Agda. Isis' legs were slightly shaking from her nerves. Frode gestured with his head towards Bylur and Agda nodded enthusiastically, her face alight with a bright and eager smile.

Frode ducked his head towards Isis, a smile on his face. "You should have just heard him. He just called you beautiful, like he had never seen such a lovely sight. Go to him. He will take good care of you."

With the encouragement from her two new friends, Isis strode forward, her movements jerky and unsure as she approached him. His outstretched arms never dropped as she came towards him. He only moved to face her as she drew close. As his hands still reached for her, Isis took in a breath, looking in his eyes to see a calm confidence within them, silently steadying her. She lifted her hands, placing them within his.

King Bylur drew her close to him, holding her hand in his left hand while his right slid around her waist. Isis felt tense as his voice boomed across the otherwise silent room. His hand dropped hers for a moment to grab his previously abandoned tankard and raised it high in the air. The room erupted into cheers and the celebration seemed to pick up where it left off, slowly at first but then easing back into the way it was before she arrived.

Her husband-to-be took a long drink from his tankard, hand still resting around Isis' waist. He then turned, pulling her with him as he sat down.

Isis was pulled into his lap as he relaxed into his high-back wooden chair with a sigh. Every muscle within Isis was strained with tension, taut and frozen.

She was in the Viking King's lap.

CHAPTER TWENTY-TWO
THE VIKING KING'S LAP

Isis felt Bylur's muscular form beneath her. His body was firm but relaxed as he looked out over his people. Isis did her best to breathe and try to calm herself, still noticing glances cast her way from people every now and then. She closed her eyes and tried to block out all of the noise around her, focusing on her breathing instead.

Isis had just gotten a hold on herself when Bylur's hand on her hip began to rub gently against her clothed skin, his thumb drawing circles upon her. It was almost painfully gentle, a stark contrast to the power she could feel beneath her. He was calm and in control, powerful and yet kind. Intimidating and yet comforting. She knew at once this was a purposeful choice on his part. He was a man who had worked hard on being in control of himself and knowing how to present himself, a man that refused to be a bloody savage.

Oh, how her idea of the Viking brutes she had learned about in school had been so thoroughly broken and ruined.

Turning back to look at him, his gaze turned away from her as he lazily looked over the crowds. When he sensed her movement, he turned, an easy smile slipping onto his face. His other hand left his metal tankard, reaching up to gently push a fluffy strand of thick, black hair away from Isis' cheek and behind her ear. Dropping his hand, Bylur turned, giving a little wave towards one of the serving people, who hurried over. Bylur's voice was quiet as he spoke to the bald-headed man, a vast difference from the voice he had used to command the entire room. The man nodded, an empty tray in his hand as he turned and departed the room.

Moments later, the server returned, his tray full of filled tankards once more. He grinned as he placed one in on the table in front of Isis before turning and disappearing into the crowd.

Bylur nodded towards the mug before pointing to Isis. *He had gotten it for her.*

Isis looked towards the tankard, golden liquid filling it to the brim, a small cluster of foam dripping down the side in slow motion as the drink threatened to flow over the tankard's grasp. She had never been a particular fan of beer, or that was what she assumed it was, considering the stereotypes about Vikings. She supposed there was no harm in trying it, especially if it meant not offending her husband-to-be. The fact that she was actually going to go through with this boggled her mind but...she tried not to overwhelm herself with that particular subject now.

She carefully brought the tankard to her lips, which was a slow and somewhat tedious process as she tried not to let it spill. How did that man manage to carry a whole tray of them without them all sloshing over in the very least?

As she took her first sip, the cool liquid swirling into her mouth, she could see Bylur watching her from out of the corner of her eye. She wondered if his leg was going asleep yet from having her in his lap. Certainly, she was not the tiniest of women, siting on him for this long.

The golden drink was far sweeter than she had imagined it to be. It was richer, with more depth of flavor than any beer she had drunk before. It was cool, crisp, the definition of refreshing. Her eyes widened as the expanse of flavors exploded on her tongue. This was actually *good*. And she liked it. It went down easily, it wasn't hard to drink. It wasn't bitter like any of the beer she had tasted before.

Frode strolled up next to her, a grin on his face and a tankard in his own hand. "Ah, I see you've discovered our mead. How do you like it?"

Isis grinned as gently set her drink back down on the table. "It's delicious! Mead? What's that?"

"It's a drink, uh...what's the word..." Frode snapped his fingers as he recalled it. "Fermented, that's it. It's fermented with honey. Lots and lots of honey. Makes it sweet, you see?"

Isis nodded. "It *is* sweet. It's better than the beer I've had. That's what I thought it was going to be."

Frode furrowed his brows. "Beer? Oh, do you mean ale? Yes, it is the favored drink of all shieldmaidens, mead. I'm glad you like it. I think our Great King is happy with it, too." Isis turned at Frode's words to see Bylur smirking at her. She contained a blush before snapping back to look at Frode once more. The Translator's face held a big, wide grin once more. "Speaking of him, how are you enjoying yourself? Tell me, is that the best seat in the house, Lady Isis?"

The blush Isis had successfully repressed now burst onto her cheeks. She leveled a glare at the other man. "I am just fulfilling my duty. Making it clear that we are...*attached* as you said earlier."

"And having a real fun time, too, while you're at it, by the looks of it." Frode snorted through his nose.

Bylur's deep voice rumbled beneath her, the sound vibrating into her through his chest.

Frode rolled his eyes. "Our Great King says I am teasing you again, and that if I do not want to be forced to give him lessons in your language so he can put me in my place when I do so in your tongue, then I should stop."

Isis chuckled. "Then maybe you should stop. It does not seem wise to anger your King. Especially when he's as buff as he is."

"Buff? What is this word? I do not recall learning it." Frode scrunched his nose up, as if he was repulsed by his own ignorance.

The blush tingled Isis' face once more. "It means muscular. Physically fit. Able and powerful in the physical sense."

Frode grinned widely as his eyes turned to Bylur behind her, switching languages as he began to speak in the Viking tongue.

Isis gaped at him. "Don't you *dare*."

"Oh, I already *am* telling him. There's no hope for you now, Lady Isis."

Chapter Twenty-Three

As the Party Goes On

Bylur's deep laugh sounded from below Isis, making her smile as well. Frode was chuckling as well, taking a long sip from his tankard, his eyes full of pride at his own jest. After Bylur finished his belly laugh, he pulled his own mead towards him and took a drink. He then spoke something, his own light and playful.

Frode snickered. "He says he likes the way you feel sitting on his lap."

Isis narrowed her eyes at him. "You liar. That is *not* what he said, is it?"

"What? Do you believe I lack honor? Integrity? Morality? You believe I am capable of such sin, Lady Isis?" Frode's eyes sparkled with mischief.

Isis rolled her eyes at him, drawing it out for dramatic effect. "If it meant that you could tease me and make a good joke about it? Have some fun holding so much power in your hand as the only person able to speak both languages? Yes. Yes, I do."

Frode laughed, smacking his free hand against his knee. "You wound me, Lady Isis."

"No, I don't, and you know it," Isis smirked, his good humor contagious.

He burst into laughter once more, shaking his finger at her. "You're right, and I like you for it. You're a good match for our people. A good match for Bylur. He needs this sharp ice you have to cool off his fire." His voice dropped to a whisper. "But don't tell him I told you that." He gave her a mischievous wink.

Bylur's voice rumbled beneath her once more, and Frode jumped to switch languages, going on for a little bit in his translation. After a moment, Bylur pulled her closer, his meaty arm snaking around her tighter. Frode chuckled and winked at her. "I admit, I didn't tell him before. I told him we were joking about drinking ale and mead, which is somewhat true. But I did just tell him now."

"You devil." Isis breathed, trying to glare at him but unable to keep the humor from her features.

"Or maybe I didn't. I guess you'll never really know." He shrugged his shoulders and took another drink from his mead and turned before walking away, a bright smile on his face.

Isis shook her head as she watched him go, the smile she had been holding back creeping up onto her lips.

Frode had barely been able to disappear into the crowd when he was grabbed and dragged back towards Isis and Bylur by Agda. The Translator looked thoroughly annoyed, rolling his eyes and whining in their language. Isis may not be able to understand what he was saying, but she could tell when someone was moaning and groaning easily enough. That particular tone was a universal language all on its own.

Frode sighed, resigned to his fate. "Shieldmaiden Agda would like to express her utmost delight in having you here." His voice dropped to a whisper once more. "She's trying to encourage the others to do the same in welcoming you."

Isis raised her brow at the man. "You thought you could escape from me, didn't you? Tell Agda I'm glad to have her. *Someone* needed to keep you from stumbling away from your duty."

"Oh, not you *too*. I don't need it from every side of things, you know." Frode sighed, narrowing his eyes into an annoyed look. Still, he turned and expressed Isis' sentiment to Agda.

Agda placed her hands on her hips, giving Frode a sassy remark if Isis had ever heard one.

Frode heaved a great sigh. "You two are going to be trouble together, I can tell. If you weren't already staying in her home, I would try my best to keep you apart, for my sanity's sake."

Isis rolled her eyes. "Then you would be selfish to do so, and weren't you just trying to say you were righteous or honorable just moments ago?"

Agda laughed, pointing towards Isis and then Frode's irritated expression.

"If it is selfish to wish away the fire and wrath of you two together, then perhaps it is so. Just look at her, she doesn't know what you said, but she can tell you are leveling jokes at me, and look how she loves it! How disturbing it is to see. I fear for our entire village, truly." Frode huffed, shaking his head at Agda, who was still laughing.

Bylur asked a question and Frode nodded his head in the affirmative, still looking quite bothered by the whole thing.

Of course, Isis could tell the entire thing was a dramatic act, a playful ruse for humor's sake, which he did successfully. At Frode's silent response, Bylur laughed, patting Isis' hip as if he approved and was expressing his pride in her.

Frode sighed again and shook his head, rattling something off in the other language, causing Bylur and Agda to laugh heartily.

Isis felt sure that she needed to start learning this language pronto if she was going to stay. And maybe it would be best that Frode didn't know, not at first, anyway. She wanted to be able to hear just what this hilarious man was saying for her.

CHAPTER TWENTY-FOUR
VISITING THE VOLVA

Isis found herself sleeping comfortably within Agda's home when she awoke the next morning, her sleep sweetened by the warm mead she drank the night before. The celebration the previous night had been pleasant, even if she had to be a spectacle on Bylur's lap the entire night. She dearly hoped the message had gotten across to the entire village. Isis wasn't sure if she could handle another dose of embarrassment like that. Not that sitting on that handsome of a man's lap was unpleasant, but being self-conscious and being the center of attention was.

And Isis still wasn't accustomed to receiving attention from someone like Bylur. Nor was she used to the flirtatious manner in which these Viking men seemed to operate, especially Bylur.

Agda helped her get ready for the day, the other woman chatting away the entire time. Isis found her easygoing nature and friendly conversation, despite the language barrier, kind and comforting. Isis' body itched with the nervousness of not knowing what the day would look like, what the rest of her days would look like.

It wasn't long before Frode came knocking, Agda answering the door with a hand on her hip. Poor Frode looked miserable. "You look terrible," Isis stated as she approached from her back room.

The Translator glared at her as he rubbed his eyes tiredly. "I drank my fair share last night."

"I can see that." Isis chuckled. "So what's the plan for me today? What...what is expected of me?"

Frode glared at her for another moment before taking in a deep breath to answer her question. "You are to see our village Volva to seek guidance in preparation for your upcoming wedding."

Isis took in a sharp breath. *So the wedding was really happening. It still feels hard to believe.* "A Volva? What's that?"

"I believe...it's difficult. Your language might use several different words. Seeress? Witch? Priestess? They are all of those and something else, I suppose. They are very important to us. A vital part of communion with the gods." Frode scratched his chin. "In any case, she has already been seen to when our Great King Bylur was thinking of choosing you. She was approached so that she might foresee if you were an acceptable choice for him. All of the omens were very favorable, so that is not what today will be about. Her wisdom and guidance are being sought for moving forward in your future." Frode yawned as if the explanation took more energy than he currently had to give.

Nodding, Isis processed his words, trying to digest the information. "I think I understand...Will anything be expected of me? Do I need to act a certain way or anything?"

Frode shook his head. "No. Just be respectful."

Isis smiled. "I can do that."

"Good." Frode returned her smile with one of his own, before gesturing out the still-open door. "Are you ready to go? It is not wise to be late to one's meeting, especially your first one, with the Volva."

Isis nodded. "I think so."

Agda grabbed her before she left, looking into her eyes and speaking cheerfully. The wisps that frizzed out of her long, braided hair blew gently in the breeze from the open door. She patted Isis' arm as she let her go, gesturing toward the door.

"She just blessed you," Frode lazily translated.

Isis dipped her head towards her future sister-in-law. "Thank you, Agda."

Agda smiled broadly before Frode even translated her thankfulness.

Frode and Isis walked side by side through the village as Agda closed the door behind them, silence settling between them as a cold breeze whipped through the longhouses. It wasn't long before they arrived at a small house at the edge of town, a thick forest just behind it. Mushrooms, herbs, and other plants surrounded the edifice, and it honestly looked just like Isis imagined a Viking witch's house to look like, which made her smile. It looked cozy and mysterious, but not scary. There was still a welcoming element to it as chimes softly sang in the breeze.

Isis took a deep breath as they approached, steadying herself. She didn't know what to expect but had to admit this was another exciting historical experience she hadn't ever imagined happening. It was pretty amazing, being here, doing these things in another time, having these incredible experiences no one in hundreds of years had the opportunity to experience.

Frode knocked on the door, and the door creaked as it opened, a woman not much older than Isis standing on the threshold. She wore a long colorful dress, gloves, and a hat, despite being indoors. Her brown hair held many braids in it, and her tone was even but polite enough as she opened her door to them.

Isis wiped her sweaty palms on her dress, gifted to her from Agda, as she stepped through the threshold of the Volva's house. *Here we go.*

CHAPTER TWENTY-FIVE

THE VOLVA'S PROPHECY

What surprised Isis most about the Volva's home wasn't anything actually about the house. Instead, it was about what was already in it. *King Bylur.* Their eyes met from across the room, and Isis felt herself grow a little more at ease, and then slightly more shy than before. How could it be that one man could stir such differing emotions within her? He helped her feel calmer and more at peace, and yet, she felt shy and nervous like a young girl around her crush.

Bylur stood as they entered, his eyes following Isis as they approached. The Volva led them into her abode, the heavy scent of lavender and other herbs Isis couldn't recognize hitting Isis' nose potently. She directed Isis and Frode where

119

to sit, all three next to each other on furs, facing a crackling fire. Isis sat in the middle between the two men, her body instantly becoming aware of Bylur's presence as they all sat down. The others spoke in their tongue for a minute before the Volva grabbed a small brown pot from a nearby table, scooping out a yellowish-white cream and applying it to her skin. She sat down and took in a deep breath, closing her eyes and beginning to sing.

The song was beautiful as it was eerie. Goosebumps rose on Isis' skin involuntarily as she watched the woman sway. The atmosphere of the room shifted, and Isis could have sworn that she could see a sort of mist seep into the room, if she looked out of the corner of her eye. The Volva was silhouetted by the roaring fire behind her, making it seem like she was one with the shadows.

The Volva lurched, her spine straight in her seat as she stopped singing. She spoke, her voice hoarse and raspy.

Bylur leaned forward towards her, his tone seeming to denote that of a question as he watched the Volva intently.

She answered his question in a slow, mumbled tone, and a slow sway took over her body once more. He nodded, asking another question, which she answered. After a few minutes of this, Bylur reached over and grasped Isis' hand without removing his gaze from the Volva. The priestess continued, her inflictions rising and lowering as if her voice was attuned to the waves of the ocean.

After a few minutes, the atmosphere shifted once more, and the Volva opened her eyes, blinking. Polite conversation happened for a few more moments before Bylur turned, gesturing to Isis and Frode. The priestess nodded, and Frode turned to Isis with a gentle smile. "The Volva has given a prophecy regarding the marriage of yours and Our Great King Bylur. I have not translated up until this point because it is disrespectful to interrupt or disturb in any way, but she has given permission for me to do so now."

Isis' eyes widened as she nodded, eager to hear.

"A lot of it is difficult to translate, so I ask for your patience, Lady Isis. But in essence, she said that the gods, goddesses, and spirits all agree that, though time tried to separate you, destiny was victorious. A fire burns deep inside you, ready to burst forth like a vicious wolf, tearing into your enemies and ripping out their throats. You will not just be a Queen, you will be a warrior, a shieldmaiden. And when war comes—and it shall—only when you and Bylur fight alongside one another, will you be able to conquer things. And you will not be able to fight together, not truly, until you win the wars inside of yourselves and vanquish the foul spirits that hurt those near you. Only when you choose to defend those in need, will you be able to win your wars."

Chapter Twenty-Six

THE RETURN OF THE WOMEN

Several days drifted by since the night of the celebration. Isis settled into her new way of life, learning new things daily from Agda, and sometimes teaching her new friend some new things in return. Isis found their relaxed way of life refreshing. No rushing around to this appointment or that, no honking of car horns, no getting stuck in the rat race that consumed so much of her old world. It was peaceful, it was simple, it was calm.

And then, just as she was getting settled in, Isis' world completely shifted once again.

That morning had been like any other as of late. Her day started with helping Agda with some chores before the two women prepared themselves for the day. Agda's baby bump grew larger with every passing day. It had been rather quiet that morning; usually, the men of the village were out and about, shouting to one another and completing their morning chores as well, which was sometimes quite the noisy thing. But no such sounds reached Isis' ears.

When Agda and Isis stepped outside of their abode, Isis knew it was too quiet. Something had changed, something was different. Agda looked excited, which brought Isis some relief. Her friend knew what was happening and didn't seem displeased or worried about it, which meant it was probably a good thing.

Little did Isis know that a good thing for Agda was quite possibly *not* a good thing for her.

The sound of many horses' hooves clattering against the ground stirred Isis' interest. The sound grew louder until the riders appeared, turning the corner of the road Agda lived on and coming into view.

The Viking men looked fierce on their horses, but what drew Isis' interest most were the women that sat behind all of them on the horses. As they came closer and Isis was able to perceive details about them, she knew at once these were the women from her village, the ones that had been kidnapped with her and brought to this time, world, whatever it was...

They were here. Which meant Violet was here.

Isis looked for her friend as the women passed through, but she never saw any sign of her blonde-haired friend. Several of the women stared at Isis as they went by, some of their expressions not so pleasant or friendly. Some even sneered at her as they passed.

How lovely it will be having them around again. Isis thought to herself as she rolled her eyes.

The village erupted with activity as the women arrived and got settled into their homes. Agda pulled on Isis' shirt sleeve to garner her attention before gesturing with her head in the direction away from where the women had ventured down. Isis followed Agda to a high hill where the Volva stood at its greatest height, overlooking the crowds of Viking men and modern women. King Bylur stood behind the Volva at some distance, perhaps so much that the people below couldn't even see him. Beside him stood Frode, the Translator's hands clasped behind his back as he watched on casually.

The two men turned as Agda and Isis approached, Bylur's expression softening from one of intense thought to a gentle delight upon seeing the two women. It made Isis' lips spread into a smile as well.

"Ah, here to see the show?" Frode grinned at Isis as he rolled onto the balls of his feet before coming back down.

Isis raised her eyebrow at him. "The show? What show?"

Frode snickered. "The mass wedding."

"The *what?*" Isis exclaimed, horror and shock spreading over her features.

"Oh, yes. These men waste no time getting their brides. They are asking the Volva for her blessing. If they get it, she will marry them at once." Frode looked quite amused.

Isis breathed in a shaky breath. "But...the women don't even know what's happening. That isn't right."

Frode nodded his head in agreement. "Oh, yes, we think it as well. It's why Bylur is in a particularly grumpy mood at the moment. But there were men that insisted—the damned troublemakers—and when they wouldn't back down, Bylur said he would allow them to stand before the Volva and hear what the gods have to say. And then when that happened, all of the other men followed these awful men's lead and are doing the same."

"How awful," Isis said, shaking her head in disgust.

"Yes, and how foolish. Patience is the sign of a strong warrior and a wise leader in our culture. Obviously, these men are not that." Frode turned his attention to the Volva as she raised up her hands, silencing everyone.

The fate of so many women, including her friend Violet's, was now in the hands of the Volva.

Chapter Twenty-Seven

THE VOLVA'S PRONOUNCEMENT

The Volva gave a deep, guttural shout, silencing all of those below her. Then with her hands raised, she looked out over the crowd, surveying them as if she were looking for the answer within their faces. She would be deciding the fate of the women who stared up at her, and Isis couldn't help but wonder if the women below even knew that. What did they think? Were they frightened of the woman? Scared by the whole situation?

They should be.

As Isis looked down at the Viking men of the group below, she saw many who looked just as unsure about the situation as the women did. Why didn't they stand up and declare their uncertainty? It was beyond Isis, but she supposed peer pressure was a powerful thing. However, there was a core group of Vikings in the middle of the group that stared up at the Volva with a wolfish grin, as if she was about them they could devour the meal set before them. They looked altogether too smug with themselves, and Isis felt sure these were the troublemakers that had instigated this entire thing.

Isis' heart nearly stopped in her chest as she spied Violet, her sweet friend, crying next to a tall man that seemed to belong to the group of these terrible-looking men, his hand firmly grasping around her upper arm. Her eyes were red and swollen, her face pale and almost sickly. She was marked by one of *them*. Her friend had been right, the man's anger and bruising of her arm the first time they met was a sure sign of things to come. In fact, by the looks of it, her arm would probably already be bruised by the way he was holding onto her so tightly now.

It made Isis sick. Her stomach clenched and churned, her head spinning for a moment. How could she have let this happen? If she had tried harder to protest against this entire thing, perhaps Bylur wouldn't have let any of this occur. Perhaps he would have listened if she put up more of a fight. It didn't matter if he was pleasant and warm and kind. It didn't matter that she was starting to *like* the idea of being married to him. It was the principle that was at stake here, her rights being questioned, and thus the rights of every single woman down below as well.

And Violet wasn't as lucky as Isis, and she was sure there were others that were also in a similar situation.

If Bylur wanted her to be his queen, then she needed to start leading and standing up for her people. Wasn't that what a queen did?

That understanding was almost enough to make her leap forward to interrupt the Volva's proceedings, but something within her told her to wait. Perhaps the Volva would shut things down before Isis had to say anything at all. Or perhaps Isis would lose any respect she had established with these people if she did something as offensive as that. It seemed like they respected this woman and placed her in a high place of power and esteem. Undermining and possibly embarrassing her did not seem like a wise plan.

The Volva launched into a speech, raising her hands high to the heavens before waving them out over the crowd. She then folded her hands in front of her, growing silent as she studied the people below her once more. The Volva gave a slow shake of her head. Isis *wished* she could see the woman's face right now to try to gleam some sort of telling expression from it.

Finally, the Volva began to speak again, her tone quiet and cold, almost sharp. Isis furrowed her brows, trying to determine what her tone of voice meant. Did it mean the Volva was declaring the doom of these women's rights, or did it mean she was refusing to give these men what they wanted?

A chill ran up Isis' spine as she imagined the reaction some of these men might have if they were told no.

The Volva dropped her hands to her sides and turned, walking down from the hill and towards Isis and the others. She stopped before King Bylur, the two speaking for a few moments, during which Bylur nodded and remained silent mostly, his brows furrowed in thought. There was a strange moment when he glanced over at Isis, studying her for a moment before turning back to the Volva. Isis couldn't help but wonder what that was about. The priestess then shared a nod with the King before turning and walking on, disappearing behind some buildings, heading towards the general direction Isis recalled the Volva's home had been in.

Isis turned to Frode. "What did she say? What was her pronouncement?"

Frode furrowed his brows, stroking his beard. "It is curious. She has decided she will take it marriage by marriage, couple by couple. She is to do prayers to ask for guidance involving each and every man and woman, so the spirits can help her decide for each one. This is an incredible amount of work for her and will take some time. She must have felt the spirits wanted this strongly, to decide to do this."

Before Isis had a chance to reply, King Bylur approached them, speaking in low tones to Frode, casting quick glances at Isis every now and then. Frode raised his eyebrows a few seconds into Bylur's information. The Translator looked quite surprised.

After the King had finished speaking, he nodded, and Frode turned to Isis. "Well, this is even more surprising. The Volva has specifically requested your help with this matter. She says she *needs* your presence and assistance, Lady Isis."

CHAPTER TWENTY-EIGHT

TO WELCOME REJECTION

I sis stood at the threshold of the large house that Frode informed her all of the women from her time would be staying in until their marriages took place, or their engagements were dissolved. Taking in a deep breath, she tried to gather her courage to knock on the door, but felt hesitation take over her once more. Agda placed a gentle hand on Isis' shoulder, giving her a small smile and a nod when Isis looked her way.

She wasn't alone. That was pleasant. But was it enough? These women didn't like her, they made that abundantly clear. Everyone but Violet had ostracized and gossiped about her, making her feel isolated and self-conscious. It had been a constant battle against insecurity during her time in that village with these women, but she never wanted to let anyone else decide how she was going to feel about herself.

Isis returned Agda's smile before raising her hand and knocking on the thick wooden door.

It opened with a jerk as a girl Isis recognized, but didn't know the name of, stood staring at them. Swallowing her nerves, Isis tried for a smile. "Hello. We've come to see that you're doing okay and to make sure you don't need anything."

The woman rolled her eyes and stormed back into the house. "The chosen one is here, fulfilling her queenly duties."

Several snickers erupted within the large room that made up the entire building, the place filled with cots, the beds forming aisles where each girl slept. Isis realized her cozy little corner in Agda's house was much more private and comfortable than this, making her neck heat just a little at the remembrance of her somewhat ungrateful attitude towards the room when she had first arrived.

Amanda sat on a nearby bed, legs dangling off of it as she propped herself up on her elbows to stare Isis down. "You don't really expect us to believe you are now some great queen or something, do you? You may have gotten a little lucky, but you really aren't any better than the rest of us. We saw you fetching well water yesterday. If you were *really* a queen, you'd have servants to do that. You're not a real queen."

"I never called myself a queen." Isis felt a stirring of anger rising up within her. For the entire time she'd known these women, they had made her feel inadequate. And now that she had finally been chosen and seen as valuable by someone outside of them, they were trying to make her out to be some prideful arrogant jerk. Would there ever be a time where they treated her with at least some respect or human decency? Clearly it was too much to ask for kindness from them.

Amanda rolled her eyes. "But you clearly expect us to treat you as such."

Isis furrowed her brows. "No, why would you think that? I would never want to make anyone feel inferior—"

"Yeah, right." Amanda scoffed, crossing her arms as she sat up. "I can already tell you will never let us live this down."

Catching herself from outright laughing, Isis settled for raised eyebrows, holding her humor in. "I think that might be your own perception, Amanda. I'm not the type to do that whatsoever. Perhaps it's guilt for how you've treated me in the past?"

The brunette scoffed, flipping her dark hair over her shoulder. "What's that supposed to mean?"

"You know full well what that means, Amanda. Violet has been the only one who has been kind to me since we all got dragged here," Isis clarified, the room stilling as their voices grew tense.

Amanda stood, keeping her arms crossed in front of her as she strode over to Isis, getting in her face. "What? Are you going to cry about it now that you think you're a pretty princess?"

"I'm not crying about it. I'm simply stating it as fact. You don't have to be so rude, you know." Isis pulled her features into a tight expression of displeasure.

Rolling her eyes, Amanda once again tossed her hair over her shoulder in a display of dramatics. "I'm not trying to be rude, sorry if it comes off that way. I just don't like when people try to make victims of themselves for pity. It's disgusting, in my opinion."

A blaze of anger burned through Isis. "I'm not trying to make myself a victim. In fact, that is the *opposite* of what I want. I'm here to try to help and see if you need anything. I'm not here to flaunt anything or complain."

"So you're here to try to act like our knight in shining armor, our savior, huh? What are we, damsels in distress? We have our Viking men. They will take care of us, we don't need you and your arrogant self-righteousness." Amanda turned, stomping off back to her cot and plopping down on it.

Isis sighed after a moment, allowing her anger to cool into pity. "Very well. I'll leave you be, then. I hope you all are happy with your accommodations and the Volva's decisions, whatever that may be. I'm done trying to convince you to act like decent human beings."

Looking back at Agda, her Viking friend was frowning, obviously sensing the tension in the room. Isis patted her arm as she passed her, leaving through the door they arrived through. She heard the footsteps of Agda following and then walking beside her.

The door of the women's longhouse slammed behind them, making both Isis and Agda jump. The Viking woman's scowl deepened, her thoughts clearly filled with displeasure. As Isis turned to head back to their home, Agda grabbed her arm, leading her in another direction.

At the end of the path was a large longhouse, and outside of its front doors stood Frode and King Bylur.

Agda was dragging her to complain about the women's treatment towards Isis. And honestly, Isis wasn't sure she minded.

CHAPTER TWENTY-NINE
HER DEFENDER

As soon as the two men noticed Isis and Agda, the latter began talking with a firm tone, clearly upset. Her arms flailed about as she complained, and Isis pressed her lips into a firm line. She didn't like to see her new friend so upset. She could only hope that she was upset by the other women's behavior and not by anything Isis did or didn't do.

After a moment, Agda huffed and crossed her arms. Frode turned to Isis with furrowed brows. "Lady Isis, is this true? Shieldmaiden Agda said that there was a woman from your village that treated you unkindly."

Isis sighed, a measure of relief filling her that Agda could tell what was going on and wasn't upset by anything Isis had done. "Yes. Amanda and I have never gotten along. I'm afraid she's kind of a leader amongst the women, so none of them took very kindly to me coming there since Amanda didn't."

Frode's scowl deepened as Isis told him this. "Lady Agda said she saw the marking on Amanda's arm. She said it belonged to an ally of Bodvar Karsson, one of the troublemakers in the village. She was afraid it had something to do with him."

"No, not that I know of. Though if she is engaged with one of the troublemakers, then they will be quite the pair to watch out for, I'd say." Isis rolled her eyes.

Frode bobbed his head up and down. "Duly noted. I will be sure to tell the King this, as well as relieve Shieldmaiden Agda of her fears. You not getting along with someone because she is an unkind person is far different than you not getting along because her betrothed turned her against you because of who you are set to marry. That could be a sign of an uprising."

Isis raised her eyebrows in surprise. "An uprising? Are you concerned of that?"

"Yes, I'm afraid to say." Frode frowned. "If you excuse me a moment, Lady Isis, I'd like to translate your information for the King and Agda." Isis nodded, and Frode switched languages, speaking rapidly in the other tongue.

Agda seemed a smidge relieved, but a bit of a frown still hung on her face. Bylur, however, crossed his arms, his face wrinkling with displeasure. He replied to Frode with a tense tone.

Before Frode had a chance to reply, Isis interrupted. "Tell him I'm fine, that it's nothing to worry about. She's bothersome, yes, but nothing dangerous or threatening. I can handle someone being unkind, it's her loss anyway, since I was there to offer help or assistance and she refused me. It hurts her more than me."

Frode nodded, a small smile on his face as he turned and translated for the King. Bylur looked somewhat mollified, but he still didn't seem happy about the situation. He began to speak again, and Frode nodded, pulling out a small leatherbound notebook of some kind and a quill and wrote something down in it.

The Translator turned back to Isis afterward. "She's been added to the list of people that has gained the displeasure of our Great King. We watch them closely."

Isis lifted an eyebrow up at the smirk on Frode's face. "I see. And what is to be done about those on that list? Are they set to be banned or something?"

"No, not unless they do something deserving of being exiled. But we observe them closely and are sure not to grant them any special allowances or assistance as we are unsure if those resources might be used against us," Frode explained. A small smirk rose on his features once more. "Our Great King Bylur has specifically said that this woman be placed on the list and receive no such kindnesses due to her mistreatment of you."

Isis ignored the heat that was flushing her features. "That seems a bit hasty but perhaps it is for the better, considering who she is engaged to."

Frode chuckled as he nodded. His attention was pulled away by Bylur, who was asking him something barely above a whisper. Agda still heard it though, and began to laugh. Her brother frowned at her, and the two began to banter back and forth. Frode simply shook his head and turned to Isis.

"Our Great King Bylur wishes to know if you would join him on a walk through the forest. Alone. Just the two of you." The Translator wiggled his eyebrows.

Suddenly, Isis felt quite nervous.

CHAPTER THIRTY

A WALK IN THE WOODS

A soft breeze rifled through Isis' thick, curly hair as she walked through the village, King Bylur at her side. Wiping her damp palms on her dress, Isis took in a deep breath, the motion drawing her companion's attention. Bylur titled his head at her, eyes studying her questioningly.

Isis tried for a smile, feeling her cheeks grow tense. She knew it probably wasn't the most convincing of a smile, but she did her best. He frowned, lifting a hand as if to touch her, but dropping her after a moment of hesitation. Isis' chest squeezed at the motion and she turned from him, her forced smile dropping from her face.

They walked on in silence for several minutes, the forest appearing beyond the houses, tall pines swaying softly from the wind. Tears pricked Isis' eyes, and she looked off in the distance, trying to turn her face away from Bylur so he couldn't see without being obvious about it.

The land truly was beautiful. The weather was mild and pleasant. The sky above blue with fluffy white clouds drifting by lazily. The trees were a vibrant green, their scent filling the air. The salt of the ocean was still present, as well, creating a pleasant mixture of earthy, woodsy, and sweet.

As they passed under the trees' canopy, the dirt path winding through the forest, Isis felt a hand gently touch her shoulder. She turned to see Bylur gazing at her with concern, his fingers brushing against her upper arm. Her tears dripped down her cheeks, sliding against her skin as the wind blew once more, making her tears feel cold.

Bylur's face tightened into a frown, his forehead wrinkling with the tension. He reached forward, watching her closely, as his thumbs brushed the tears away, one by one. His hand pulled back as he continued to observe her, and suddenly Isis realized his problem. Without being able to communicate, there was no way for her to communicate any discomfort or dislike of something he did. All he had was her facial expressions and body language, so he watched closely with every move he made.

He hadn't been abandoning her by pulling back his hand, he had been respecting her. After all, he knew somewhat of how she felt about this entire situation. Now that she thought about it, if he *wasn't* hesitant and careful with her, especially with touching her, she would probably be concerned.

With all these thoughts swirling in her mind, she reached out grasping his hand with hers and giving it a squeeze. He returned the squeeze, smiling as he did so. The two looked into each other's eyes for a moment before he broke the gaze, continuing to hold her hand as he began to resume their walk through the forest.

Isis looked back at the barely visible village through the trees, watching it disappear as the path turned a corner, the trees blocking the view. They were now alone, and yet Isis did not fear Bylur. She knew that if he had wanted to do something forceful, he would have done it by now. His character was different than she'd ever known. He was King, but he was a respectful and kind man. She had no reason to fear him, she felt it in her soul.

With entwined hands, the pair continued on the path until the sound of a trickling stream sang to their ears. It wound its way through the trees, the sparkling waters glittering with the few rays of sunlight that managed to break through the canopy of leaves.

It was a beautiful sight, and pleasantly reminded her of the first time she had met Bylur while washing dishes that early morning. How strange it was to think upon that day that felt so long ago, and yet, was barely a few weeks past.

A raw yearning in her soul erupted within Isis. A desire to connect, to feel, to be bound to someone. Turning to look at the man next to her, Bylur smiled, his well-groomed beard lifting with the action. A childlike excitement sparkled in his eyes, as if he were giddy to show her this place. Isis couldn't help but smile with him, his joy contagious. Tears continued to flow from her eyes, making his smile drop as he frowned once more.

Isis kept her smile and shook her head, reaching for his arm with her other free hand. Grasping it, she could feel the strength beneath her touch. But all she could see was the gentleness in his eyes. So sweet, so kind, so worried.

And she wanted it for herself. Reaching for him, she drew close, looking into his eyes, that yearning for connection bursting forth in her chest stronger than ever. He tilted his head, eyebrows pinching together in confusion. Isis reached up, gently touching his cheek with the pads of her fingertips.

Understanding seemed to dawn upon him as his eyes widened, his eyebrows raising with comprehension. His free hand reached up to cup her cheek, Isis resting her head in his hand. He lifted his hand to stroke her hair, pulling her into his embrace.

He whispered a word in the Viking tongue, one that Isis recognized from the celebrations not so long ago. He was calling her *beautiful*.

Warmth filled her chest, making her heart race in anticipation for what was to come.

CHAPTER THIRTY-ONE

THE VIKING KING'S TOUCH

Hearing Bylur's heartbeat underneath his soft clothing soothed Isis' anxiety. His arms wrapped around her, his hands rubbing her back in a gentle caress. Isis felt his lips kiss the top of her head, waiting a moment as if to sense her reaction to the display of affection. When she did not tense or pull away, he kissed her hair once more, this time a little lower.

Isis looked up at him, reaching up underneath his beard to touch his neck. He titled his head to the side, searching her eyes. She could practically feel him trying to read her thoughts.

That raw feeling took over her, filling her until all her doubts and fears vanished from her mind. Lifting herself on her tiptoes, she brought her face closer to his, watching him closely for any signs of discomfort. When his lips slid up into a smile, a chuckle escaped from his chest, and she dove forward, brushing her lips against his.

Pulling back, she searched his eyes and face for his reaction, suddenly feeling quite bashful about her forwardness. But all she could see was the wide smile of Bylur before her, a sparkling joy and gladness glittering in his eyes. He slowly moved forward, inching his lips closer to hers until they met again, this time under Bylur's guidance.

This meeting of their lips was much more sure and steady, their lips locking and moving against each other, joining in a passionate embrace. Bylur pulled her closer to him until their bodies were touching as his tongue began to delve into her mouth, the feeling foreign but delightful. Isis allowed him to lead, feeling her body erupt in the sweet sensation of electric tingling as it became attuned to his body against hers.

Breaking the kiss, Bylur pulled back searching her face once more. Isis smiled, nodding her approval, pushing her body against his. He lifted an eyebrow, flirtatious amusement flickering in his eyes. Isis ran a hand down his chest, and he drew close again, kissing her once again with more fervor.

Isis ran her hand back up his chest and tangled her fingers in his hair, pulling slightly. A small growl escaped from his throat, making all of the air vanish from Isis' lungs as her entire body responded to the sound.

Bylur's lips left hers as they began to kiss down her cheek and then onto her neck, the soft hair of his beard brushing against her skin, a delicious sensation as his lips relished her. He grasped her shoulders, turning her, so her back was up against a nearby tree. Isis wrapped her arms around his shoulders, holding him loose as she continued to play with his beautiful black locks.

Bylur's hands moved down, grasping her waist, taking his time to feel every curve and bump of her body. A feeling of nervousness rose up in Isis at the sensation. It felt strange for someone to touch her with such tenderness, especially there, when she was accustomed to a world that found her body disgusting. But if the eager way Bylur was touching her, pulling her closer, he evidently didn't feel that way.

As he pushed up against her, Isis could feel his erection straining against his leather pants, making her gasp. He chuckled into her neck, before taking a moment to suck on her sensitive skin there. His hands moved lower, taking a firm hold of the tender flesh of her butt and squeezing it before one trailed lower, grasping her thigh and picking up her leg, wrapping it around his hips.

Feeling his hard member against her aching mound made Isis take in a ragged breath, he pushed against her, feeling the friction build between them. Bylur released a low, breathy moan, causing an electric sensation to shoot straight to Isis' vagina. She gave a moan in response, and Bylur thrust his hips into her once again.

The King stepped away, both his and Isis' chests heaving. He unclasped his fur cloak, laying it down nearby, between a large oak and the trickling stream. He gestured toward it with one hand as he undid his belt with the other. Isis gave him a soft smirk as she went to the cloak, sitting down upon it as she watched him stalk toward her, eyes full of fiery desire.

Bylur threw his belt to the side, kicking off his boots before pulling down his leather pants. His erection greeted her proudly, and Isis moved to remove her own clothing, shoving off her shoes before grasping the bottom of her dress and pulling it over her head. Bylur kneeled before her, running both hands up her legs, opening them wider.

The fur of his cloak was soft beneath her, tickling her skin with pleasant comfort, feeling its embrace beneath her as Bylur settled in above her. The air was crisp and cool against her heated skin as her lover reached down between them, brushing the pads of two fingers against her sensitive clit, making her gasp for air. Bylur continued his gentle touching as he leaned down to resume his kissing of her neck.

His kissing trailed a path down to her breasts, where he spent a significant amount of time, giving sweet attention to each one. With one hand rubbing in circles against her aching bud, his other grasping her voluptuous hips and love handles.

A single finger gently delved inside her, making her cry out. It had been some time since Isis had sex, and her entire body buzzed from his attention. She felt her own slickness with every movement of his finger. Soon, her internal muscles relaxed and grew as her pleasure mounted, and Bylur added another finger, and then another.

By the end, Isis was gasping and giving him soft whimpers, and Bylur leaned forward to kiss her once more. Isis grabbed his brown tunic and practically ripped it off him, moaning at the sight of his firm chest and tattooed arms. He chuckled before kissing her once more as she ran her fingers down his bare skin, the gorgeous man above her shivering at her administrations. She began to trace the curves of his tattoos, trying to memorize them and this moment in her mind forever.

Bylur retracted his fingers from her, her body pushing towards him instinctually at the loss of contact. Throwing his brown locks over his shoulder, he picked up her hips, aligning himself and easing himself in. He closed his eyes and threw his head back, a guttural moan coming forth from his lips. Isis couldn't catch her breath, the feeling of him entering her almost too much to bear. It didn't feel like anything she had felt before, no man had felt like this. It felt like their souls were entangling just as much as their bodies were, if not more.

He stilled within her, bending down to plant a soft kiss against her lips. Pulling his face away from hers, they looked into each other's eyes as Bylur began to move, thrusting in and out of her. They gave each other moans and sweet cries of pleasure as their connection only grew and strengthened, their bodies making their own sounds as they joined, the sound of skin embracing over and over again.

Isis raked her fingers down his back as he nuzzled his face in her neck, his hot breath fanning against her skin. His fingers pressed into her lower backs as he held her hips aloft, pushing and pulling in and out of her, her legs wrapped around him.

With the sound of the creek creating sweet music for their joining, the pressure built within Isis, feeling it grow, especially when Bylur reached down, circling around her sensitive nub with the pads of his fingers. Isis moaned out, feeling her muscles tighten around him at the sensation. Bylur gave a ragged moan as he stopped a moment, Isis still constricting around him. After another moment, he began again, thrusting his hips against hers.

The two sensations of him inside her, brushing against her walls over and over again, combined with his fingers rubbing against her clit, made everything build all the more. Isis began to huff and squirm, her hips thrusting upwards against him in unison with his thrusts. Her hands continued to roam all over his skin until she finally grasped his sides, feeling herself grow close to climax. Bylur grunted, seeming to take notice as his pace quickened, his own resolve breaking as his movements grew erratic and wild.

His grunting continued, turning into desperate moans as Isis finally cried out, feeling herself explode with pleasure, lights popping behind her eyelids as her orgasm took over.

Her entire body was ablaze with pure bliss, and she felt every inch of Bylur's skin against her all at once. She felt herself pulse around him, coaxing him to give in.

Three more thrusts was all it took until Bylur gave a wild gasp from deep within his chest, throwing his head into her neck and wrapping his arms tightly around her as he plunged as deep within her as he could. His member began to pulse and twitch within her, exploding as his cum filled her. Isis gasped at the sensation, another jolt of pleasure filling her.

The two stilled, and Isis raised a hand to gently caress the back of his head, his soft hair feeling comforting underneath her palm. Bylur gave one last moan before he gave soft kisses to her neck, raising up onto her cheek and finally resting upon her lips.

Isis felt like she was home.

CHAPTER THIRTY-TWO

A NEW CONNECTION

Isis skipped on clouds for the next few days, or so it felt. She had forgotten the fulfillment that came from two people coming together, but more than that, she had never experienced such a passionate connection with someone prior to that day in the forest.

She missed Bylur. It hadn't been that long since she had seen him, but she had been kept busy with her work with the Volva. It had been interesting but rather simple work, sitting with Frode, who'd been asked to step in as the Translator, the Volva, and the couple in question. Frode mostly spoke to whatever Viking man was present that day, while Isis focused on the American woman. The Volva simply sat back and observed the entire thing, occasionally praying. But for the most part, she kept silent. Later, she would deliver her pronouncement before the couple left her home. Isis would only find out from Frode after they left.

So far, they only had acceptance of the marriages from the priestess. Not that Isis minded, because so far, she also believed each marriage was okay. The men seemed meek but excited about the prospect of marriage to the women and were quite respectful as far as Isis could tell. And the women weren't opposed to the idea of marrying them. Each had explained to Isis, in their own way, that while they would have never expected to marry a Viking man, they found themselves drawn to the idea. Perhaps it was unwise since they didn't really know to whom they would be married, but they were too curious for their own good to pass up such an opportunity. Besides, who else were they going to marry around here? Was it smart to hold out hope of returning to their homeland, or should they try to adapt? Most were choosing to do the latter, which involved going through with their marriages.

Isis couldn't judge them. She felt the exact same as them. Perhaps it wasn't all that smart to marry a man from another time and culture that couldn't speak the same language, but sometimes your heart can carry you where your brain cannot.

And Isis could do these women one better in terms of foolishness. Whereas they freely admitted they did not know the men they married, for better or for worse, Isis felt as though she did.

And furthermore, she felt as though she was committing the most foolish and dangerous thing of all: falling in love. Her heart was at stake now. What else could be more dangerous than that?

Isis did have her concerns regarding the future of her work with the Volva. Namely, she was concerned about how she would feel when the woman wasn't desiring or willing to get married. Obviously, it would go against her moral code. It would be wrong not to stand up and say something. But how would the Volva react when she did such a thing? Would she refuse the marriage or ignore the woman's feelings and wishes entirely?

Because the truth was, they were not in their culture anymore. All of the power rested in this one priestess' hands and what she felt their gods were saying. That meant that if she and a member of the couple was unwilling and not consenting, she would still wed them if the gods wished for it. A fact that felt like a stone sinking to the bottom of Isis' stomach and sitting there, weighing her down.

Several days after her blessed time with King Bylur in the forest, the time she feared came upon her. She journeyed to the Volva's house as she had every day in that week, greeted the priestess and Translator Frode, and watched as a proud-looking Viking man stomped into the Volva's house, dragging behind him a whimpering woman, her eyes red and puffy.

Isis felt like standing up and yelling at him already, just from the smirk on his face. She felt like tearing at him with her nails until he let the poor girl go. She felt like rescuing the woman from him, pulling her away and hugging her until she felt safer, reassuring her she never had to return to him or see him ever again.

But she couldn't. She was trapped where she sat, watching the display unfold as the man practically threw the modern woman onto her seat, making her whimper once more as he sat down next to her. Isis took in a deep breath before she turned to greet the woman, introducing herself.

"Hello, my name is Isis. I'm here for you, okay? I'm here to help as much as I am able. We'll get through this together, all right?"

The woman looked up at her with wide eyes, her brown hair a frizzy tangled mess. She didn't look like she had been taken care of or properly groomed in a while. "What do you mean by that? Does that mean you can get me away from him?"

Isis hated that she couldn't immediately promise her that yes, she could save her from this man. But she felt a resolution rise up with mighty strength inside her heart. A resolution to bring justice to this situation, to break these women out of the prison they had been thrown in, to free these captives from these enslavers of men. She would do it, even if it meant risking her standing with the Volva, with Agda and Frode, with the entire village, and yes, with King Bylur. She would do the right thing, for herself and for these women. She refused to be burdened with regret because she sat by and did nothing.

She would help these women, or die trying.

CHAPTER THIRTY-THREE

INSIDE BYLUR'S MIND

Bylur had never seen a woman like his bride-to-be before. Her dark skin took his breath away. Her eyes seemed to be so full of life, her very soul peering back at him. Whenever he looked into them, he was reminded of the earth underneath his feet, the nature that thrived all around him. And seeing how Bylur was raised to respect and admire nature with great passion, he couldn't help but be in awe of Isis.

Her hair was like a crown of curls, her smile felt like home, her voice reminded him of a beautiful song. She was exotic, she was foreign, she was a mystery he was drawn to, and yet, she felt familiar and comforting. Her easy jesting with his friends and sister made him smile. Everything about her felt right.

Bylur had observed the women in that village for days, sighing at the prospect of being married to any of them. But then he had seen her, her hard work and dedication, how she never looked to anyone to lead the way or take charge of her own life. She was her own leader, she took control of her own life and never looked back. Despite the circumstances that had befallen her, which he had only learned to be far worse than he had known before, she was determined to be strong and refused to be a victim.

She was beautiful. She was worthy of being a queen.

He had thought it strange when she was so fearful and wary of him at first, that initial time they met in the woods near the river. After all, weren't these women supposed to be here to be wives for them? Didn't they volunteer?

Discovering they didn't volunteer, or even know that being wives was what they were here for, felt like a cold slap to his face. His heart broke for Isis, and her fearful eyes had haunted him more than he ever let on. He was determined to be careful with her, to guard his own actions and movements carefully, so he did not hurt her or cause her more fear in any way. And he had accomplished this so well, until that day in the forest with her.

He did not regret a single thing. He knew that she was pushing past the careful walls he had built to protect her. She wanted him. She wanted to be close, to feel him...and it was intoxicating to him. The desire in her eyes had been too powerful to refuse. He wanted her, and perhaps he should have waited until they were wed, but...her skin had been so soft under his fingertips, her hands so alluring as they tangled themselves in his hair, and her lips gave him a taste of Valhalla itself.

Bylur wondered if her terrible interaction with her own people had caused her to seek out his affection. The thought of what Agda had described made his blood boil with rage. He had a tight rein on his anger, but the cruelty of these women made him want to forget how to control himself. How *dare* they insult and wound his beloved. Who did they think they were? Simple women, with their place next to Viking men still unsure. Even if it was confirmed and they were wed, his Isis would be the *Queen*. They would not. They would be regular women compared to her.

He wondered if Isis knew what role she would take on, or if she understood that this village was only a temporary home. His true home lay not far to the east, a castle surrounded by an expansive village with a harbor and a fine trade route running through it. This outer village was selected due to its proximity to the foreign women's village while still remaining rather close to his town, in case his duties as King needed immediate attention. Did she know of the beautiful things that would soon be hers? He couldn't wait to give her the greatest of spices from the far east, or the finest of silks, or glittering jewels. He wondered what she liked. He knew she was a hardworking woman, but did that mean she would put aside all desire for riches?

All Bylur knew was that she deserved the best. And as King, he was proud to be able to provide her with that.

He watched her walk next to Frode towards the Volva's abode. He could tell she had mixed feelings regarding the situation with the women. He understood her pain, the idea of forcing any of these women to marry someone they did not want to was disturbing to him. It was a tense situation, with Bodvar Karsson and his men sending Bylur a list of demands, a threat hidden underneath them. That man had stirred up trouble for him time and time again, even at one point making a claim for the throne. He had been dismissed by all accounts, but he held some level of power by making allies with some of the warriors.

The last thing Bylur wanted was a fight with his own people, especially with this foreign power that came to them with an offer too great to refuse. He didn't trust them, not since Isis told them about how they treated her like cattle or horses.

Anger flickered through him once more at the thought of Isis being mistreated in such a terrible way.

He watched as wind rippled through Isis' hair, blowing it back off of her shoulders. It reminded him of that day in the forest, how she had felt underneath him. The sounds he had made against his shoulder, her hands roaming his torso...

Bylur swore under his breath as his member gave a small throb in his trousers. He didn't have time to be distracted by Isis' beauty, although that was a damn impossible task. But she was more than beautiful, she was intelligent, brave, powerful...

With a grunt he turned, focusing on the important thing he needed to find a solution for. Which was...he shook his head, trying to get his head out of his pants. He needed to be King, to protect Isis. It was just that he had not felt this way for anyone, ever. Their wedding couldn't come soon enough. Having her close would soothe his soul in ways he couldn't describe. He didn't know how he knew this, but he felt it deep within his bones.

But this was for Isis. To protect her. To protect his people, which would be *their* people soon. He was excited for that day to come, but for now, he ought to figure out what to do about Bodvar Karsson before that man came for everything that mattered. He threatened to destroy everything Bylur had. So perhaps it was more important to figure out how to save everything he had instead of dreaming of giving it to Isis. That time would come, but not if he sat on his haunches daydreaming all day, instead of protecting it from this bloody brute.

Bylur turned, casting one look at where Isis had long disappeared into the Volva's house. His gaze then drifted to the forest not far off, where his soul had joined with hers. It made sense for them to join in such a way, surrounded by nature, just as she reminded him of. And considering they had met by a stream in a forest, it had been perfect. Better than he could have ever planned. He had not planned it, certainly not. He had only meant to have a quiet moment with her, hoping to bring her some peace and comfort.

But he wouldn't trade it to gain his entire kingdom back. If he had lost it, that was. Which he wouldn't.

Bylur broke his gaze from the trees, returning to the shelter of his home, where a quiet fire crackled. The words of the Volva rolled around in his brain, her warning that Bodvar Karsson and his men would have their turn soon in her home. She had been putting them off, much to their displeasure and anger, but soon she would be unable to put them off any longer. She began with those she felt were safe and easily approved, but what would happen when Bodvar arrived and was inevitably rejected?

It was possible he could try to stir up trouble. A fight. A bloody *war*. The man was a brutish fool. He would never let himself be humbled, his pride was far too great for that.

Bylur took in a breath. Perhaps such a thing was inevitable.

CHAPTER THIRTY-FOUR

THE BEGINNING OF TROUBLE

Isis had known the moment that the Volva opened the door that today was going to be different. The priestess was usually serious, her features relaxed into a calm, neutral expression. But today it was entirely different. It wasn't just serious, it was downright solemn. There was even a flicker of anxiety in her eyes, concern in how the corners of her eyes wrinkled.

Clearly, the Volva knew something that Isis didn't. And whatever that was, she was worried about it. Which meant it was likely to be something for Isis to be concerned about, too, since she would probably be here in the middle of whatever it was.

The Volva ushered Isis and Frode inside, hurriedly closing the door behind them. She spoke in low tones to Frode, her voice tense, her throat tight as she swallowed. Isis watched the two Vikings carefully, casting glances between the two of them as they conversed.

Finally, Frode sighed and turned to Isis. "It seems that the meeting we have today is with one of the men we have listed as...*troublemakers*. The Volva fears that—given the harsh demeanor of most, if not all of these men—the woman will be unwilling, which opens many troubles for us. She says she needs you and me more than ever. The gods do not like men with hands that hurt the innocent. She says it is unlikely they will approve of such a union if the woman is in fact scared of her betrothed. However, we are all concerned about denying these men. Their attitudes regarding these marriages have been more like demands than the requests that they should be."

Isis frowned, furrowing her brows as she crossed her arms in front of her. "What do you think they will do? Steal the women away? Or do you think they will attack the Volva, or someone else?"

"All of the above and then some." Frode sighed, scratching his beard in thought. "Bylur is also concerned they might try to revolt against him."

Isis' eyes widened at the thought. "You really think they would do that?"

"They would be foolish to, but these are not the wisest of men. They are arrogant, foolhardy, greedy, hungry for power. They might think of themselves as capable by their overinflated egos. Which means they are trouble. And, truth be told, attacking King Bylur while he is in this outer isolated village is a good plan. Doing it in the city would be suicide." Frode turned and began quietly conversing with the Volva once more.

When their conversation came to a breaking point, Isis interrupted, her patience barely withstanding as she waited for them to finish their discussion. The question burst from her mouth as soon as she opened it. "Frode, what do you mean by outer villages and the city? I don't understand."

Frode's eyebrows lifted slowly in surprise. "Oh, you haven't been told, have you? I suppose not, since I haven't told you. It seems so foolish of me to assume...forgive me, Lady Isis. This is purely an outer village we are staying in. King Bylur reigns from a much bigger city. You will see soon

171

enough. Once this whole marriage debacle is settled, we will set off for it at once. We came here because it was close to your old village, where you were dropped off, and because the Volva lives here. Volvas often enjoy being out in the isolated wilderness, you see. Nature better connects them to the gods. And since your village was right there, it seemed foolish to trek all the way to your village and then all the way to the city without stopping to allow the Volva to handle things. Or we could have done that and summoned her to the city, but that seems inconsiderate and just as foolish."

"...city? There's more than this?" Isis gawked, caught off guard.

Frode laughed at the expression on Isis' face. "Oh yes! You did not think your King was a simple farming Viking, did you?"

"Actually, yes, I did. And I was quite fine with that." Isis sighed, wondering just how extensive this city was going to be.

Frode patted her arm. "You are a good woman, Isis. Now, I believe the Volva would like us to prepare. Our...*guests* will be here at any moment. Please, come sit."

The trio waited for several more minutes, the three of them remaining mostly silent the entire time. Heavy anticipation hung in the air, and Isis felt like they were waiting for their mother to walk in after they had just disobeyed her. Surely they weren't going to get yelled at and punished by this man, so why were they acting like it? Surely he had no authority in this place.

When the man and his would-be-bride arrived, Isis understood their anxiousness. For it was not that he had any authority, but that he *acted* like he did, and demanded it. Their dread stemmed from knowing they would have to tell him no, reminding him that he actually *didn't* have any authority, and thus deal with his angry reaction at such a denial.

He was a man-child that would throw a tantrum if told no, basically. Isis hated these types of people, but it was especially unpleasant when the person was an extremely tall, muscular man that knew how to wield an ax, and had the temper of a raging bull.

The man strutted in like a proud peacock, dragging a teary-eyed woman behind him.

Isis knew everything was about to change.

Once it was confirmed that the woman surely did not wish to marry this man, and Isis felt her strong feelings of protectiveness for her, she cast a glance towards Frode. The

Translator met her eye and nodded, glancing towards the Volva.

The Viking man seemed so preoccupied with telling the Volva some long, drawn-out monologue that he missed the Volva pressing her lips into a thin line and nodding at both Isis and Frode.

The priestess interrupted the man, making his face scowl for a moment before he brightened up a bit, nodding. The Volva gave him a tense smile before producing her incense and oils, things Isis now recognized as components of her prayers. She began as she always did, the atmosphere shifting with her singing. Isis still found it eerie, but she no longer feared the customs of this time or the priestess. Instead, she waited patiently, more eager to hear the outcome of this prayer than ever before.

The woman gripped Isis' hand like Isis was life itself she was desperately clinging to. Isis' heart squeezed. She could only hope in her heart that whatever god or gods that were out there, if there were any, were listening and willing to help this woman, and all of them, really, get out of this mess without anyone getting hurt.

CHAPTER THIRTY-FIVE

THE THREAT

Bylur could hear the shouting across the entire village. He flew out of his longhouse, running down with other people that were coming to see what the commotion was about.

His blood froze when he realized it was coming from the Volva's house. He had one thought on his mind as he began to run towards it. *Isis.*

The shouting seemed to come from one man only, which meant that whoever was meeting with the Volva today was not happy. Seeing as the Volva had warned him that the first man was from Bodvar Karsson's little group of troublemakers.

As he drew close to the Volva's house, he could hear the man's words loud and clear. "You will regret this, you pathetic witch! Rejecting me like that, who do you think you are! Bodvar will hear of this, and when he does, he and all of us who follow him will bring down wrath and fire on any who oppose us, which is you now, Volva. You think you have power, but you have none. You will see what happens when you cater to the King."

The Volva's voice was calm, much quieter than the yelling man's. "I cater to no man, not the King, and certainly not you. I am simply a messenger of the gods. If you cannot handle their pronouncement, then you should take it up with them, not me."

The man scoffed, and even from this distance, Bylur could see he spit everywhere as his tongue lashed out. "You do not speak for the gods. Why would the gods choose a woman to speak for them?"

The Volva frowned, looking more annoyed than upset by his words. "They do as they have done for many generations. Go now. I have nothing left to say to you."

The man spat at the Volva's feet before turning and storming off. As he left, Bylur could see Isis, who had been blocked by the man's large figure. She clutched onto a weeping woman, who was cowering by her side. Isis had her arm wrapped around her, comforting her as she watched on.

Their eyes met once the man left, and they gave each other a nod of understanding. Bylur turned towards the Volva, furrowing his brows. Stepping towards the priestess, he crossed his arms. "Did he hurt you?"

The Volva shook her head. "No. He tried to be intimidating, but I think he was more scared of me than I was of him. He might say he does not believe I speak for the gods, but the fear in his eyes betrayed him. He knows I am a holy woman. I doubt he would dare to lay a hand on me. If he had a wife, however, that might be a different story. The gods were clear, those two are not to be wed. I am not surprised."

Bylur let out a long breath. "Neither am I." He turned back towards Isis and the crying woman. "Will she be all right?"

Frode stepped forward this time. "I believe she is in the capable hands of your future wife, my King. Isis did not let her face him alone. She was determined to be by her side the entire time."

Bylur smiled, letting out a soft chuckle. "I am not surprised by that, either."

"Neither am I." Frode grinned.

"Bylur!" The shout ripped across the village, silencing every other voice. Bylur slowly turned around, already knowing what was heading towards him.

Bodvar Karsson was striding towards him, his entire body tense with fury. Bylur had hoped this wouldn't happen, that Bodvar wouldn't make a scene like this, at least not on the very first man's meeting. He suspected it would happen eventually, since the brute had an inflated ego. It was only a matter of time before he took things personally. But within a few minutes of his first man being rejected? Things were worse off than Bylur had thought.

As Bodvar approached, two men flanking either side of him, he felt Frode tense and put a hand on the ax that hung from the Translator's belt. Bylur held out a hand without looking his brother's way, signaling him to be careful and slow down. He didn't want to trigger bloodshed if it was possible to avoid it.

"Every man gets accepted until mine. You want to tell me that is a coincidence? And now I see you standing here, consorting with the Volva. Tell me, priestess, are you truly loyal to our gods, or are you a whore for hire now?" Bodvar growled, his face twisted into a snarl.

Bylur stepped in front of the Volva. "You will watch your tongue about our priestess, especially in my presence, Bodvar. I understand you might have some frustration, but you will give her the respect she is due."

Bodvar snorted. "Is she really due that much respect? Not when she is handing out pronouncements based on your wishes, she is not."

"I am only here because one of your men caused a scene. He was yelling. Of course, I came running, it is my duty as King to protect this village, is it not? If there is a disturbance, wouldn't I be going against that duty by ignoring it? He just left, so I have barely gotten a handle on what happened here." When Bodvar was about to retaliate, scorn evident on his frowning face, Bylur continued in a heavy tone. "The Volva carries out the wishes of no one but the gods. You know this, Bodvar. It is blasphemy for her to do anything but. Do you really think she or I would risk getting struck down just to deny your man? No." Bylur stared the man down, the two holding eye contact for several tense seconds.

Bodvar took a step closer to Bylur. "I think you don't like that I am opposing you, Bylur. I think you feel threatened. And thus, what wouldn't you do to make sure I don't get what I want? Marriage is important to our people. And yet, at the present time it is a difficult thing for us to acquire. Why wouldn't you try to make sure we never get it?"

Bylur did not stand down. Instead, he crossed his arms and maintained eye contact with the man. "You are correct in that you have questioned me and tried to undermine my authority at every turn, Bodvar. Of course, I do not want this. But if you think I would disrespect the gods and commit blasphemy against them in order to attack you, then you think too highly of yourself. I am not a fool that I would anger the gods, especially not to be petty against you."

As he took a step closer to Bylur, getting right into his face, Bodvar gave a low growl, his lips curled into a snarl. "That better be the case, *Oh Great King,* because if I find that it's not, I will make sure the people see what a pathetic excuse for a Viking you are, not to mention a King. You will wish the gods had never allowed you to be born when I am done with you." The snarl shifted to an animalistic grin. "And your woman will be full and satisfied."

Red hot anger burst through Bylur at the mention of Isis, and it took everything within him to control himself from brawling with the man right then and there. "I would watch your mouth if I were you, Bodvar. Someone might take you seriously."

Bodvar laughed in Bylur's face. "And? Would that be you? Do you really think you could best me in a fight, not to mention me and my men? The gods know who to support, and who is the strongest. Is your Volva going to protect you when I am slamming you into the ground, hmm?"

"Go. Now. Before I decide to show you just how far your head is up your own ass," Bylur growled, lips turning upwards into a snarl as his eyes raged with fury at the hubris of Bodvar.

Bylur would be damned if he let this arrogant fool have his way.

CHAPTER THIRTY-SIX

WATCHING HIM FROM AFAR

I sis tried to stand tall when the man began his shouting. The woman who would have been his wife, whom Isis learned was named Jenny, jumped from her seat and cowered on the other side of Isis, hiding behind her.

It seemed that the Volva did indeed care about the woman's feelings in all of this. *Thank heavens.* While it was not pleasant having this man scream about and stomp his feet, Isis still felt relieved. Knowing that these Vikings would not throw her or any of the women to the wolves felt like breathing again, after holding it for so long.

The man took a step towards Isis and Jenny. His eyes were wild with fury, a vein bulging from his forehead. Isis began to feel a bit worried. She stood strong in the face of the man, but Frode stepped in, getting in between them, and pointing towards the door as he rattled off a firm yet calm command in their tongue.

Frode escorted him out as the Volva followed, her demeanor calm, but Isis could see her hands shaking ever so slightly before she clasped them in front of her. Isis wrapped her arms around Jenny, walking her out as the man screamed and raged. Frode kept a close eye on him as he stepped towards the Volva, who lifted her head high.

People began to emerge from their homes, his shouting disturbing the peace of the village and drawing them forth. Cresting over a hill, Isis saw a figure approaching, and even at a distance, she knew it was Bylur. His broad shoulders stood strong in his silhouette, his long hair pulled back. He wore some sort of leather vest today, and *god* did it look good on him. The big angry Viking turned towards him as he approached, blocking Isis' view of her King.

His voice cut through the furious Viking's ranting, making Isis intake a sharp breath. His voice was like a calming force to the storm, a bright light breaking through the darkness. Even though Isis could not understand what he was saying, she could feel the weight of power that they carried, the authority that he so easily exerted. It was exhilarating to hear, and her heart began to hammer in her chest, just from hearing his power.

The things Frode had told her just before the Viking man and Jenny had arrived popped back into her mind. *A city.* Just how much did Bylur preside over? And what would Isis' life look like as his wife? Suddenly the idea of becoming a queen seemed much more daunting when it wasn't just a little village she would be helping to lead. Would she even be helping to lead? What would her responsibilities and duties even be?

Her thoughts were cut off when the Viking man stormed off, revealing Bylur who had been standing on the other side of him. Bylur and Isis met eyes once he left, a calm certainty swirling within his gaze. Did he realize how much strength he passed to her with just a look? Butterflies danced in her chest as he gave her a small smile before turning to the Volva, a serious expression taking hold of him once more.

The priestess and the king talked for several minutes as Isis clutched Jenny, who was slowly calming down. Isis simply rubbed her back soothingly, waiting for a calmer moment to speak with the woman.

But no moment would come, not for a little while longer.

Three men stormed towards them, the middle one yelling things at King Bylur. Isis felt herself tense as he walked right up to Bylur, getting in his face. *This must be the man they say leads the troublemakers.* Bylur stared the man in his eye, his shoulders straight. He did not back down or cower, not even for a second. It was honestly quite attractive to Isis.

Just when Isis thought things might turn into a full-out brawl, or worse, considering all of the men had weapons on them, and after Frode stepped up with his hand on his ax, the center man snarled once more before turning around and leaving. Jenny had started crying more somewhere in the middle of the confrontation, and Isis was nearly holding her up so she didn't fall to the ground.

Finally, when they were gone, it felt as if everyone let out a collective sigh of relief. The Volva spoke once more to Bylur, who nodded, following her inside of her house and shutting the door behind them.

Frode walked up to Isis and Jenny, letting out a literal sigh as he did. "They are discussing what to do. Bodvar is going to insist on causing trouble. He just threatened Bylur and the Volva that they better start approving his men and their selected women for marriage or else. Obviously, they cannot guarantee that. It depends on what the gods declare. They

185

are trying to decide what to do when he inevitably decides to pick a fight, is what I believe your people would say."

Isis lifted her eyebrows. "Inevitably? What do you think he is going to do?"

Frode shrugged. "Hard to say. We need to prepare for the worst. But come, let us take care of you and this lady. I am not sure it is safe for her to stay with the other women at this point. We will have to figure out another living arrangement for her. Can you help me with that, Lady Isis?"

"Of course." Isis nodded, feeling Jenny calm down next to her. "Come, Jenny. Let us find a safe place for you to stay, hm?"

CHAPTER THIRTY-SEVEN

THE CONCERNS OF THE VOLVA

Bylur stepped inside the Volva's house per her request, shutting the door behind him. His blood was still pumping, his mind buzzing with adrenaline from his confrontation with Bodvar. Something had to be done, and it seemed that the Volva agreed.

"He will not be kept at bay, my King. He has made it clear that he holds no respect for my position or yours. The will of the gods is not important compared to his will. He has already convinced himself that the gods are on his side no matter what. He will not cease his pursuit of what he wants until he has it and he is willing to trample on anything or anyone that stands in his way, which at this present moment, is us." The Volva paced in front of the fireplace, clenching her hands at her sides.

Bylur nodded, crossing his arms, finding himself impressed at the priestess' ability to maintain her composure up until now. She had shown a single sign of stress or anxiety until this moment, in the privacy of her home. "I agree with you. Something must be done, we must be prepared. He will take this as far as he can, which means we have to be ready for an uprising, a battle, even. Do you have any suggestions?"

The priestess paused her pacing, her back turned to the crackling fire. She stood still, blinking in thought. "My mind is a mess of emotions. I am angered by his utter disregard for the gods, for the holy ways. I need to think, to pray. The gods will have an answer to this, I am sure. I would not usually approach them about the petty squabbling of men, but this has to do directly with someone's disrespect for them and their pronouncements. They will want to be involved, to help, to set him straight."

"I am glad. It would seem foolish for them not to strike someone down that is attempting to inhibit their commands from being carried out. In fact, he is trying to go beyond that and make sure that the *opposite* of their orders takes place. As a king, if someone did that to me, I would deem it treason. It would become a top priority to ensure not only that they were stopped but also that they were made an example of." Bylur studied the Volva for any signs of distress or anger at his words but found none. He felt relieved, she was truly on his side.

The Volva nodded, resuming her pacing. "Yes, I understand that perspective. I suspect the gods will feel similarly. But you should go. Speak with your council, make a plan. Leave me to my prayers. I will beseech them to look down upon this situation and support those that loyally follow them, while inflicting their wrath on those that oppose them. This is the way of the gods, to interfere where it matters most."

Bylur nodded, taking in a deep breath. "Yes, I shall gather the council and see what they have to say. We will get prepared to handle whatever Karsson throws at us. But there is another issue, Volva."

The woman paused her pacing once more to look at him with furrowed brows. "What is it?"

"The foreigners that brought the woman here. Now that we have learned of their trickery and kidnapping of the women, I suspect that is not the end of their deceit and manipulation. Depending on how you look at it, they were almost enslaving these women by selling them off into marriages, trapping them in another place and another time. If they are willing to do that, what else are they willing to do? Where are their morals? And if that is the case, can we really trust them not to commit worse sins, much less uphold their side of the deal?" Bylur clenched his jaw at the thought of Isis screaming as she was dragged away to this foreign place. How terrifying it must have been.

The Volva stood silent for a moment. When she spoke again, her voice was quiet. "And do we really want the kind of power we offered them in their hands?"

Bylur nodded. "Precisely my thought."

"We must discuss this with Isis in time. She might have wisdom to offer us. But for now, we should focus on the threat on hand—Bodvar. He is the greatest danger at the moment, the foreigners can wait." The Volva furrowed her brow in concern. "So many threats facing us..."

Bylur gave a long sigh. "Too many. But I will be sure to see it handled. It is my duty."

When the Volva was silent for a long while, Bylur took this as a dismissal. Respecting the priestess' wishes, he turned to open the door and depart. Her voice stopped him. "My

King, some wisdom for you. Protect your Isis. Watch over her and make sure she is safe. I suspect Bodvar's anger and jealousy will only grow for you. He will want what you have, especially her when his own selection of a wife is taken from him. And when that time comes, she will need you, and you will need her. There is a reason why the gods have put you together."

With his hand on the handle to the door, Bylur stood still, soaking in her words. "I will protect her with my life."

CHAPTER THIRTY-EIGHT

AMANDA'S CONFRONTATION

I sis felt relieved to find that, for the next few days, the Volva had arranged meetings for potential couples that did not include any of Bodvar Karrson's men. This meant that most of them went smoothly, with only one case where it seemed neither member of the couple was really interested in each other or the marriage, but the Viking man felt pressured into choosing a lady. The Volva quickly relieved them of this pressure, and they both went about their merry way, and everyone was happy.

She knew that feeling probably wouldn't last, but Isis still held onto the hope that it would.

How quickly did that hope become shattered.

THE VIKING KING'S LOVE

It was a rather gray and overcast morning as Frode and Isis walked to the Volva's house as they usually did. Ever since Bylur's tense encounter with Bodvar, Isis noticed that her favorite Translator seemed much more on edge, his eyes darting around, checking behind every corner as they walked on. His hand seemed perpetually on his weapon as of late, ready to pounce into a fight at any given moment. It was somewhat distressing to see him this way, his jokes not quite as witty or quick as they once were, not when he was so distracted with staying on guard.

The wind whipped around the longhouses, biting its chilly breath straight through the layers of Isis' clothing and into her skin. She shivered, feeling her feet move a bit faster towards the Volva's house. But once she made it within the line of sight of the priestess' home, she stopped in her tracks.

Standing at the front of the house was Amanda, batting her eyelashes up at a Viking man who was wearing a frown. Isis sighed. She did not think this was going to be very pleasant for her.

Frode stopped beside her, crossing his arms in front of him. "That is strange. They are very early for their meeting with the Volva. We usually are here before the couple. I wonder what provoked them to journey out into the cold this early? Surely they know the Volva is strict that they should be on time. Not a moment too soon or a moment too late, it is one of her rules."

"That is Amanda. She is the one that has caused trouble for me in the past. She does not care about any rules except the ones she instills." Isis sighed, looking towards Frode, who raised a brow in interest. She simply shrugged, rolling her eyes before resuming her approach towards the house.

Amanda tossed her dark brown hair over her shoulder, raising her once perfectly plucked eyebrows at Isis. "Well, look who it is. It is not time for your meeting, you know. It is *our* turn." Amanda giggled, reaching out and grabbing the Viking man's hand, who nearly flinched at her touch. "So you and your little lowly man better get out of here. It is our turn, not yours."

Isis did not grow angry at her words, more annoyed than anything. But mostly, she was, at this point, numb from the woman's stupidity.

But just as she was about to open her mouth to tell Amanda that she was coming off stupid and desperate in dissing Isis—as they both well knew whom Isis was betrothed to—Frode stepped forward, clearing his throat. "Good morning. I believe you have the wrong impression.

I am King Bylur's brother, I act as Translator for the Volva
in these circumstances. I am not courting Lady Isis, I do
not have that honor. That esteemed privilege belongs to my
brother, King Bylur himself. Only the best for the King,
after all. But the Volva has requested Lady Isis' help with
all of the couples, regarding the women of the relationship
especially. The soon-to-be *Queen* helps make the decision
on whether or not the marriage will come to fruition."

All of the color drained from Amanda's face. "I-I am aware
who the King is. But she—"

"Will be the Queen, yes. You have a remarkable
opportunity to make a good impression on her today, I
suggest you do so. But you two are very early, we are
supposed to be here before you. If you would step aside
so that Queen Isis and I might get through, that would be
very wise of you." Frode's lips tilted upwards into a tight
smile, his gleaming eyes clearing conveying the threat he was
bestowing on her.

With her face still blanched, Amanda nodded while
pulling on the Viking's arm, which she still clung to, trying
to drag him to the side. The big man did not move, lifting
an eyebrow up at the woman.

Frode gave a quiet chuckle Isis was sure only she could hear, before he switched languages, greeting the man. The two conversed for a while, the man frowning the entire time while it looked like Frode was trying not to laugh. Amanda was trying to yank on the man's arm, even growling and stomping her feet at one time in frustration at his lack of movement.

After a few more moments, in which Isis was trying not to make eye contact with Amanda or laugh, Frode finally nodded before dipping his head towards the other man, the Viking doing the same. The man stepped to the side, nearly bowling Amanda over in the process. She huffed, her hands stilled, wrapped around his forearm.

Isis and Frode walked past them, knocking on the door and waiting. Isis sniffed, her nose a little numb from the cold. After a few moments, the Volva opened the door, her face plastered with an annoyed expression, making Isis raise her eyebrows. She had never seen the priestess show any sort of emotion, her face usually a carefully crafted blankness at all times.

Upon seeing Isis and Frode, her face relaxed, and she stepped to the side, welcoming them in. She closed the door behind them with a little more aggression than needed, the door nearly slamming.

Frode burst into laughter as soon as they were inside. "That poor man. He is regretting all of his choices right now."

Isis lifted an eyebrow at him. "What do you mean?"

"That woman went and fetched *him* this morning, far earlier than what was needed, and dragged him all the way here. He feels embarrassed on her behalf, as he should. She is something else. No wonder why you two do not get along, you are opposites. I am *so* glad that our Great King did not choose someone like her, thank the gods." Frode smirked, before turning to the Volva and rattling something off in the Viking tongue.

The Volva sighed before replying, rubbing her temple.

Frode burst into laughter once more before turning to Isis. "She says that woman has been knocking on her door over and over, complaining and demanding things of her. She does not know what specifically, but that kind of voice is in every language. The Volva was ready to cancel the meeting just to get rid of the woman."

Isis joined Frode in laughter. She simply couldn't help herself. "I don't blame her. I have felt similarly. But the man really said he regrets choosing her?"

"Yes, he said that. Apparently, she was rather infamous during the choosing process, throwing herself at all the men as they came to make their selections. Poor Svan did not have much of a choice. He was lower on the priority list as far as choosing goes and did not have much of a selection left when he went to make his decision. He had hoped she would calm down after she was chosen, but it seems not to be the case." Frode snickered once more.

The Volva waved a hand towards the door and turned around towards her chair, crossing the room to sit in it as she let out another long sigh. Frode laughed and elbowed Isis. "She wants to get this over with. I guess we should, hm?"

Isis nodded. "I think that is for the best. The sooner this is over, the better."

Frode nodded his agreement as Isis left his side to take her seat, the Translator opening the door and speaking to the man in the Viking tongue, presumably welcoming them in. Footsteps ensued, and Isis watched as Amanda gave her one glance before choosing the furthest seat from her, which was usually the seat the Viking man sat in. Svan, her betrothed, looked rather put off by her behavior, but said nothing as he sat next to Isis, lurching as Amanda reached out and grabbed his arm, pulling him closer to her.

The Volva, looking a little more bothered than usual, began her prayer, burning incense and swaying in her song. Isis watched on, now having learned to enjoy the woman's hauntingly beautiful music.

There was a slight interruption when, in the middle of the Volva's song, Amanda leaned over and began to giggle in Svan's ear, whispering flirtatious words the man couldn't even understand. The Volva's singing paused, her lips pursing as she heard the interruption. Svan frowned at Amanda, giving a gentle shove away from him before pointing at the Volva, shushing her. Amanda immediately crossed her arms and began to pout like the absolute child that she was.

But after a time, the Volva was able to complete her song, breathing in deeply, allowing the calm serenity that was usually over her to settle over her once more. She spoke in a quiet voice, and Svan sat up a bit straighter, his eyes widening as he listened to her words.

Looking over at Frode, Isis could see the Translator was trying not to laugh. After another moment, the Volva stood, prompting the rest to stand as well. Svan bolted up from his position, yanking his arm away from Amanda and grinning, dipping his head respectfully towards the Volva first, then Frode, before finishing with Isis. He did not give Amanda a second glance as he strode out the door, disappearing into the chilly morning.

Amanda sat there, a dumbfounded look on her face as she called after him. After a moment, she looked between Frode and Isis, anger trickling into her expression. "What just happened?"

"The Volva has pronounced that your marriage is *not* to take place. The gods do not wish it to happen. You are free to go now," Frode calmly explained, his expression containing a bit more smugness than maybe it ought to.

Amanda let out a high-pitched noise from the back of her throat, gawking at the Translator in horror. "That can't be right! It was already established! W-we are betrothed!"

Frode's lips twitched with the need to grin. "Not anymore."

Amanda bolted up from her seat, nearly stumbling over in the process. She stared at Frode for a hard minute, and Isis was scared she was going to slap him for a moment. She then turned to Isis, her lips curled into a snarl. "You *bitch*. You had something to do with this, I know it. You convinced the witch to absolve our blessed union just to get back at me! It's because you're jealous, isn't it!"

Isis blinked at the woman before saying deadpan. "What am I supposed to be jealous of? Your fake face, your fake boobs, or your fake personality?"

Amanda let out a screech, throwing herself towards Isis, claws extended. Before she could reach her, however, Frode grabbed her, tossing her towards the door like he was tossing a small bag of flour. She landed on the floor with a thud before beginning to cry. Frode moved to stand between Isis and Amanda, despite the latter still laying on the floor. "You have just tried to assault the Queen. You will have to stand before the King and his council for such actions."

Tears streaking down her cheeks, Amanda's eyes looked past Frode, glaring at Isis with a raging fury. "You'll pay for this, Isis. I'll make sure you get what you deserve."

"And a threat, too, eh? I'll be sure to tell the King that. You might want to keep your mouth shut. The King is very protective of his betrothed." Frode was no longer smiling, his chest heaving with what Isis thought might be anger. She couldn't blame him. This woman was infuriating.

But still, as Frode escorted Amanda from the building, Isis couldn't help but feel that Amanda would make good on her threat if she had the slightest of opportunities.

CHAPTER THIRTY-NINE
FAMILY SUPPER

I sis needed a nap after the drama of the past couple of days. Frode escorted her to her temporary home at Agda's house, and Isis retreated to her small room, separated from the rest of the house by a simple black curtain. She nearly fell into her small cot, falling asleep within minutes. Apparently, she was more exhausted than she realized.

As sleep encompassed her mind, Isis began to dream. Her imagination transferring her to a dark forest. She now associated forest with peace and serenity, but this place was far from that. A heavy fog blanketed the scenery, obscuring her view. She felt like this forest was endless, like there was no escape from it. And to make matters worse, fear raised the hair on the back of her neck, telling her she *needed* to run, that she desperately *needed* to escape from it.

Something was coming. Something was after her, watching her even now, some evil being, obscured by the fog, hidden behind some tree...she didn't know what it was or where it was, but she could feel its eyes on her, waiting to strike...

Isis awoke with a gasp. Agda stood over her bed, her brows furrowed in a concerned expression. Isis blinked, trying to shake off the fear that had ensnared her mind. With a deep breath, she swung her legs over the side of her cot, a shiver running through her body from the cold sweat that had coated her entire being. Agda stepped back, worry still lining her features. She pointed towards the front door of the cabin before turning back to Isis expectantly. *Apparently, they were supposed to be going somewhere.*

After making herself as presentable as possible in a short amount of time, Isis followed Agda out of the house. Darkness settled over the village like a heavy blanket, hushing it into a quiet slumber. Only she and Agda moved about, everyone else presumably off having their last meal for the day as they usually did about this time. The evening's darkness made Isis raise her eyebrows in surprise. She did not realize how long she had slept. It had only felt like a few minutes, but clearly, it had been hours. It would seem she had needed the rest, although not all of it had been very restful.

The blackness of the night reminded her of her nightmare, making Isis shiver. Thankfully, it wasn't long until they reached their destination, a large longhouse on a hill. Isis had never been here before, but Agda opened the door almost as if she owned the place, strolling in with a casualness Isis only saw around her when the shieldmaiden was with friends and family.

Following in behind her, Isis shut the door as she entered, barring the cold night air from entering any longer. A large table sat next to a fireplace, although not as big as the table that resided in the massive building that the celebration had been held in. The place bustled with activity, people zipping about with trays and platters in their hands, setting the table for a feast for a handful of people, it would seem.

"Ah! Isis! Welcome!" Isis turned to see Frode smiling brightly at her, arms spread, displaying his broad set of shoulders underneath his brown tunic. "It should be fun tonight. The food looks very good."

Isis raised an eyebrow at him. "What is going on? I just followed Agda here."

Frode chuckled, pointing towards the table. "We are having supper together. Just the family. Bylur wanted some relaxed time together amidst the chaos that has been surrounding the village as of late. A time just to breathe and enjoy each others' company, you know?"

"That does sound pleasant." Isis felt her shoulder lose some of their tension already. "Who is all here?"

Both Isis and Frode turned towards the table, which was nearly finished being prepared. "Not many. You and I, Agda, of course, and her husband. And then a little surprise for you." Frode winked, making Isis raise her eyebrow.

"A surprise? Of what kind?" Isis asked, but Frode shook his head, refusing to answer. "Come on now, Frode, you know you want to tell me."

Before Frode could verbally refuse, another voice interrupted them. "Isis!"

Turning to look past Frode, Isis felt her stomach leap into her throat with excitement. "Violet!" She ran towards her best friend since arriving in this time. The two women hugged one another tightly. "What are you doing here?"

Frode chuckled behind them. "That is your little surprise, Lady Isis. You can thank your betrothed for that. Bylur has been working very hard to come up with a plan to bring her here without *him* finding out."

Isis turned back towards the Translator, furrowing her brows in confusion. "Who is *him?*"

Violet sighed next to her. "He means Bodvar, the man I am set to marry."

"*What?*" Isis' jaw dropped, tightening her grasp on Violet's arm. "No, you cannot be serious."

Violet's lips trembled a bit. "I'm afraid so, Isis. I hate him. He is terrible, everything that is wrong in the world. I'm...I'm scared of him." She said softly, looking down at her feet as tears began to drop.

"The Volva will not allow the marriage to go through. Don't worry Violet," Isis reassured her, lifting a hand to rub her friend's shoulder.

"She may not have a choice, Isis. He is dangerous and adamant about marrying me. He could become violent if he is refused." Violet bit her lip.

Frode stepped forward, anger flashing in his eyes. "Then let him become violent. Bylur is prepared for that to happen. That wimp will be put down within an instant."

A commotion at the other side of the room distracted them as King Bylur stepped into the room, no longer adorned with any sort of fur coat. Instead, he wore a simple tunic and trousers, a soft smile on his face as he hugged his sister Agda. His eyes lifted, and his smile grew as he noticed Isis standing near Violet. He turned his attention to Frode, asking him a question in their tongue. Frode nodded before gesturing to another man that had stepped in behind Violet, a man that Isis recognized as Arne, Agda's husband.

Violet stepped towards Frode, gaining his attention. "Could you please tell this man who helped me thank you? He was very careful about escorting me here. He did an excellent job."

Frode nodded before relaying her message to Arne, who gave her a gruff smile before dipping into a small bow. He then walked across the room, greeting his wife and sitting next to her. Frode looked back towards Isis and Violet. "Well, shall we begin this delicious feast?"

Chapter Forty

"ISIS. STAY."

I sis was seated at Bylur's right hand. It seemed she didn't have much choice in the matter. Agda only giggled when Isis tried to sit elsewhere, and the shieldmaiden even pushed in the other chairs, so Isis couldn't sit in them.

Violet sat next to her, and Frode across from her. The three of them chatted easily, Bylur politely listening for a change. It felt nice to not be the one who didn't understand anything that was going on for once.

"Tell me about how things have been since I left. I want to know what your life has been like with all of the women moving into this village." Isis sipped her mead, trying not to look too concerned as she waited for Violet to answer.

Violet sighed, shoving some food around on her plate. "It's been interesting. A lot of fighting between the women,

209

especially with Amanda and some of the others. We've been trying to settle in and find our place here, to make ourselves useful. A lot of us don't want to just be pretty little wives. We want to be helpful to the village in more ways than that. But sadly few of us actually have skills that are useful here. I suppose that makes sense since we're used to electricity and such in the modern world."

Isis sighed. "I should have thought about that, too. It's a good idea, making ourselves useful. But I agree, I'm not sure what I could actually help with...I worked with computers before I came here. That's not so helpful here now, is it?"

Violet chuckled, shaking her head. "No, it isn't."

"Computers? What are those?" Frode frowned, looking between the two women, especially when they started laughing.

"What is our lives, Violet? This feels like straight out of a movie." The two women started laughing again as Frode looked confused once more. "It's hard to explain, Frode. They are new things...new inventions. I think it would be impossible to try to help you understand. Not that you are incapable of understanding, it's just that you have nothing close to it, so it would probably be hard for you to comprehend without us just showing you, which obviously we can't do."

Violet nodded along as Isis spoke before adding on, "But movies are stories. That's the context of what she was saying, that it's like a story we have heard before."

Frode's eyes widened a bit before he nodded. "I see. Many new exciting things in that future world of yours?"

The two women nodded before looking at each other.

Finally, Isis turned back to Frode, leaning her elbows on the table as laughter came from down the table, where apparently Arne said something funny to Agda. "Tell me, Frode. What can we do to help the village and settle in here? To make ourselves useful?"

Frode wiped his mouth and beard with a napkin. "There's not much until we go back to the city. Then we will help you all find a role you can fill."

"The city?" Violet asked, eyes darting between Frode and Isis.

Isis nodded towards her friend. "This is only a temporary place for us to stay. A small village for farming, I heard? Most of the people here, including Frode and Bylur, live in a much larger city. Is that correct, Frode?"

"Yes, that's right. It's only a few hours' ride from here. Not that long to get to. But we are really here for the Volva, since she lives here. Once things are settled with the marriages, we will go home," Frode replied, explaining the situation.

Violet cringed at the mention of the marriages. "I see. That is...unexpected. But welcome, don't get me wrong. So we'll be given ways to be helpful once we arrive there?"

Frode took a big bite of chicken as she spoke, nodding as he finished chewing. "That's right. It would be foolish to begin teaching you here, as things will all change once we return home. We can get you settled into our lifestyle once we arrive there."

Violet's shoulders sagged with relief. "That is good to hear. A lot of us were getting nervous and frustrated on why we weren't being allowed to help with anything."

"Yes, I can see why that would be frustrating. But that is the reason why. I am sorry that was not communicated to you all earlier. That is my fault. I should have realized that would be an issue." Frode scratched his head, a frown growing on his face.

Isis bit her lip, thinking. "Maybe it's not all your fault, Frode. I should be trying to help out as a sort of ambassador with the women. It only makes sense. That way I can come to you with any questions or concerns they might have. Maybe I can solve a few on my own without your help, even. Agda will help me."

Frode raised an eyebrow. "You have been busy with the Volva. You have been helping with the women in that regard. Besides, look how it turned out last time you went to visit the women. That awful woman yelled at you, Agda said." Frode scrunched his nose up in disgust at his mention of Amanda.

"I know, but you have been helping with the meetings with the Volva as well. I just think it could be better if we worked together," Isis replied with a sigh, enjoying her meal as they chatted. She cast a glance at Bylur, who seemed to be watching each person as they spoke as if he were trying to read them to understand what was being said.

"You make a good point, Lady Isis. I think working with you would be delightful." Frode smiled before turning and nudging his brother, saying something in their tongue in a teasing tone.

Violet cleared her throat. "I can help, too. I would very much like that. Our days can be long and empty, since we came to this village from the one we were placed in when we arrived here. We don't have much to do."

Frode lifted an eyebrow. "Very well. That can be arranged." The Translator tried not to smile as Bylur gave a playful punch to his arm. Clearly, those two were playing a separate game all on their own. "Hopefully this marriage matter with the Volva will be completed soon and we will be on our way."

Dinner continued on. A relaxed and easygoing atmosphere filled the longhouse as they ate and sipped their mead. Frode translated things with ease, switching between the two languages like it was no issue. Isis noticed that Bylur was not talking much about halfway through the night. As things continued on and still he did not speak, she furrowed her brows as she turned to Frode. "Is the King all right?"

"Bah, he's fine. You'll see." Frode chuckled into his tankard.

"What do you mean? He isn't talking much, Frode." Isis wished the Translator would quit joking around. She was beginning to get worried.

Frode waved her off once more. "He has a good reason to be silent and just listen. You'll see."

Finally, as the night drew to a close and Bylur still hadn't spoken up much, Isis felt a weight on her chest. She was concerned. She couldn't pinpoint exactly what her feelings were, but something about his silence bothered her. She was a confident woman, but something about his lack of addressing her made her feel almost insecure. Which bothered her, really. She shouldn't feel like a little schoolgirl desperate for his attention, even if she was falling in love with him...

As Agda and Arne stood up to leave, Isis felt her stomach sink to the floor. She turned, preparing to stand up and leave herself when she felt a gentle hand on her arm. Turning back, Bylur's eyes were fixed on hers, an intensity she hadn't seen within them since that day in the forest. "Isis. Stay."

Isis raised her eyebrows in pure shock. Had she heard that correctly? Had he just said an English word? Her gaze flew to Frode, who looked quite smug. He nodded once her eyes landed on him. "That's right. We've been working on learning your language. It has been fun. The choice of words he has wanted to learn first has been very interesting... Frode's eyes twinkled with mischief.

Isis looked between Frode, Bylur, and Violet, the latter of whom was still sitting next to her with a small smile on her face. Her friend finally nudged her with her elbow. "Well, what are you waiting for? Tell him you'll stay!"

"I...but Agda—" Isis directed her gaze towards the shieldmaiden, who began scolding her in her tongue, the words unfamiliar to Isis but the tone and body language clear enough.

Frode laughed. "She says you aren't allowed to use her as an excuse. She is perfectly capable of handling herself. She doesn't want you bringing her into this."

Isis flushed just a bit. "Sorry, Agda." The room grew silent as Isis looked nervously around. "What, am I supposed to announce to the entire room that I'm staying the night? That's a bit embarrassing, don't you think?"

Frode snorted through his nose. "Not in our culture. It is normal, especially in a family setting like this. What's there to be embarrassed about? The only thing that kept Bylur from moving you here into his house from the start was respect to the gods and the Volva. He wanted to make sure he had their blessing before doing that. And there was the matter of your consent to the marriage...but we all know that is no longer an issue." Frode winked at her, making her blush a bit more. "And so now it would just be a hassle to move you since we will be leaving for the city soon. You will get settled into your permanent quarters there."

"Okay, well...you can all quit waiting for me to say something. I am staying."

Frode laughed and clapped his hands, saying something in their tongue. It must have been the translation, because Agda burst into a cheer at once, rushing over to give Isis a pat, and messing up her brother's hair, who looked quite put off by the display of sibling affection. She then began to usher everyone out, giving Violet and Isis a moment to hug and say their farewells.

"Are you sure you'll be all right?" Isis frowned at her friend.

Violet gave a shrug before smirking. "Not as all right as you will be tonight, I'm sure, but..."

Isis gave a gentle smack to her friend's arm. "I'm trying to be serious here, Violet!"

"So am I!" Violet laughed. "Okay, okay...Yes, I'm sure I will be fine...I hope so, anyway. Let us hope your soon-to-be husband is able to handle the man I'm currently ensnared to, hm? I think he's pretty strong and capable. I'm willing to trust him."

Isis took in a deep breath. "So am I."

Violet smiled with a nod. "Good. Then I'll be all right, won't I? Well, it looks like I might anger the shieldmaiden if

I don't get out of here, so I best be going...besides, the longer I'm gone, the more chance there is for Bodvar to find out I'm missing and where I'm at. Let's hope he doesn't." The two women gave each other one last tight hug before Violet was off, being led into the shadows of the back door by Arne and Agda.

It was so silent in the house after they left. Frode had gone, too, so it was just Isis and Bylur. Isis turned back to find Bylur observing her, a small smile on his face. She took a step towards him. "How much English did you learn?"

He seemed to concentrate on her words before nodding. "Little." He showed his pointing fingers and thumb almost pinching, indicating a tiny amount.

That made sense. She raised her eyebrows. It was impressive he understood her question at all. It was hard to learn a language, especially one from a far future. She smiled at him. "Thank you."

He chuckled, taking a step closer towards her. He didn't seem to quite know what to say, and after a few more moments of comfortable silence—the two looking at each other as if trying to read one another's thoughts—Bylur slowly closed the gap between them until he stood just in front of her, raising a hand to a curl, tucking it behind her ear. "Beautiful Isis."

The words nearly took her breath away, her eyes widening as the words echoed inside her mind. His eyes were trained upon her as if she was the most beautiful thing he had ever looked upon, his gaze studying her every feature, as if he wanted to memorize her face. It felt almost as if time didn't exist at all, as if the Viking world and the modern world had faded away just the same.

No man had ever looked at her this way, with such eager adoration. Isis had always felt like either men looked at her as if she were the exact same as every other woman, or they saw that she looked different—too different—and wanted nothing to do with her. There had been no in-between.

But this...this look in his eye spoke of deep reverence. He looked at her as if she were special—one-of-a-kind—the only woman who looked like this for all of eternity. Like nothing could compare to her, that she was a masterpiece. She neither blended in with the others to him nor was she too different to be liked. He *enjoyed* that she looked different from him, and from the other women in his village.

And when he lowered his head down to kiss her, his lips only communicated that same message further. And then his hands joined in on that chorus, gently grasping her arms and pulling her close.

She kissed him back until she could think of nothing else except him. His lips, his hands, his warmth. His kindness. His strength. His leadership. His smile. How he protected her, observed her, how he made her feel. His dark hair, reaching his shoulders, his long beard, well-groomed and kept. His pale skin and blue eyes, how they never should have met, how impossible this moment was, and yet, as fate would have it...

Was this what it was like to have a soulmate? To be connected with them, against all odds? To find the place where you belonged within their arms?

Chapter Forty-One

STAYING WITH THE KING

Bylur broke their kiss, and Isis' chest heaved in excitement and longing as he began to lead her to another room. Isis could see a large bed of furs splayed out near another fireplace. The fire cast a flickering golden glow over the soft furs. Isis nearly felt like she was floating as they entered the room, the firelight dancing over Bylur's face as he turned to her, his eyes wild and wanting.

As he reached up and caressed her cheek, the expression within his eyes shifted, changing to one of absolute adoration. To be looked upon in such a way made Isis feel whole, like it was something she had been searching for her entire life without even realizing it, and had finally found it when she least expected. It made Isis' head swim and her heart flutter with bliss. To be wanted and admired in such a way, it truly felt like a gift she had not been expecting.

Within a moment, Bylur reached back down to join his lips to hers, their lips merging in a passionate dance. Their kissing was a delicate and slow song, with sweet, soft notes. But as they continued on, that song intensified, building in vigor until their song hit its crescendo, Isis' hands twirled within Bylur's thick mane of hair. His strong arms were wrapped around her waist, holding her, caressing every inch he could as if he would never get a chance to do so again.

Grabbing her by her thighs, Bylur launched Isis onto the bed of furs like she was barely a sack of grain, the man not even breaking a sweat. It left Isis breathless as she fell into the bed, barely feeling the furs tickle her skin as her focus was entirely upon her lover.

As the fire in the hearth danced, casting light and shadows over Bylur's form all at once, he pulled off his simple black tunic, revealing his strong physique underneath. Isis had been so lost in the passion of their union the first time they made love in the forest that she had never taken the time to study his gorgeous form, but her eyes drank in the sight now like she had been lost in the desert for days and had just found an oasis of water.

THE VIKING KING'S LOVE

His muscles were very evident, but he was still lean and trim. His abs were only highlighted by the shadows of the fire. His heaving chest displayed his pecs with every breath he took. But what captivated Isis the most were the black tattoos that crawled down his right side, covering his shoulder before trailing down his arm all the way to his wrist. The tattoos were swirling lines, weaving together like a patterned cobweb, or perhaps a tapestry of design, creating a beautiful piece of art upon his skin. Isis didn't know almost anything about this historic culture before she came here, but it almost reminded her of Celtic design, but not quite. It was unique in its own way, and it was breathtaking, a work of art most definitely.

As Isis raised her eyes from Bylur's body, she found his eyes trained on her, watching her study him. A smirk had found its way onto his lips, his eyes twinkling with pleasure at what Isis was sure was an awed expression.

While their union in the forest had been a blazing hot fire that burned hot and quick, this moment was a slow and steady flame—though perhaps not as bright—would still burn for hours on end. They knew they had time, there was no need for haste or desperation. But as Bylur stepped towards her, unbuckling his belt, the look in his eyes promised all of the fiery heat she could ever want or need.

Breathing in deep, Isis raised herself up, untying the back of her dress and beginning to undress, her eyes locked with Bylur's the entire time. At once she saw the appeal of watching him as he watched her, seeing his eyes widen at the revelation of her naked skin. As his eyes soaked in her image, his mouth fell slightly ajar. His chest only increased in its heaving.

Isis exhaled as she noticed at once Bylur's member stirring to life, creating a tent in his pants. It was addicting, seeing this incredible man from another time, another *world* entirely find her alluring and desirable. As his eyes raked down her body as she continued to peel off her Viking attire, Isis involuntarily shivered underneath his weighted gaze, bringing a smile to his lips once more.

His eyes lifted to meet hers. "Beautiful." His thick accent made the words feel accentuated, as if his effort in speaking her tongue, a language unfamiliar and new to him, made it all the more heavy with sincerity. Heat blossomed in Isis' chest, spreading up her neck and sending waves into her face. Not knowing what else to do, she smiled. She didn't know how else to express her appreciation and return the sentiment. Isis realized at once that she needed to follow his lead and begin to learn his language as well. She'd have to talk with Frode about it, but that was a thought for another time, as her mind returned its full focus to the gorgeous man in front of her.

Isis reached for him, and he smiled again, shrugging off his trousers before climbing on top of her. As their lips joined once more in a sweet embrace, Isis ran her hands down from Bylur's shoulders to his lip, feeling his skin underneath her fingertips. He pulled back, gazing into her eyes with such warmth and adoration. Isis' eyes flickered to his tattoos once more, lifting her hands back up to trace their marks on his skin, following the swirling patterns that decorated his ivory skin. He chuckled, the deep sound sinking into Isis' chest until she captured the sound within her heart.

Bylur reached back down, giving whispers of kisses on her ear and down her neck, speaking in his own tongue as he went, his voice low and husky. Isis breathed in a sharp intake of air at the sound, his voice heavy with want and desire. Goosebumps arose on her skin, and Bylur seemed to take notice, continuing to speak in his Viking language, whispering his sweet nothings against her skin in between his kisses.

Isis lifted her leg, feeling her skin brushing against his leg and up to his hips. Bylur chuckled, mumbling something in his language as he shook his head, his eyes filled with amusement as a smirk played on his lips. He reached down, his fingertips dancing against her skin as he traced down from her waist to her hips, then from her hips to her thighs where he grasped her skin, squeezing it within his large hands.

Looking down, his eyes focused on her breasts, and he leaned forward to kiss them, swirling his tongue around her dark nipple, sending electric jolts of pleasure throughout Isis. She released a breathy moan, and Bylur stilled, his eyes flickering back up to her face. His expression was covered with dark desire, his eyes filled with lust.

Clearly she was not the only one who enjoyed the sounds each other were making. His expression made her want to become louder, more vocal, to whisper every utterance of pleasure that he made her feel. She would do anything to be rewarded with that look once again.

Isis smirked, enjoying the heat of the moment as she reached down and grasped the flesh of his ass, causing him to chuckle once more. In a flash, Isis moved her hand to his member, softly running her hands over it. His chuckle quickly turned into a shuddering moan.

Bylur's eyes flashed with dark mischief. Isis raised one of her eyebrows, realizing she had just started something. She could only hope it was as earth-shattering as his lustful gaze seemed to promise.

Isis had no doubt that it would be. Bylur was an honorable man of his word, after all.

CHAPTER FORTY-TWO

THE FIRES OF LOVE

Bylur couldn't contain his moan as Isis ran her fingers across his sensitive skin. With the way she looked up at him, she knew full well what she was doing. Seeing her grow playful with him was a delight, it was everything he could have wished for and more. It made him grin down at her, enjoying the view of her beneath him.

She was beautiful. Everything about her. She lit up this room brighter than the fireplace that roared in its hearth, and every fiber of Bylur's being yearned to worship her in every way. He planned to give in fully to that yearning, now and for as long as he had breath within his lungs.

With Isis smirking up at him, Bylur felt himself relax for the first time in a long time. He became lost in the moment, without a single thought of anything else other than her, and her soft skin against his. He didn't realize, until that moment, how much leading his people weighed on him, ensnared him with thoughts of the future, making him unable to live in the present moment most of the time.

Bylur stepped back, chuckling at the disappointment and surprise written on Isis' face. Instead, he stepped to the side, choosing to lay down beside her instead. Before Isis had a chance to look too perplexed, he grabbed both of her hips, lifting her on top of him. His gorgeous Isis ran her hands over his chest, pure pleasure spreading throughout him at her touch.

Running his hands over her bare skin, he focused on her breasts once more, relishing in their full nature. With one swift movement, Isis grabbed his member, making him gasp, before sinking down on it. The two moaned at the pleasure of their physical union. It had been like his soul had missed hers ever since their time together in the forest, and now it sighed, finally at peace as they were reunited once again.

Despite his enjoyment of Isis' bold taking of initiative, he wasn't about to let her have full control. Bylur grabbed her hips, picking her up with ease and setting her back down, feeling the spike of pleasure course through him.

Their gasps of enjoyment filled the room, their lovemaking creating a sweet song of rhythm and unity. Bylur knew that this was how it was supposed to be, that such great passion for one another was a sign that the gods had blessed them and brought them together for a purpose.

Isis leaned down, her dark hair tickling the sides of Bylur's face as she kissed him, her full lips embracing his. At this moment, you could have convinced Bylur that Isis was an angel sent to bring him joy and love with ease. In fact, it didn't even take any prompting for him to think such a thing. As his hips continued to rise and fall, their hands explored every inch of one another. Isis pulled back, her face contorting in sweet pleasure as she breathed out his name.

"Bylur." She threw her head back, releasing an airy moan. The sight of her on top of him, experiencing pleasure, combined with the blissful sounds she was creating, calling out his name with such devotion, was nearly enough to send him over the edge.

Quickening his pace, Bylur removed one hand from Isis' hips, and instead, he snaked it down her body until his fingers connected with the soft flesh between her legs, making her entire body shudder as she released a ragged gasp. Beginning a slow circular pattern on her bud, Bylur watched her closely. He didn't want to miss a single moment of pleasure on her face.

"You're so beautiful, do you know that? Do you know how insane you make me? For your body, for your smile, for the comfort of your soul? If you don't know yet, you soon will, my love..." Bylur spoke into her neck, his lips speaking her praises against her skin. When he pulled back to look into her eyes, he recognized that Isis didn't understand a word he said, unsurprisingly, but understood the sentiment, the sparkle in her eyes telling him how she relished every syllable he spoke.

He chuckled as he leaned down to kiss her lips. "You are like a warm fireplace on a cold day. I only feel relief and comfort whenever I am near you. I wish to wake up every single day just to bring pleasure to you as I see on your face now. My very being cries out to keep you safe, to protect you from all harm...to vanquish those that threw you to the side as if you were not the Queen you are. Fools, all of them. You are the sharpest of swords, the most valuable of treasures..."

As he continued the precise circling between her legs, he drank in the expression on her face. Each moment fluctuated its nuisances, the slightest change shifting it from pure bliss to delighted agony. From excited elation to eager anticipation.

Bylur felt her body steadily begin to tense as sweat began to form on her brow, her sweetness beginning to tighten around her until pleasure exploded within her, causing her to cry out and grab onto his shoulders, pulling him close as if she was desperate for him. It took every ounce of Bylur's willpower not to give in to his own climax as her body gripped onto his member as if it never intended to let him go. Pleasure spiked through him, but he held onto his sanity, sweat dripping down the crevice of his muscular back from the control he was exhibiting.

Isis gasped and writhed on top of him, nearly collapsing onto him. "Oh, Bylur..." she breathed out, rattling something further off in her language, something that sounded suspiciously like a curse word to Bylur's ears.

The sweat glistened against her skin in the light of the fire like small sparkling gems all across her body. Isis blinked, settling down from the euphoria she had just experienced. Bylur had slowed his pace, still encouraging her high to course through her for as long as it could, but he did not wish to hurt her. If the wild days of his youth had taught him anything, it was how to precisely pleasure a woman.

Bylur raised his eyebrows as Isis pushed his hands off of her hips. He let out a moan as she began to rise up and down, setting her own pace as she took control of the situation. Not one to discourage someone who was eager to step up and show initiative, he watched her change her focus to pleasuring him. Her hands caressed him, as she reached back on either side of her and touched his thighs, running them up, past her own legs, before connecting again on his lower abdomen, and then rising until she cupped either side of his face tenderly.

Looking into her dark brown eyes, Bylur felt an emotion rise in the core of his chest. An intense knowing that this was *her*—the woman his mother used to speak to him about, the lover of his soul, his wife, his queen, his everything. Up until now, he had thought making Isis his queen had been a logical decision, but he realized now that his heart had been leading him the whole way.

His soul had been calling to hers ever since he had observed all the women of her village, looking for someone to choose as his spouse. He had noticed how diligent and purposeful she had been about everything she set her mind to, how intelligent and bright she was, how strong and hardworking she was, despite everything he now knew she was enduring.

His mother had always said *find the one your soul belongs with.* He never quite knew what that meant, but at this moment in the firelight, everything settled together like pieces of a puzzle solving itself in his mind. He had never felt like he belonged more in his entire life than he felt at this present moment in time. In his house, with this incredible woman, with a loving future established between them.

It could only be better if they were in his quarters in his childhood home, in the great castle that never felt quite as big to him as it did to everyone else. It was home, the only true home he had ever known. And everything within him yearned to share that with Isis Lozada in the same way that he now shared his heart with her. He wanted to see her settle in and change things until it was clear it was her home, too.

Flashes of scenes emerged in Bylur's imagination as he leaned up to kiss Isis. Roaming the fields with her, looking over the ocean with their hands entwined. The two of them talking long into the night, switching between their two languages as they conversed. Isis' stomach large with child, and Bylur leaning down to kiss their unborn child that grew within her. And then, finally, Bylur skipping over the green hills of his homeland with a young one on his shoulders with two others running around him. They were beautiful children and looked so much like their gorgeous mother.

Bylur could hardly wait for that future to unravel before him.

His thoughts were interrupted by Isis chuckling as his member had slipped out of her. Her laugh was glorious, her calm and cheerful demeanor filling the room as they made love. As she settled everything back into position, her giggling quickly switched back to the sounds of pleasure that had come before, but Bylur's heart still felt stuck on her soft laughter as he reached up to caress every inch of her skin.

Their love lasted late into the night, finishing and picking up again after some time. When they finally fell asleep, the fire had dimmed down into mere embers glowing in the hearth.

Isis' head laid on his chest, her hair brushing against his bare skin with every intake of breath. Her breathing was slow and heavy, lulling Bylur like the sweetest of lullabies as he drifted off into a sleep of his own, whispering into the air one final promise. "I will do anything for you, my lovely Isis."

Peaceful slumber washed over him like the many waves of the ocean, pulling him with its strong currents into the bliss of dreamless, comfortable sleep.

CHAPTER FORTY-THREE

VIOLET WEEPS

The warm sunlight of the morning sun bathed Isis in comfort and joy. Nothing was as blissful as this moment when Isis realized how bright of a future was ahead of her. Walking outside, she felt the fresh air caress her face. Waking up in Bylur's house had felt like waking up in a dream. She realized it was only the beginning, many wonderful things were ahead of her if last night was any indication.

"Good morning, Lady Isis. A fine day out, is it not?" Frode waltzed up to her, a giant grin on his face. "Although, I suspect it is especially fine for you."

Isis rolled her eyes at her friend. "You really enjoy trying to embarrass me, don't you? "

Frode laughed, his eyes sparkling with delight. "There's a special joy in causing your cheeks to redden, yes. What is a little playful teasing between friends?"

"Mighty bold for you to assume that we are friends, Frode. I have not declared that as of yet." Isis winked at him, a smirk on her face.

"Oh, dear. My apologies for being so thoroughly incorrect. How rude of me, to assume such a thing. Will you ever forgive me?" Frode gave her puppy dog eyes, his lips twitching with the urge to smile. It was clear he was trying to hold back a laugh.

Isis' smile grew to encompass the entirety of her face. "Perhaps. I shall consider it if you remain on your best behavior."

Frode laughed, wrinkles forming at the edges of his warm brown eyes. "I shall endeavor to do so, my lady. Although, I admit being on my best behavior is quite difficult for me. I like being mischievous too much for that nonsense. But alas, for you I shall try my hardest. Until then, you and I should discuss the matter of what will be happening today."

Isis raised an eyebrow at the serious expression that had suddenly fallen over her friend's demeanor. "What is going on today?"

"Today is the day we have all been dreading. Bodvar and your friend Violet are set to meet with the Volva today at our usual time. Preparations have been going on all through the night, including at the King's house." Frode said with a wink. Frode's humor sparkled for a moment before dimming once again. "But in all seriousness, we don't expect today to be pleasant. Bodvar will put up a fight if he does not get exactly what he wants. And we all know that is doubtful the gods will give him what he desires, not if they have any fairness or justice at all."

Isis clenched her eyes shut, feeling the dread of the day washing over her. "I see. This should be interesting at the very least. Is there anything that you need from me? Can I do anything to help?"

"Just to be on guard and to be yourself. We also suspect that your friend Violet will need you today. But other than that, no. We simply ask for your trust, as things might get...*heated*, but I assure you, I will let no harm befall you or Violet as long as I am physically able to protect you. You have my promise that I will do so until I am dead." Frode's eyes creased with intense sincerity.

Isis sighed, looking out over the village. "Well, let us hope that it does not come to that. I know that Bylur would be very upset should you die, which means things would become very bothersome to me. So do not annoy me by going out and getting yourself killed, hmm?"

Frode gave a hearty laugh, amusement finding its way back into his face. "I will do my best to honor that request, Lady Isis. And I request you do not go out and get hurt in any way if you can help it. It would be equally bothersome to me should anything hurt you. I know that Bylur would be quite furious with me, if such a thing should occur. "

"Yes, I believe he would." Isis scrunched up her cheeks into a smile.

"Well, shall we be off? No time like the present to deal with unpleasant matters such as these, I say. After all, we do not want to leave the Volva on her own for too long before such a tense meeting. I have heard word that she is already quite nervous enough as it is. Perhaps you and I can provide some solace for her. I can only imagine what she is going through at this present time." Frode lifted his arm for her to link hers through, as they did most mornings when they were heading to the priestess' house.

The walk to the Volva's home was brisk and rather pleasant. The pair shared kind conversation and playful banter the whole way there. For a moment, Isis could forget of the possible terror that lay before them if things should go awry. The spell was broken as soon as the priestess' house came into view. The sight reminded both of them what they were in for in just a short while.

A curtain was pushed aside in one of the windows on either side of the priestess' door, revealing the Volva peeking through, her face twisted in fear and anxiousness. At the sight of them, her expression relaxed ever so slightly, and the curtain fell back into place as she quickly moved to open the door, greeting them at once. She and Frode began speaking in the Viking tongue, exchanging comments back and forth until she ushered them in.

The trio made themselves comfortable as they waited, the priestess giving out some sort of dried fruit tea to her visitors, as she and the translator conversed quietly. Isis could do nothing but sit and wait, enjoying her tea in the meantime.

They all jumped when a knock arrived on the door, all three of them standing up in a rush. The Volva approached the door after they stared at it for a moment. The time that they had been anxiously anticipating had finally come.

Bodvar was a tall and hefty man with shoulders that filled the entire doorway, his long hair tangled in knots, with bits of food and debris still caught in his beard. His eyes burned with a threatening fire, as his lips stood upturned in a cocky challenge.

Leaning over to Isis, Frode whispered near her ear. "Remember, there are men waiting to storm this house in the case that he tries anything untoward. Breathe deep, relax, and help your friend as much as you can. We will get through this together. "

Isis nodded, breathing deeply in an attempt to calm herself down. She trusted Frode and Bylur to take care of her and to do the best for their village. They weren't going to let this man burn everything down just because he wasn't going to get what he wanted. This man may have followers, but was he as strong of a leader as Bylur? Isis doubted it. Bodvar was an emotionally charged man in his anger, and that desperation would cause him to be a weak leader. Bylur had no such insecurities driving him to prove himself.

Violet appeared once Bodvar fully entered the house, her smaller form had been hidden by his large stature. Upon seeing her friend, Isis rushed forward, embracing Violet in a tight hug. Bodvar clicked his tongue, pulling the two apart after a moment. He spoke in the Viking tongue, something that sounded suspiciously like a reprimand.

Frode grunted, turning to Isis with pursed lips. "He recommends not trying anything funny, and not being too friendly with his *wife*," he said with a look of disgust when the last word was in his mouth.

"Why can't I be too friendly with his...*wife*? We have been friends ever since we came to this time. We were neighbors and have been close ever since. Why would her new impending marriage change that?" Isis asked with a frown.

"I am not sure, Lady Isis. I do not want to question him at this time, either. I do not think he has much logic behind his actions, if you understand my meaning." Frode copied her frowning expression with one of his own.

The priestess interrupted their conversation with emotion to the chairs—a gesture that Isis was familiar with—to note that she wished to begin the ritual by asking the gods what their decision was regarding the couple. They all moved to join her in sitting, Violet following meekly behind before being yanked into Bodvar's lap with a squeal. Isis had never seen her friend so nervous and frantic, the blonde girl's limbs were trembling with fear. Though the other unwilling women had been unpleasant to witness before, seeing her dear friend like this upset Isis all the more.

As the Volva began her chanting and singing, and since filling the room with a sickly sweet aroma, Isis found herself praying along—to whatever might be out there, any merciful being that might listen to her pleas—to free Violet from this horrid man and to shut his violence down before it even started. She prayed for peace for all in the village. But most of all, she prayed for peace for these women who were forced into the situations of which they wanted no part.

The room grew silent as the priestess grew quiet, her eyes shut as she listened for the gods to speak to her. Isis recognized this as it was something she had always done in previous meetings. But Isis did notice that the priestess seemed especially intent on this occasion, her eyes shut tighter than ever before, her fists clenched at her sides until they turned ivory white. After what felt like an eternity to Isis, the priestess' eyes flew open, nearly startling Isis.

As the priestess began to make her pronouncement, Isis felt her palms grow sweaty as her stomach turned with anxiety. She knew within mere moments that the gods had rejected this marriage union. The priestess' voice held strength and anger that Isis had never heard from her before. Not only that, but she saw Bodvar growing redder in the face with each passing second, his fingers squeezing into the soft flesh of Violet's arms, her friend whimpering from the pressure.

Her desperate pleas to the divines grew more insistent with every passing moment.

When the Volva grew silent, her steel-gray eyes staring at Bodvar with a fierce intensity, the brutish man launched up from his seat, growling before beginning his tirade of yelling. Shoving Violet off of him, he dashed towards the priestess who looked at him with a serene firmness. Isis tried to catch Violet as she fell, but was unable to fully do so. Thankfully, her friend landed on the soft cushion of one of the seats. When Isis looked up once more she gasped, seeing that Bodvar had the Volva by the throat, her feet dangling several feet up in the air. Within seconds, Frode was at their side, tearing Bodvar away from the priestess and getting in between them.

Isis turned to Violet, who was shaking by her side. "We need to get help, and we need to get out of here. Now." Her poor friend could do nothing but nod as she followed Isis out of the house as quickly and quietly as they could. When Isis looked back, Bodvar was now tussling with Frode, the two men aiming for each other's throats with their respective weapons.

Opening the door and stepping out, she looked around for any sign of the warriors that Frode had been talking about before, or for her beloved Bylur. She found them in a group talking on a hillside not far away and immediately began to wave her arms in the air to draw their attention as subtly as she could. Her plan worked, drawing the men's attention right away as they had been looking for such a signal. They began striding towards their house with a determined gate. But within moments, Isis realized with horror that they were not the only ones watching the house for such a thing to occur. Out of the shadows came a dozen or so men, several of them Isis recognized as Bodvar's men whom she had met on other disturbing occasions.

It happened so quickly, and yet Isis felt like she was watching it all happen in slow motion. She could do nothing to stop any of it, she was helpless as she looked on. Bodvar's men and the strong warriors that followed Bylur began to clash, starting with fists flying through the air, and then leading to axes and swords clashing in the fresh air of the morning.

Isis knew she had to get out of here and get Violet to safety as well. Being in the middle of this would only result in both of them getting hurt or worse. Sneaking around the side of the priestess' house, she held tightly onto Violet's hand as they crept alongside by side.

With her heart hammering inside of her chest, Isis looked around the village for any place that could provide sanctuary for her and her friend. She could still hear the shouting and the clanging of metal echoing throughout the entire village. The sounds made her feel sick, and panic began to rise up into her throat, making it hard to think clearly. She considered fleeing to Agda's house but knew at once that if they were looking for her and Violet, that is one of the first places they would look, as was the king's house and the house for all of the foreign women. But unfortunately, those were the only places she was familiar with, other than the priestess' house.

Violet pulled on her shirt sleeve. "Look! There's a barn on the outskirts of town! We could lie low there until things are safer."

Isis nodded, following the line of sight that Violet was pointing to. There stood an old wooden barn, used to house horses from the looks of it. It wouldn't be a pleasant experience probably, but it was better than being caught up in the fighting.

Creeping in the shadows as much as possible, the two women made their way to the barn's door, opening it with a loud creak. They opened it slowly, trying to minimize the noise as much as possible, looking around for any sign that they have been followed or noticed. When no such sign appeared, they entered the barn, shutting the door firmly behind them and barring it.

"Should we find a hiding spot in here? In case they search the barn?" Violet asked, looking around the somewhat empty barn with fear.

"I think that would be best, yes. " Isis greeted one of the few horses that remained in this stable before looking for a good hiding spot big enough to house both of them. She found a wooden ladder that went up into the loft of the barn soon after, but Isis hesitated, biting her lip in worry. "I feel like if they were to search this barn, the first place they would look is up in the loft, don't you agree?

Violet nodded. "Oh, absolutely. That is the first place I would go to hide. It's the most obvious location to go if you were trying to remain undetected. Perhaps we should find something a little less obvious than that."

A few torturous minutes went by before another solution presented itself. Violet exclaimed as she pointed out a large trough that was filled with hay. "What if we pulled out half the hay and hid underneath the hay so it covered us?"

Isis bit her lip as she considered that option. "I don't know if it'll work, but I think it's a better idea than hiding in the loft, so I think we're going to have to try it. Maybe I should go in first and you can tell me if you can see me through the hay or not."

"I think that's a good idea. I hadn't thought about the amount of hay that could fully conceal us. Good thinking, Isis." Violet nodded, and the two girls set out to scoop the hay out of the trough as quickly as they could.

Soon enough they had finished their task, and Isis climbed in, Violet covering her with hay in a matter of seconds.

After another moment, Violet sighed. "I think it'll work. I'm just nervous about covering myself up good enough once I get in there as well. It's better when someone from the outside can do it for you."

"Do you want me to try to find another hiding spot, so I can conceal you properly? After all, it's more important that you are concealed and remain hidden than it is for me," Isis volunteered, her voice muffled by the hay.

Isis could hear Violet's disapproving tone loud and clear despite the barrier of hay that muffled her ears. "Are you serious? There is no way I'm letting you do that. After all, who says that it is more important for me to remain hidden? You are going to be the queen, Isis. He can use you as leverage or ransom. He can do so much with you, the future queen."

Isis admittedly had not thought about it like that before. Another element of becoming queen that Isis had never considered. There were now risks and threats to her life simply because of whom she was marrying. It was a concept Isis had never once thought would be happening in her life, this sort of thing just didn't happen in the modern world. Not to someone like her, anyway.

Isis sighed through the hay. "You have a very good point there." Despite the revelation, Isis knew there was a more urgent matter at hand. "Just get in and let's work together to do our best to conceal us both properly. And then we can hope that even if they do search this barn, they don't think to look in a hay trough. That's all we can do, right? Our best. That's all anyone can do."

"You're right, Isis. That's all we can do. Let's hope it's enough." Violet's voice was quiet when she finally spoke again. Isis could tell from the cracking of her voice that she was crying, holding back her tears from turning into hysterics.

Within a matter of minutes, they had properly concealed themselves underneath the hay, anxiously listening for any sounds of someone approaching. They waited for what felt like forever before Isis picked up on the sound of footsteps outside of the barn.

Someone was coming.

CHAPTER FORTY-FOUR

VILLAGE IN CHAOS

Bylur could see Bodvar in the priestess' home, fighting with Frode like two bloodthirsty animals. He looked frantically around for his beloved Isis, but as people flew about, warriors from each side fighting on the hillside, he saw no sign of her. Fear began to pound within his veins making him eager to finish this. He rushed into the house, giving a firm nod to the Volva, before pouncing on Bodvar.

Before his hands could lay upon Bodvar's form, his entire body was tackled to the side by one of Bodvar's men. A big ugly brute that had followed him into the Volva's house. The thirst for blood raged in the man's eyes with the same intensity as the sun, and Bylur was forced to will all of his desire—to keep his village and soon-to-be wife safe—into a fight with this brute.

Chaos continued to erupt all around them as they fought, and when he finally laid a good blow to the other's face, it knocked him unconscious onto the ground, but swiftly, another man stepped up to take his place. Minutes ticked by, and all Bylur could do was focus on making it through this next battle, overcoming his opponent.

When the dust cleared and all of Bodvar's men lay unconscious or were restrained, Bylur furiously looked around, calling out in the village for his beautiful Isis. When no answer reached his ears, he switched to calling for her friend Violet, hoping that she could understand him with his heavy accent. When still no answer returned to him, he instead switched his focus to finding Bodvar. When this proved to be difficult as well, he sought out Frode, whom he found rather easily, thank the gods.

Racing up to his adopted brother, he embraced him, both men covered in sweat and blood. "I'm glad to see you made it through, brother. What happened to Bodvar?" Bylur clenched his jaw, eager to hear his brother's answer.

Frode shook his head with a sorrowed expression upon his face, stroking his beard, matted with blood and dirt. "I do not know, my king. I fought with him for a little while before three of his men stormed us. In my desperate attempts to fight them all off, I lost Bodvar. I've been looking for him ever since with no good fortune. This is quite the issue we have on our hands."

"We need to find him, quickly. He knows he is cornered now. He will fight like a wounded and desperate animal, which means there will be no morals on the table for him. We need to find Isis and Violet immediately, he will seek them out first since the Volva is safe." Bylur gestured to the priestess that stood some distance away, talking with Shieldmaiden Agda. It was a relief to at least see his sister here and well. Bylur could use all of the familiar and helpful faces he could get at this present moment, with Bodvar standing against him, and the villagers causing a stir.

Frode nodded, his lips pressed into a thin line of concern. "I agree. However, I fear Bodvar is going to go after your queen first and foremost. And since I surmise his desired wife is with her, they are an easy target to collect together. Wherever those two ladies are, we can be sure that Bodvar will be. Which begs the question, where would Isis and Violet go?"

"My apologies for interrupting. But did I hear you say you were looking for Lady Isis?" The priestess stepped forward, drawing both of the men's attention to her.

Bylur felt his heart begin to race at the prospect of the Volva being able to provide an easy solution. "Yes, that is precisely whom we are looking for. We believe Bodvar will use her and her friend as ransom in the very least. Wherever they are is most likely where he will be, or at the very least will be trying to find them. We must find them first. So anything you can tell us would be greatly appreciated and helpful, priestess."

"Certainly, my King. I saw Lady Isis and her friend leave my home and sneak around the side, in the direction of Shieldmaiden Agda's home. And speaking of, here is the brave shieldmaiden herself." The priestess nodded towards an approaching figure, who Bylur recognized as his sister at once. "We may want to look in that direction first." Upon seeing Bylur's unconvinced expression, the Volva let out a laugh. "That is right, my King, we are not letting you and Sir Frode do this on your own. I think you need all the help you can get in the situation, and I can feel the gods on our side. They wish me to take part in assisting you."

Bylur felt his lips pressed into a thin line, allowing his displeasure at the prospect to show on his face. It was not that he did not trust the priestess, but that he feared her safety in the midst of it all. Bodvar had shown much aggression and violence towards her today already. He could only imagine what the man would do if he was left to his own devices given the opportunity. "Is that best, my priestess? You are a valuable member of our community. If anything should happen to you..."

"Trust me, my lord, I feel strongly about this. And I trust you, Frode, and of course, perhaps most of all, Shieldmaiden Agda to protect me if anything should go awry. I would not be doing this if I did not feel this strong urging to do so from the spirits above."

Bylur dipped his head in a show of concession. "Very well, Volva. I shall trust you and the gods to know what you are doing. And, of course, I know that they will take care of you, as they have always taken care of all of the priestesses that have come before you. Your feats are legendary and I shall not forget that. I am only merely concerned, as your king, to protect you and keep you safe. Your wisdom and insight are what keep our society safe and in line with the gods' wishes."

"I recognize that sentiment, my King. And I believe the gods do as well. Your respect and desire to protect have not gone unnoticed or been misinterpreted. I appreciate your looking out for me," the priestess said with a small and rare smile.

Next to her, Agda crossed her arms, a small smirk playing on her lips. "You are not thinking about trying to convince me not to come now, are you? It would be foolery to do such a thing, brother. You have to know that I am as determined as ever to be by your side and protect you wherever possible. Just because I am a woman does not mean that I cannot take care of myself. If you even attempt such a thing, I'm afraid I will have to demand that you do the same to Frode."

Bylur gave a bright, hearty laugh at his sister's words. "No, my dear sister. I would never dream of doing such a thing as trying to leave you out of anything. I know how fierce and strong you are, and how valuable you are to have at my side. I do not doubt your capabilities or skills, trust me. I need you more than ever, Agda. My queen is out there at risk of falling into the hands of my enemy. I shall not risk her further by denying you your right as a shieldmaiden to protect and be by my side. And even more so as my sister. I need you, I make no qualms about that."

"Very good, brother. You never have put me down for my femininity before, but I am always scared that you will start acting as many men have that came before you. I am always pleasantly surprised when you deny their masculine insecurities and allow me to serve despite my gender. I will be by your side no matter what, and we will find and protect Isis, together. Speaking of which, shall we?"

Bylur nodded, eager to begin his search for Isis. "Yes, let us begin at once. We need not waste time on such matters, as we see each other as equals. We have each other and we need each other, that is all that matters. Let us show Bodvar the foolery he has committed by attacking our family." Bylur turns to the priestess after he and Agda share nods and assuring small smiles. "Thank you, priestess, for your knowledge. We shall check your Agda's home first. I suppose it makes sense that she went somewhere familiar."

As they rushed to Shieldmaiden Agda's house, Bylur could not help but feel like a storm was brewing inside of him. One void of air to breathe, causing him to suffocate and his brain to grow foggy with uncertainty and fear. Everything he had set his hopes in was on the edge of falling off a cliff into the raging sea. He did not want to lose this. He did not want to lose *any* of it, but most of all he did not want to lose the one chance at love he had felt for the first time in his life. Isis was the only woman he had ever felt connected to, like their souls were intertwined and meant to be together.

And so he would fight for what was his. He would fight for all of the blessings the gods had given him. No other woman could serve as his queen like he knew Isis would. And with all the struggles and hardships that he would face as a king, Bylur knew resoundingly in his heart of hearts that he needed a steadfast and wise queen by his side for as long as he reigned and then beyond. He was confident Isis could fulfill that role like no one else ever could, seeing as she had been only so capable, strong-willed and unwaveringly brave.

The village was eerily silent as they arrived at Agda's home. The door creaked as they entered, the only sound in the vicinity. It was not a large home to search, and it only took a minute or two before the group felt assured that no one was hiding here. There was no sign of Isis, Violet, or Bodvar himself. This fact was neither calming nor alarming. The neutrality of finding nothing made Bylur feel rushed to find someone—anyone—to lead them to his enemy or his love.

It was quickly decided between them that the next place they should search through was at Bylur's own home. It was further past Agda's, but still in the same direction. Their walk was brisk and hurried, but it took everything within

Bylur not to sprint to his destination. His muscles ached and burned to run at full speed, rushing to find any trace of his beloved. The fact that he didn't find anything so far was nerve-wracking and caused him to feel so helpless.

As they walked on, shouting drew their attention away from their mission. Changing their course, they found a house that was on fire, people scrambling to try to put out the flames with piles of water. The process had been slow going, from the looks of it. Though, the people looked ragged and tired already. Bylur and his companions rushed to assist them as quickly as they could, forming a line from the well to the house, passing buckets of water back and forth as hastily as they could.

Once the flames were properly extinguished, Bylur turned to what he believed was the father that was surrounded by children, for this edifice seemed to belong to a family. "What happened here? We have not had a fire in our village, or our much larger city, in years now. We have always taken precautions to prevent such a disaster from striking. What happened today to make things different?"

The man bowed, signaling to the rest of his family to do likewise. "My King, we are not exactly sure. But I do have my suspicions. I saw a man wandering around our home shortly before the fire began, lurking about as if he had no good intentions. I tried to chase him off, but he simply ignored me with a smirk on his face. After some time I did not see him anymore, so I thought everything was back to normal. It was only a couple minutes after that when I noticed the flames had begun to grow on the side of my house."

Bylur raised his eyebrows at the alarming prospect of someone setting the fire. "And did you recognize this man? Most everyone knows each other in this village. There are not many of us living here, surely you knew the identity of this fellow?"

The man exhaled slowly as he nodded his head. "Yes, my King. It is one of Bodvar's men. His name is Hjalti. But I think that the fact he is a known ally and follower of Bodvar speaks loudly enough."

Bylur gave a grim nod of his head. "That it does, I'm afraid. It tells me everything I need to know, in fact. Thank you for your information and I'm sorry you had to endure this. We will help you rebuild and recover anything that was lost from the flames just as soon as everything's calmed down in the village. You are not alone in this, I assure you. Is there anything else I can do for you before I go on? I'm afraid we have another crisis at hand at the moment."

The man shook his head with a sorrowful look upon his face. "No, my King. You have done so much already. I thank you for your assistance with putting out the flames. We could not have done it without all of you. You have my thanks. Please, go attend to your other situation. I hope it turns out even better than ours. May the gods carry you swiftly to a solution regarding Bodvar. I can sense he has angered them fiercely already. Good day, my King."

Once they had left the man and his family's company, heading towards Bylur's own abode, Agda strode up beside him, an angered look upon her face. "What are the plans for dealing with Bodvar, brother? Surely something must be done to stop this terrible beast of a man. He has gone too far already and I believe that man was right. The gods are angered by his prideful and selfish actions. He has disobeyed them now, at least once that we know of, and he has turned this village into a place of chaos and turmoil. He has caused division and rebellion against you and the gods. This cannot stand, he cannot be allowed to carry on like this. Tell me that you have a plan and a course of action you will take against him."

"Sister, I ask for your trust as your king and your brother. You know that I trust you as a shieldmaiden and as my sister. It is why you are by my side now. I am asking for the same in return. I believe I will know exactly what to do when the time comes to carry out the will of the gods and put a final stop to Bodvar and his antics. At this moment, I cannot think of anything else other than protecting Isis. Until we have her safely among us again, and her friend as well, I cannot think of a future beyond that." As the party walked on, Bylur took note of his companions, listening to carefully heed to his words. Agda regarded him with an agreeable yet weighty look. Frode looked onwards and sometimes around, ever the vigilant watchman, yet nodding his understanding of Bylur's words. The priestess remained quiet, but would supply a slow nod as Bylur continued to speak. "We will sit down as a council and a community to decide Bodvar's fate once things have settled down and Isis has been recovered. As of right now, if we find him, I plan to capture him and restrain him for the time being. I think it should be decided as a united people what should be done with him. And then I will have the final word as the king. That is the way I want to lead, with my people, not against them. So, sister, do I have your trust?" Bylur laid a hand on his sister's shoulder as they walked, peering into her eyes and sharing a look of respect with her.

Agda gave a final nod of her head, a look of concern still written strongly upon her features. As they trekked, Agda replied, "Yes, you have my trust. I understand why you would not want to rush into matters. Having your community's input and support for the whole matter—especially since this issue arose from someone in the community itself—makes sense. Making sure everyone is included on that decision makes it rest on our people's back as a whole and not just on yours. It leaves little room for anyone getting upset over the matter and blaming you for whatever comes of Bodvar after all of this. You are a wise man, Bylur. I am proud to be your sister and your shieldmaiden."

Bylur choked back the emotion that had suddenly gripped his throat as he nodded toward his sister. All the while, they approached his house.

It was evident before they even stepped a foot into his house that something had happened here. The door was already ajar, and within, they could see furniture on the floor in shambles, many pieces broken and splintered. It took several minutes before they realized no one was here, although the place had been tossed as if they were looking for something.

"Bodvar was definitely here. But now the question is, did he find his quarry or did he leave disappointed and empty-handed?" Frode observed, a grim expression on his face as he looked around the house.

Bylur shut his eyes for a moment, breathing deeply and exhaling slowly as he searched his soul for an answer. He knew his heart was connected to Isis. He needed to trust his gut on the situation to know what to do moving forward. His gut had never pointed him in the wrong direction before, and he knew in this scenario, where it mattered most, it would not let him down.

Continuing to breathe deeply, he slowed his racing heart and mind to seek out an answer. His intuition perked up almost immediately, and soon, a strong sense hit Bylur—that Bodvar had not found what he was looking for here. Isis had never come to his house. A small relieved smile spread over Bylur's face at the calm reassurance that Bodvar had not found Isis here and had wasted time searching for her where she was not to be found. That meant there was still hope to catch up to Bodvar before he ever discovered where Isis and Violet were.

"No, he did not find them here. I feel this strongly. I'm afraid I have been mistaken to lead us here, as my Isis would know the first places anyone would look to try to find them. She would know that he would possibly search for her." Bylur's mind felt drawn to recall all of the many moments when he had watched her in awe before he decided to mark her as his. The moments when she showed she was beyond proficiency, ingenuity and grace. "She's incredibly intelligent enough to know these places would not be safe, which means she would flee to somewhere she felt no one would look for her." Bylur flickered his eyes open again to find the priestess smiling at him.

She nodded. "You are wise, my King. The spirits guide you now, as they should. I feel you are correct on the matter. Do you have any other inclination on where she might go? Trust that feeling you are having. Let it guide you wherever it wishes to lead."

Bylur frowned, thinking about the priestess' question. He was not sure, no sudden and certain answer came to mind about any possible location she might have fled to. "I am not sure. Give me a moment to think about it and sense what may come to me."

The group nodded as they gave him time as he requested. After several moments, Frode crossed his arms leaning against one of the walls. "If she would have selected somewhere in this village that no one would have thought her to flee to, then that means it would have been neutral ground for her, somewhere probably unfamiliar, and someplace unexpected. This means we only know of a couple of places it would *not* be and many, many places it *could* be, meaning it could be almost anywhere in the village and perhaps even beyond. Searching at random seems unwise and inefficient. It turns this into a game of chance instead of logic and strategy. This means there would be just as much chance that Bodvar could find her and escape with her hours before we ever even find out, just as much as there is a chance that we find her immediately and Bodvar never does. It seems unwise to take such a risk."

A brief moment passed wherein the group silently thought to themselves, before Bylur spoke. "You are right, brother. It does seem unwise to do such a thing, and it is not a gamble I am willing to take, not when my future wife is on the line. She is too valuable to risk like that, which means we need a better strategy than that. I have no inclinations towards anywhere she could be. If anyone does, please speak up immediately as soon as it comes. All of your insight and skills are welcome and valued here. But for now, I say we leave here, as we know neither Bodvar nor Isis is here, and go where the wind takes us, I suppose." Bylur declared the end with a sigh. It was as if his intuition from the gods were short-lived, but he would not be deterred by that, if it were the case.

The entire group agreed as they left Bylur's house, and as they did, a cold wind blew into the village, chilling their bones. As they arrived outside, a group of people approached them, unhappy expressions on all of their faces.

One of them quickly raised questions. "My King Bylur, what have you to say about this entire Bodvar situation? Do you have no solution for us? No answer to why any of this happened? Is it not your responsibility as king to solve this? Was it not your fault to begin with why an uprising would even begin? Please, my King, we need answers. This is not the time for silence but for taking responsibility. We need you to step up and admit that you are at fault here."

A flash of anger burned through Bylur's entire body. It felt terrible, to feel so helpless against Bodvar's actions against him, helpless to find and protect Isis in this moment, and to be accused of being at fault for it all made everything amplify. Were they correct? Was it his fault that any of this has occurred?

If he had been a better king, would Bodvar have rebelled against him as he did?

Was Isis' endangerment his fault?

CHAPTER FORTY-FIVE

BODVAR'S HUNTING

Bodvar felt his anger grow, like an aching hunger building in his belly and burning through his entire body. Sitting in the Volva's seat at her house and observing her performance of prayer, he felt the heat rise up his neck and into his cheeks. He knew already that she was no real priestess, but a charlatan that worked for the so-called King. She would do exactly what he wanted her to, as the two had clearly already come to an agreement. She would sell out her religion and play the part of a priestess but deny the gods their actual wishes, and Bylur would give her something in return.

The king had become her god now, and Bodvar could not stand for such blasphemy. The blonde girl that shivered in his lap was neither here nor there for him. It wasn't like he loved her or desired her specifically, but it was the principle of it all. He had chosen her over other women, yes, for she physically appealed to him. But he would do just as well with any other woman. However, if he was denied his selection, it would be a personal offense, and he could taste the affront that was heading his way on his lips already, for all this time the king and his minions had been against him so foolishly and without sufficient reason.

The priestess would deny him, of this he was sure. But it was not because of the gods' will like she claimed. It was not even because of the girl that sat in his lap. No, it had everything to do with Bodvar himself and the threat he posed to the king. He was not totally sure how the king managed to get the priestess over onto his side, but there were many ways to do such a thing. Wealth, opportunities of power, or perhaps she had feelings for the puny king. Bodvar did not know, and frankly, he did not want to know. It was irrelevant to him, the true facts remained the same. She was a deceiver, and the king was feeding her the lines of lies she was supposed to tell. This girl would be his wife, out of the pure principle of the matter. He had chosen her, and his honor would not be denied.

271

Weeks of built-up anger burst through him when the priestess finally pronounced his denial. All he could think of doing was snapping the filthy liar's fragile neck. And when the big bad translator stepped in to defend her, Bodvar wanted to laugh in his face. Frode had chosen this pathetic path of scholarly inquisitions and had set himself up as the king's right-hand man without so much as a battle to prove himself. In Bodvar's opinion, Frode was too weak to fill the position he was in. He spent more time reading books and learning new languages than he did honing his fighting skills or practicing any talents for strategy. If he had any, that is. So it came as a surprise to Bodvar when Frode put up far more of a fight than he imagined, though he would never admit this out loud.

As both Bylur's men and Bodvar's men stormed into the house, and one of Bodvar's warriors got in between him and Frode, Bodvar was able to step back and observe everything that was going on around him. That was when he saw the King's chosen woman, the one that they called Isis, the one that would be queen if Bylur got his way.

Bodvar had always found Bylur's choice of women to be interesting. Isis was not the one Bodvar would have ever selected. Indeed, he had once looked upon her before he knew that Bylur had chosen her, and had dismissed her without a second thought. He did not even recognize her until some time after being reintroduced to her. He had laughed out loud when he finally understood that the woman he had evaluated and had found lacking was supposed to be the future queen. It spoke of Bylur's incapability as a leader, for him to choose such a woman.

But now his interest had been sparked by that revelation, that Bylur had chosen her. What did the king see in her? Or perhaps he had chosen at random, although that did not seem likely to Bodvar. Something drew the king's attention, and Bodvar wanted to know what.

And so when Isis slipped out of the Volva's house, dragging behind his own selected wife behind her, he felt the heat of anger burn brighter in his chest as it condensed down into one singular, focused ember that blazed like the sun within him. A fire spread out and burned too hot, and too quickly extinguished easily. Bodvar did not want that for himself or this goal he was trying to achieve. With renewed understanding of what he needed to do, he allowed his anger to focus on one place, one thick coal of enraging fire that would not be put out so easily.

He focused on that singular point of anger as he was forced to resume his fighting, as Frode came at him once more with a battle cry. He was able to push off Frode's attention onto another one of his warriors before he was intercepted by one of the king's warriors, much to his frustration. It was several more minutes before he was able to free himself and leave the battle, huffing with labored breath, as he went in the direction he had seen the two women go towards. There was no sight of them as he looked around the village, much to his further frustration. He could only think of one place that she would go. She would flee to where she felt safe, a sanctuary where she had been promised solitude and security. There was no other such place than in the king's house itself.

Charging into the larger house, he felt bitter disgust at the level of wealth that the king held. He also felt something he refused to acknowledge, the undeniable pain of jealousy, which he suppressed as he had many times since he met Bylur. His mind had to remain a steadfast source of righteous indignation or else he feared he would crumble and crack under the weight of his selfish motives, though he would never admit that to himself.

There was not a sound to be heard as he entered the house, and his own labored breathing seemed loud in the midst of the otherwise silent atmosphere. His ears refused to pick up any sound as he strained to listen, hoping to hear even the slightest scratch of a noise to lead him to where the two women must be hidden.

"Come out and play, two little pretties. There is no use in hiding from me, I am one of the most prestigious trackers in all of the Great City. I have traveled many seas and many continents on our longboats. There is no one who can hide from my perceiving eyes. Come and give me what is mine, little women. Or else I shall take what is currently *not* mine and make it my own." Bodvar could not help but grin as he stepped through the house, beginning to throw furniture around like they were weightless toys, breaking them in the process.

He stepped over the shattered remains as he continued on, his frustration building with every passing moment that he did not find them. It was an impossible notion that anyone could conceal themselves from the Great Bodvar, especially two foreign women from their strange and pathetic time. He had never seen any of these women have any of the womanly duties that Viking women usually were taught to have.

It was a bit of a hassle, but Bodvar knew how to make do. He had not been raised to whine and complain, but instead to do what needed to be done and to be resourceful at all times. This would be no different.

As it quickly became apparent to him that there would be no finding the two women here, Bodvar roared, cursing loudly as he began to thrash about the house, breaking as much as he could in his anger. His lungs burned from the exertion once he had finished, his chest heaving from the effort. Storming out of the house, he looked around the village, unsure of where to go next. If the woman did not hide in the security of her lover's home, then where would she go? He could go to that blasted shieldmaiden's house, but he felt that if she had not fled to the king's house, she would not go there, either.

Bodvar stood outside of the King's house for a minute, feeling the cold wind whip around him, cooling his heated body. It seemed a cold storm was coming in over the skies of the village, enforcing the feeling that the gods were truly on his side. And if that was the case, would they not lead him directly to where he was supposed to be? Would they allow him to fail now when he had risked everything for them? He was not a fool to hold such disbelief. His faith was strong, as was his will to finish this.

As he looked about the village a flutter of movement caught his eye. The barn door to the old horse stable had flung open in the strong wind and was now whipping back and forth from the unseen force. A wolfish grin spread over his features as it nearly beckoned for him to come closer.

The gods had not abandoned him after all. He knew that they never would.

The creaking of the barn door screeched like an owl as he approached, calling to him like an angry old woman. As he stepped into the barn, he noticed immediately that someone had attempted to bar the door closed, but had fastened it incorrectly. A chuckle emitted from his lips at the revelation. No Viking would ever make such a simple error, as they all spent much time in barns like these as children, doing chores and other tasks that were assigned to them, such as riding the horses or milking the cows. No, only someone who had no familiarity with stables such as this would fail at something as simple as this, especially if they moved with haste. This was a sign that he had been looking for. He knew in his very bones that the two women he looked for were in this barn.

The sound of his leather boots hitting the hard-packed dirt ground of the barn echoed within its walls. He could not help the ever-growing wolfish grin that spread over his features, not when the thought of the two women quaking in their boots at the sound of him entering filled his mind. He was a predator that loved to be feared, and he was in his element, stalking his prey.

The wooden ladder creaked with a strain of his weight as he made his way up into the upper loft of the barn. Hay was strewn all about, although most of it was in neat bales. Several minutes went by as Bodvar peeked behind every single square bale of hay, tossing them about as his muscles burned. He soon realized no one was up here. Feeling a cold sweat breaking out over his body, the fear that he'd been mistaken about the location of where they were once again crept upon him.

He had not risked everything to fail now. And so, he would not do so.

He began to search every single stall of the barn, throwing open every door with a loud bang as he thoroughly searched the barn from top to bottom. Clenching his hands at his sides, he gritted his teeth as he stepped back into the main aisle of the stables. He stared at the main barn door he had entered, which was now properly closed. He had made sure to shut it behind him as he entered, in the case that King Bylur somehow managed to track him. He did not want him seeing the open barn door waving about like an invitation as Bodvar had.

Charging over to that door, he removed the bar from its place, reaching to open it and depart from this place. Right before his hand met the wood of the door to push it open, a thought itched inside his mind, causing him to stop where he stood. As he had approached the door, he had not even realized something he had observed. A strange sight returned to him in his mind's eye, something that did not belong. Taking a few steps back, he looked over to the second stall on his right, which stood empty. He had already searched there to no avail, as the stall was completely empty other than a trough filled with hay.

A great big grin stretched his lips wide as his eyes focused on the site that had bothered his mind enough to stop him.

A singular brown leather boot peeked out slightly from beneath the hay in the trough. Now that he considered it, the vessel was big enough to possibly hold two grown women if they squeezed together uncomfortably. And if they covered themselves with hay, who would think to look there? He nearly had not, and he was the best there was when it came to finding prey trying to hide themselves from predators such as him.

But unfortunately for them, he was the finest of hunters, and no prey outsmarted him. He figured it out eventually, as he always did.

CHAPTER FORTY-SIX

PARALYZED

I sis felt paralyzed in the cold wooden trough she was curled into. Time seemed to go in slow motion, every beat of her heart felt like it took three minutes to happen, even though she knew it was pounding in her chest. Hay poked and scratched into her skin all across her body, but she ignored the urge to itch that was trying to consume her. The adrenaline of watching and hearing Bodvar walk around and search the barn was enough that she was able to control herself. The fear of being found was far too strong to allow any foolish mistakes such as that.

Isis watched him from a small crack in the trough, her heart racing as he looked all around, looking like a bloodhound on the hunt, sniffing them out. He looked this way and that, but could not find them. Her lips curved in satisfaction as the horrid man growled in frustration, storming towards the barn door to leave. It pleased her to see him become so emotionally distraught at his loss. His red face felt like a reward to Isis for a job well done. *They had done it.* Now, all they had to do was wait for Bylur and the others to come to find them, preferably after they restrained Bodvar from causing any more trouble.

Everything was going to be okay. They were safe from this beast of a man, and Bylur was going to stop him, once and for all. It could only go up from here.

Isis nearly allowed herself to breathe a sigh of relief as she heard Bodvar unbar the door. But she would not take such a risk just yet. But her heart slowed, and the smile was wide upon her face. A burst of delight warmed her chest at the thought of besting the horrible brute.

The barn stood still and quiet for a moment, leaving Isis straining to listen for any sounds of his further departure. Where had he gone? Why was he hesitating in leaving?

When a sound finally emerged once more, Isis' stomach churned with horror, her heading spinning with fierce terror.

The sound of footsteps was growing louder, not quieter. And when he came into view once more, Isis felt like screaming, her legs itching to run away with all their might, her heart feeling like it was going to explode in her chest.

The grin the man had on his face felt like that of a demon, like a bloodthirsty animal who knew he had cornered his prey. Isis did not want to be treated like a little mouse, easily caught and quickly devoured. The fear that had swelled up inside of her at being hunted like this was nothing like she'd ever experienced before, and something she never wanted to experience again. There was nothing worse than feeling like prey, especially not the prey of this monster.

Her mind raced to find some way to escape, to conquer him, to save herself, but there was no solution, certainly not one she could think of in time. She was caught, with no hope of escape or salvation. She wanted to scream for help, but she was frozen in fear, her vocal cords iced over in terror, her body stiff and unmoving as her brain was bogged down with panic.

As Bodvar stalked towards them like a grinning wolf ready to feast, Isis felt her fear grow anew in ways she had never thought possible.

He was a greedy, bloodthirsty hunter, and she was just a meek little prey, unable to even beg for mercy from a man who was merciless.

KENNEDY THOMAS

They had been found.

CHAPTER FORTY-SEVEN

PROTECTING ISIS

Bylur was about ready to scream at these fools, unleashing all of his anger upon them with a single stroke of his fist. He could contemplate their accusations another time. The matter of finding Isis before Bodvar did was far too urgent for this. Even if they were correct that he was at fault in all of this, he could not take the time to consider such things now. He could deal with the guilt or the lack thereof another time. He could not afford to consider such things when they could cost his beautiful Isis her life.

He took a deep breath, closing his eyes and trying to focus. "Are you even listening to us, King Bylur? We are your loyal people, whom *you* serve as King. You should be patiently listening to our every word and taking heed of what we have to say. We have great wisdom to offer, you know, and to refuse to listen is a mark of arrogant foolery."

Bylur's eyes flashed open at the angry man's words. He knew what he had to do, and it was *not* to listen to these people and their complaints at this very moment.

He took a deep breath before regarding the crowd forming around him, Frode, Agda and the Volva. To speak over the worried whispers of the crowd, Bylur spoke loudly and firmly. "I respect you and will gladly take heed of what you have to say another time. I am afraid, as of right now, we have a more urgent matter on our hands, which needs to be dealt with immediately.

"I understand you are concerned for yourselves, your family, and our people overall. As am I. Bodvar will be stopped and taken care of at once, and the council and I will work hard to resolve the issue peacefully. We will also discuss why it may have happened and what we can do to prevent it from ever happening again. If it is my fault, I assure you it will be dealt with and I will change matters accordingly. I asked that if you cannot trust me, you will trust the elder council and their wisdom. Any further concerns you have can be brought before them when we are all brought together.

"We would love for you to present your concerns at that time. Until then, I have important concerns of my own to deal with, so I must be going now. I thank you again for your wisdom and will see you at the gathering of the council."

With that, Bylur scanned his eyes over the village, barely listening to the growing yells and accusations that the people were now pestering him with. Trying to not focus on their outroar, his eyes wandered and began to notice the subtle outlines of large footsteps in the mud, those belonging to the boots of an extremely large man, and they led both to and from Bylur's own home. He knew his own footprint, these did not belong to him.

There were many men in this village, but none quite as large or brutish as Bodvar. A deep stirring inside of Bylur's chest confirmed that this was indeed what he was looking for. He gave final nods of his head towards Frode, and the other to the people, despite their pointing fingers and red faces. Frode would do well in his task to appease the crowd.

Turning away from them, he began to follow the footsteps, which led to the old barn on the outskirts of the village. He was keenly aware that Agda was close behind him, making sure the crowd did not follow.

Bylur tuned out the sounds of the villagers shouting after him as he approached the old structure. His entire body leapt into action once the sounds of voices and a struggle reached his ears. His entire body vibrated with the need to defend his Isis as he heard her voice cry out.

Throwing open the barn doors, he stepped inside to see Isis dangling off of the floor, gasping for breath as Bodvar held her in his grasp. Unleashing a brutal war cry, Bylur charged towards Bodvar with all the fury of a man in love. Grappling onto Bodvar's outstretched arm, Bylur twisted it until Bodvar released Isis with a ragged cry of pain. Isis dropped onto the floor, coughing and choking as she tried to regain her breath.

"Do not lay a hand on her, you son of a wench." Bylur growled as he threw a fist into Bodvar's nose, throwing his weight into it until the other man toppled to the ground.

Before Bodvar could even stand to his feet, King Bylur was on him again, attacking him with a viciousness only a Viking could produce. Perhaps Bodvar had been furious in his denial before, but he did not have the pure wrath and fury that Bylur had at this moment. Everything within him was that of a man desperate to save the woman he loved and angered that any other would lay a hand upon her.

Bylur did not even feel the aching in his fists as he pummeled the other man. He did not realize how long they had been fighting, either.

All he knew was he had to keep the other man down in order to protect everything he loved.

And when his siblings joined in on the fight, assisting him and keeping the other man down, he was thankful for their support. Violence was a necessary thing, but it was not pleasant for him in the slightest, even in his anger.

Agda gathered leather reins that were used for the horses and used them to securely restrain Bodvar. As they settled down and the fighting stopped, Bylur finally realized just how exhausting this day had been already. He turned around to see Isis, Violet, and the priestess talking in one of the stalls. Their words were quiet, barely reaching his ears as he approached them.

"Isis, are you all right?" he asked as the beloved woman rushed into his arms.

She nodded, seemingly understanding his question in spite of it being in his tongue. Her embrace of him was tight, an indication that she was not as strong as she was trying to present herself as, which was to be expected. He would be more concerned if she *wasn't* shaken after this experience.

He stroked her hair gently as he held her, feeling her tremble in his arms, making his anger burn all over again. There was nothing he wouldn't do for her, nothing that could stand in between him and his beloved queen. He pulled back, cupping her face tenderly, stroking her cheeks with his thumbs. "Thank the gods you are safe, my love."

Isis spoke something in her tongue to him—her voice tender and sweet—before she grabbed his face and kissed him. Bylur melted into the kiss, enjoying the incredible passion which she embraced him with. Now that they were reunited, Bylur never wanted to be separated from his Isis.

He clutched her close, breathing in deeply of her scent, feeling her heartbeat against his. This was home. This was where he belonged, with her and only her, and together, he knew they could do great things. Perhaps the Elder Council was right and he was a great king, but he knew that he could only be the very best of rulers with Isis by his side.

After several long moments, where nothing else mattered but the fact that Isis was safely in his arms, Isis pulled back, tears streaming down her face, which Bylur quickly but gently wiped away. They nodded towards each other, an understanding of their love for one another passing between them; an expression that spoke a thousand words, and yet none at all.

Bylur turned, observing the scene around him and sharing a respectful nod with the Volva, who had her arm around Violet. It was not long before Frode joined them, his brother reaching for the blonde maiden but pulling back before anyone noticed it. Unfortunately for him, Bylur had the perception of an eagle, especially when it came to his brother's behavior, meaning he did not miss the gesture.

Frode spoke in the rapid tongue of the modern women, his question seemingly directed to Isis, who had returned to Bylur's embrace, holding him tightly. She pulled back slightly at his voice, wiping a few more stray tears that had managed to escape from her eyes. She replied to him, her voice cracking slightly with emotion, making Bylur want to pull her into his embrace once more. Everything within him was begging to keep her safe and at ease, to comfort her and take on her pain if he could.

Isis held on to him for several more long moments before she eventually pulled back, giving him a sad smile and patting him on his arm. She then turned to embrace her friend, who seemed much more upset than even Isis was.

The two women held each other for a long moment, crying in each other's arms.

Bylur felt helpless as he watched, wishing he could save both of them from the anguish they were currently experiencing. The fact that they had been taken from their time and home, only to go through this terror, which Bodvar had inflicted upon them, felt wholly unfair and left a sour taste in Bylur's mouth.

He would never let something like this happen again.

CHAPTER FORTY-EIGHT

A BROTHER'S LOVE

Bylur watched as Isis and Violet went over to a hay bale and sat down, with Violet speaking in soft, sad tones as Isis nodded, listening. Bylur turned to his brother, observing the conflicted look on Frode's face, which Bylur knew exactly was about. He felt the same thing in his heart, but he was able to pour it out by loving and comforting Isis. His brother could not, or at least, that was most likely what Frode was thinking.

He was wrong, and Bylur needed him to know it.

Bylur turned to Frode, placing a gentle hand on his brother's shoulder. "You should comfort her, Frode. She has need of all the support she can get at this time. Do not be afraid of further upsetting her. Have no expectations and simply try to comfort her. Be a friend first and foremost.

Do not let fear hold you back." Bylur recalled his own experiences of befriending Isis back in those woods, having no expectations other than getting to know her and helping her if possible, such as when he joined her and helped her as she was washing in the stream.

Frode raised his eyebrows at Bylur's insightful advice. "I see I have been discovered. I shall have to keep it in mind that very little gets past you, brother. Yes, you are correct. My fear holds me back from taking steps towards even considering such a thing as romance with your queen's friend. However, you have exposed me just a little. You are right, I should be focusing on comforting her in this sorrowful moment, not for any reason other than the fact that she needs comfort and support. If anything further should develop, it should be once she is recovered from this ordeal. I once again thank you for your honesty and guidance."

The two men turned to observed Isis and Violet. The two women hugged, laughed, and cried together, almost as two sisters might. The sight made Bylur's heart ache, especially as his own sister stepped forward, embracing the two other women with tears in her own eyes. It was amazing how quickly Bylur's family had quickly expanded, for which he would be eternally grateful.

The priestess chuckled from where she stood a small distance away. "You are wise, King Bylur. There is nothing a woman despises more than affection with an agenda. Freely give your comfort to her, and she will not be quick to forget it. But if you tie ulterior motives to your every action like reins on a horse, you should not be surprised when she rears up in defense, for a woman is not a horse to be owned."

Frode gave a small grimace as he listened to the Volva's words. He nodded his head with a pain-filled smile. "You are right, of course, priestess. I would never wish to attempt to control any human being, much less someone I held feelings for. I will remember your wise words and keep them into account moving forward. Even if my motives are to try to simply develop something with her, it is not fair to impose that on her at such a vulnerable time. Being a comforting friend is better than being a despised reject. Thank you both for your guidance. I will not put it to waste."

"I knew you would not, brother. This is why I said something. Because I knew you would listen, even though it is hard for a man's pride to sometimes listen, especially when love is involved. But I know you are stronger than to let your ego stand between you and the truth. I applaud you for your courageous teachability." Bylur chuckled as he clapped Frode on the shoulder once more. He nearly felt like applauding his brother for how easily he took the gentle reprimand. It took a brave and strong individual indeed to welcome correction in such a way.

After a few moments of silence in the stable, Frode let out a long exhale as he looked over his shoulder towards where Agda was keeping a careful eye on Bodvar. "So, I suppose a question is now, what to do with this blasted troublemaker? How do we move forward from here?"

Bylur grew solemn, furrowing his brows as he stared Bodvar down. "We let the Elder Council decide. And, in the meantime, we take care of ourselves, our people, but most of all, these women that have been terrorized by his beastly behavior."

Frode chuckled, nudging Bylur in the side. "I have a few guesses how you will take care of Isis."

Bylur turned, leveling his brother with an icy glare. "Do I need to inform you where you can stick those guesses, brother? No? Then keep them for yourself. Perhaps, in time, you will need them. Trust me, I have plenty of ideas of my own. You should concern yourself with your own love life, not mine."

His blasted brother gave a dramatic roll of his eyes. "But why would I do that when your love life is *so fun* to meddle with?"

Bylur narrowed his eyes at Frode. "I will throttle you."

Frode cleared his throat, trying to appear serious, but a shadow of a smile remained upon his lips. "Yes, of course, *my King*. Whatever you wish."

Bylur sighed, nudging Frode towards where Violet and Isis sat. "Stop being a fífl and get your ass over there. Your sass isn't helping anyone, including you. Go comfort her."

Frode stumbled forward, glaring at Bylur over his shoulder. "Yes, your Highness. Heavens above, you are bossy..."

"I'm your king," Bylur challenged, his brow arched even as he smirked at Frode.

Frode rolled his eyes once more. "You're my brother. We all know it's not my king that is giving that command, now is it?"

Bylur's smirk only grew. "Perhaps. Still, it's solid advice. *Go.*"

For the next few minutes, Bylur contained his laughter, sharing humorous looks with the priestess as Frode slowly inched over to stand beside the three women. Agda paused as she noticed Frode, who was awkwardly shifting his weight between his two feet, looking around the room as if it wasn't the most obvious thing in the world.

After a few moments of Agda looking at him in confusion, she spoke up with her brows arched in amused confusion. "Frode? Is there something you want, brother? You are standing strangely."

"Well, no, I...no." Frode cleared his throat, and Bylur could barely contain his laughter. His usually composed and charismatic brother was suddenly clammy and shy.

Agda arched her brow for a moment, looking over Frode's shoulder at Bylur. Frode stepped in front of her gaze, trying to block Bylur, but it was too late. Bylur hastily pointed towards Violet, drawing the attention of Isis and Violet. Agda laughed, tapping Violet on the shoulder before pointing towards Frode.

Violet turned fully to face Frode, her blue eyes wide as she questioned Frode softly in their foreign languages. Bylur enjoyed the bright smile of slyness that burst onto Isis' face, watching the light that sparkled in her eyes as she observed the scene. Could she be more beautiful?

Frode answered, shifting nervously on his feet once more, reaching a hand to scratch his head as he fumbled over his words, causing Agda to giggle again, a few chuckles escaping out of Bylur's own mouth. Isis covered her hand with her mouth as she too tried not to laugh, and Bylur found himself enraptured in awe of her.

Whatever Frode managed to say, it seemed to work, for Violet smiled brightly and stood, and the pair walked out of the barn together, talking quietly back and forth, having only eyes for each other. Bylur watched them go, chuckling at the sweet, budding love that he saw in both of them as they looked at each other.

A clearing of the throat caught Bylur's attention as he turned back to the Volva, who was smiling. "I shall return to my home and begin my prayers to our Goddess for our people, but you especially, King Bylur. Know that you have my support, and hers as well. I feel it strongly."

Bylur bowed his head to the priestess. "I thank you, and the Goddess, for that. We could not have done it without her."

The volva nodded, her smile growing, reaching well into her eyes. "I will be sure to pass on your gratitude to her." And with that, she turned and left, following the path that Bylur knew led to her humble but sacred home.

Agda and Isis stepped forward, both women smiling brightly, even if both of them looked quite tired. Bylur understood the feeling all too well, it echoed the same in his chest. Sometimes victories were the most tiring. "Brother, well done today. I am so proud of you, as my brother and as my King."

Bylur bowed his head to his sister, feeling a great gratitude building in his heart for the numerous incredible women in his life. "Thank you, sister."

"You are most welcome. Well, I am going to take my future queen here to rest and bathe, gods above know she has earned it. And then, once I get her taken care of and fed, I will be sure to send her your way." Agda winked, and Bylur felt his cheeks flush red. It was one thing to be teased about such things from Frode, which he was accustomed to, but Agda rarely teased him about such romantic matters.

Bylur cleared his throat, standing a bit straighter. "Thank you, sister, you do me a great honor, taking care of my love."

Agda gave him a cheeky smile, leading Isis out of the barn, her arms wrapped around his future wife's shoulders. "Oh, I know."

Bylur laughed as they left, shaking his head. That could only mean trouble, but it was trouble he would gladly have.

THE VIKING KING'S LOVE

His heart felt full and warm, a stark contrast to the cold fear and anger he had felt not an hour before.

Gods be praised.

CHAPTER FORTY-NINE
ALONE AT LAST

Bylur watched the fire dance in his hearth, finally sitting down after such a long day. He had returned home only to remember that Bodvar had gone on a destroying rampage within it, so he spent several hours cleaning and fixing what he could.

He appreciated something to do with his hands to keep him busy. Otherwise, he knew he would be pacing the length of his house, wringing his hands with worry, mind consumed with thoughts of Isis. Even now, despite his exhaustion and weary bones, he was tempted to stand and begin to pace. He wondered how Isis was feeling. Was she okay? Did her trauma linger, like a festering wound? Did she wish to run away from this place, this time, from him even?

He wished he could be there for her, to calm her, to bring her safety and security. It drove him mad that he was separated from her, even if it was just for a few long moments. After the hardship this day had given them, all Bylur wanted was to hold Isis until the sun rose, and then maybe still a little longer after that. He needed to know she was safe and felt loved. Everything else could wait.

Yet Bylur knew she was in excellent hands. He trusted his sister with his life, and her words and tone had been clear—*I will take her to rest and breathe for a bit. I will return her to your side whenever she is ready.* Bylur certainly did not ever wish to rush his beloved, even if it drove him to madness to be apart from her during this time. Isis was the priority here, not him. If she needed space and time to process the terror she had experienced today, she would have it, as much as she wanted.

He just hoped that she wanted him, too.

Even as his mind raced, his body relaxed, and Bylur felt heavy, as if he couldn't lift his body even if he wanted to. The day had taken its toll, and his body had reached its limit. Even so, the moment that he heard a soft knock, and then the creaking of his front door opening, Bylur leapt to his feet, spinning around to see Isis, in all of her calmness and beauty, standing serenely in his doorway.

"Isis," Bylur breathed out, his mind spinning in a haze of wonder. She looked like a dream, and the moment felt like one, almost as if this was a spiritual moment, and their love was prophesied, orchestrated by the gods themselves.

"Bylur," Isis almost sang, her voice reminding Bylur of moonlight, of the shining stars breaking through the darkness of the night. The moment went by so slowly, watching Isis turn to shut the door behind her. He knew that, in reality, she moved quite quickly, and yet it still seemed too slow for his aching heart. The next movements were swift, gone by in a blur, as they hurried to embrace one another.

Bylur nearly cried at the sensation of having her in his arms again. It felt like he had been holding his breath in the few hours she had been gone from him, and finally air rushed back into his lungs now that she had returned to him. She smelled of flowers, a woodsy scent, and home, and an immense relief filled Bylur, so much so that it almost scared him. Scared him to be this in love, scared to have something so precious that he could lose.

If today taught him anything, it was that he could not bear to ever lose Isis. The world threatened to take such precious things like the pure love they shared, but such evilness could not win, *would* not win, not if Bylur had anything to say about it. He would rather die than any evil to befall her, would sacrifice everything he had to keep her safe. Together, they could brave any storm. Together, they could make their worlds a better place.

They stood there for quite some time, soaking up each other's love, warmth, and affection. There was nowhere to go, nothing to prove, nothing needing to be tended to that was more important than each other.

And when they did finally relent, pulling apart to share a gentle kiss, they shared a sense of belonging that knitted their souls together, joining them forevermore. Bylur felt it in his chest, everything within him felt electric with the revelation of the union. Isis ran her fingers through his beard, making him shudder and laugh, the sensation tickling him. Isis pulled back, eyes alight with amusement and awe for a moment, before her expression turned into a wicked wonder, full of mischievous plans.

Bylur had a feeling he might come to regret allowing her to have that particular revelation.

Isis dove in for another kiss, this one a bit more fiery. Their kiss deepened, and it did not take long before Bylur was scooping her up to take into the bedroom.

Perhaps a wedding was a special occasion for most, but it would only be a celebration of what had already happened within Bylur's heart, soul, and mind. For everything within him already promised itself to Isis, he belonged to her, wholly and completely, like the darkness belonged to the night, like the mountains belonged to the earth, like salt belonged to the sea.

His heart was already entwined with hers. A wedding was just a formality.

CHAPTER FIFTY

SETTLED

Bylur groaned as he looked out over the village, the last of the troublemakers having been dealt with. It had been quite the mess to clean up over the past several days. There had been many fires to put out, both literal and metaphorical. Including a *certain woman* from the future time having tried to steal things in the panic of the battle, and then upon being caught, trying to blame Isis.

This Amanda woman had already caused trouble for both Bylur and his future queen by being cruel to Isis and trying to hurt her at every possible turn. She had made sure Isis had been rejected by the other women in the village before any of them were chosen. She then yelled at Isis when she attempted to help all of the women once they came to this village at Bylur's request, and now she was trying to commit thievery and thought she could get away with placing all of the fault at Isis' feet.

Bylur was frankly sick of the woman and her antics. It was getting quite ridiculous, and he had had enough. And since her potential marriage had been dissolved due to the man not wanting anything to do with her, Bylur felt she had no real attachment to them or their village.

He was seriously considering throwing her to the wolves, though it was quite possible she would die out in the wilderness. She was even worse off than most of the other women in regard to being able to defend herself and survive in this world. Bylur had requested she be looked after, which really meant more of her being babysat than her being watched over and protected. The reports he received back made things clear. Amanda had no wish to do any hard work and had no concept of earning her keep. She expected everything to be handed to her on a silver platter and thought she was owed everything. When she didn't get her way, she threw fits.

This was not the way of the Vikings. And her cruelty towards Isis was not something he would ever allow. No one treated his Isis like that, not without consequences.

Bylur was still contemplating what to do about Amanda when the elder council meeting regarding Bodvar was arranged and the day for it arrived. He was considering bringing the subject of Amanda up for their wisdom during, but all depended on what else happened in the meeting.

He was not particularly looking forward to the possible complaints he was going to get from those upset villagers that had confronted him days prior. He knew they were not happy with him after his treatment of them and his search for Isis. And although he was not particularly eager to hear their red-faced accusations again, he had no regrets for what he did. He would do it all again if he had to choose. Their complaints were not an emergency, and although he loved his people and cared for them deeply, at that moment their needs did not come close to outweighing Isis' needs. He wanted to be a good king for them and would do his very best to do so, but he would not sacrifice his wife on the altar in order to appease them. If they threw his crown away and yanked him off the throne due to his actions, then he would gladly take that punishment.

Isis was worth such a sacrifice.

Being a king was a great responsibility and honor, but loving her was far more important. His commitment to the crown was not nearly as strong as his commitment to his future wife. He would feel the same about her when he did marry her, and he would feel the same for their children and grandchildren that came after as well.

So when the time for him to arrive at the elder council meeting came, he held his head high and relaxed any tension from his shoulders. He had made the correct choice and done the right thing. If they felt differently, then that was on them. He would take any consequences of his actions in stride for he was not ashamed of the choice that he made.

The entire elder council looked ragged and worn. It had been a rough week for all of them and he knew many of them had been extremely busy with all of the aftermath of Bodvar's uprising. Most of the men on the elder council were far older than Bylur. Their wisdom and experience had served his father well before Bylur had become king. These men knew what they were doing and had many wise things to say about most things in existence. But even they had never experienced something like people from the future offering women in exchange for knowledge. He remembered how baffled all of them had been at such a prospect. Even now most of them, including Bylur himself, had no idea what to fully make of the people that had approached them.

However, luckily for Bylur, they *did* have experience with a rebellion uprising many times over. The actions of Bodvar were not unique or special. He had not been a genius in constructing a following and trying to claim the crown. In fact, when Bylur first became king, the wise men on this council informed him that he would be tested by someone eventually. Every King went through such an ordeal at least once. Some of these men had even been through one with Bylur's father when he had been king.

This had been the moment Bylur had dreaded for many years now. Even though dealing with Bodvar had been difficult, it was dealing with the aftermath with any upset villagers that was the true test. Even though Bylur's father had been king, the crown had not been handed to him simply because of who his parentage was. They chose him to be their king, and it was now Bylur's duty to prove to them they had been wise in selecting him as their leader. He had to show that they had not misplaced their trust when electing him.

The elder council was having quiet conversations between themselves, many of them giving a silent nod of greeting to Bylur as he sat down at the head of the table. When the double doors to the Mead Hall opened, and a swarm of villagers entered the room, taking their proper seats on the outer edges of the large room, their murmuring slowing down. Once everyone was settled, they looked to King Bylur to begin the meeting.

Bylur stood, bringing the entire room's attention upon him by doing so. "Welcome to the elder council meeting. I thank you all for your attendance and everything you have to offer to us today." Bylur went on to explain why they were there, and that they would be weighing all evidence brought forth equally to determine whether or not Bodvar was guilty, and if so, what his punishment should be.

Bylur knew that the meeting would be long and tedious. Such meetings had always taken quite a long time, but this particular situation called for an even longer occasion. Hours went by and the elder council themselves had not finished their prior discussion. Bylur's brain started to feel tired and worn as he listened to the different debating parties as they presented evidence and discussed the severity of Bodvar's actions.

Drinks were brought forth when the outer council finished their discussion, with the overall opinion seeming to lean towards Bodvar's guilt and harsh punishment, which was a relief for Bylur, although he knew it was as it should be. He knew that Bodvar was guilty and such behavior should not be dealt with lightly. He would have been shocked if they had gone in any other direction.

The entire time the meeting was taking place, Bylur's mind couldn't help but continue to drift to thoughts that perhaps weren't appropriate for such a meeting. He knew he should focus on the serious matters at hand, but thoughts of Isis kept consuming his focus, the feeling of her skin against his, how delicious her face looked when overcome with pleasure, just as it had the night prior, and how it would be every night for as long as Isis would have him.

How he would far prefer to be experiencing that now rather than this boring meeting. This was the mundane of life, the trivial inconsequential things. Isis was the opposite of that, she was heaven itself, paradise, the best thing he could imagine.

But this council meeting took precedence. While the elder council had been fair in their assessment, trying to consider

Bodvar's behavior from every possible angle to give him a benefit of the doubt, it was still clear that they had seen his actions as wrong and harmful.

Now came the time where the villagers were given the floor to speak. It was quite possible there were those that had not followed Bodvar's ways, but perhaps had agreed with him in some aspects, making them more likely to fight against any punishment coming against him.

Bylur fidgeted with his hands nervously under the table as he waited for the villagers to step forward.

The first few villagers that came forward presented evidence of theft and some kind of harm that came to them due to the fight that had broken out between the warriors of the village and Bodvar's men. No one seemed to consider that anyone was to blame other than Bodvar himself, making Bylur relax just a little. Perhaps he had worked things up in his mind to make himself believe matters would be worse off than they really were.

But then a woman stepped forward. Somewhat older, she was married to a man that was a known drunkard in the city. She had decided to come with them as she claimed she wished to help the new women that would be arriving. She had put forth the notion that a kind older woman would bring comfort to her fellow females in this new environment.

At the time, Bylur and many others had agreed with her at that point. Thus, she was given permission to join them in their journeying to this village, leaving her husband behind. It was not until after some time spent in the village, just as the foreign women began to arrive in their own village, that it came to Bylur's attention that something suspicious was going on with her. Rumors began to bound that she was having an affair with one of the men. It would not be a difficult thing to do, as many of the men were desperate for female companionship as they sorely lacked women in their village, thus came the solution to bring new women in.

But as she stood before the elder council and leveled Bylur with a glare of fury, Bylur sat back in his chair, fully realizing just who she had been cheating on her husband with. All of the stars aligned in the king's mind to make sense for him. Clearly, she had been sleeping with Bodvar himself, and as she opened her mouth to begin laying blame on Bylur for all of what had happened over the past few days.

It was abundantly clear that she had gambled that Bodvar would win the fight and overthrow Bylur to take hold of the throne. And now that he had lost, she was going to fight tooth and nail to try her best not to lose everything.

As the woman droned on for nearly an hour, the entire elder council looked as if they grew more exhausted with every passing minute. Bylur himself felt his eyelids grow heavy with the sound of her nasal voice filling his ears. Now, more than ever, he wished for his future wife's touch, for her presence, for the ability to observe her keen mind conversing with Frode. This was getting ridiculous.

Perhaps this woman's furious accusations and slander against him should have enraged him, but after all of the energy he had spent over the past few days, Bylur truly had nothing left to give the woman. Perhaps he looked defeated, but Bylur just didn't have the strength to care as he slumped in his chair listening to her rage about the sins of the king.

As the woman approached far beyond a long moment of speaking with no sign of slowing down, one of the elders raised his hand to silence her. When she ignored his gesture, he stood, leveling her with a blatant stare to stop. When she picked up her speed, talking faster and in a higher-pitched voice, as if she wanted to get every possible word she could squeeze out before they stopped her, another elder stood up and barked at her to stop.

Finally, with no choice but to stop, she stood as straight as a board looking out over the entire table with a facial expression that was very nearly a snarl. She seemed to be trying to hold a neutral expression upon her face but was failing miserably.

"I thank you for your time and the evidence you have brought forth today, my lady, but there are many people who have come to bring forth evidence as well today, and they are waiting patiently. You have begun to repeat yourself unnecessarily, and thus I must politely request you to take your leave and return to your seat, so that another may take your place and present their evidence." When Agnes was about to protest, the elder continued. "We must not dally in making this decision as each moment we sit here and talk idly, we may be restraining an innocent man unnecessarily. We must bring forth the final conclusion swiftly so that we do not punish him by holding him captive when he may be deserving of no punishment at all. Since it seems you are against any punishment of Bodvar, I should hope you would take this concept with enthusiasm and wish us to gather all the evidence and make a decision as efficiently as possible as well," the elder spoke firmly, his voice echoing throughout the room.

The woman gave little more than a frustrated huff as if she was a little child who had just been reprimanded before storming off back to her seat. As the next person stood to come up and present their case, Bylur watched as she gathered all of her belongings and stomped out of the double doors leading out of the Mead Hall, making a big fuss as she went.

It almost felt as if the entire room gave a sigh of relief once she was finally gone.

Over the next long while, many people came and stood before them to present evidence and their story of what had happened the past few days. They gave their opinion calmly and firmly, despite most of them being quite passionate about what they were stating as things had become personal.

While no one had taken the approach that that woman had by taking all of the blame off Bodvar and placing it solely on Bylur's shoulders, several of the villagers, including the ones that had confronted him several days prior, did make strong suggestions that Bylur had at least partial blame in all of this.

That old creeping feeling that their words were true bit into him, making his mind swirl with the possibility. It was frustrating and somewhat disconcerting that some of his people had opinions that were ill of him. The fact that anyone would believe he would purposely provoke someone out of pure pride bothered him, but as King, he had no time to fear what anyone thought of him.

Still, he liked to be in partnership with his people, and having someone even seem slightly against him was somewhat jarring. But he knew it was something he would have to learn to contend with as a leader. People were often aggressive with leaders just for the sake of it due to their jealousy and envy of their position. He knew it was most likely not personal. It was easy to blame him for their own misfortune.

If the elder council came to the conclusion that he needed to make ramifications and take responsibility for something he had done in this matter, then he would gladly do so and learn from their words. He trusted that they were not against him so that anything that they said about his behavior would come from a place of wanting him to improve and only become a better version of himself. He did not fear them or their words, as he knew it would come from a place of respect and strengthening. They did not wish to tear him down in the slightest as some of the villagers might.

Bylur looked out the windows to see that the day had grown dark while they had sat in this meeting. It was not long after that the last villager came forth to present their case, and Bylur was pleased to see it was the man he had helped extinguish the fire that had been attacking his home. The man smiled and gave Bylur a nod as he stood at the end of the table, as the man drew in a deep breath. He immediately jumped into what he had seen before the fire had started, and identified the man he thought might be behind it. The crowd murmured at the suggestion that Bodvar might direct someone to do such a terrible thing to an innocent bystander only to cause more pain and chaos.

And when the man hurried to tell the part where Bylur and his companions rushed to his aid and helped him successfully put out the fire, he added much enthusiasm and praise for his king. So much so that Bylur nearly felt like standing up and proclaiming that the man exaggerated things slightly, but he knew better than to try to act humble at this time. It may even backfire and come off as false humility. The council would measure the man's words and cut off any unnecessary praise if need be. They were well versed in weighing someone's account and shedding any exaggeration from it.

When the man gave his final words and gave the outer council a small bow and took his leave, Bylur stood to his feet, his legs and bottom sore from sitting for so long, and called an end to the meeting, saying they would continue the deliberations on the morrow.

Bylur felt hopeful about tomorrow's tidings, but still, he went home with plenty dwelling on his mind. He did not get much sleep that night as thoughts circled around his head like vultures around a carcass.

CHAPTER FIFTY-ONE

THE ELDER COUNCIL DECIDES

T he dawn of the next morning arrived for Bylur like an unexpected house guest. He rushed to prepare for it, feeling lost and not ready for its arrival.

His sister, Agda arrived shortly after the sun fully made its way into the sky, bearing gifts in the form of breakfast. She embraced him once he answered his front door, a concerned expression on her face. "I heard yesterday's meeting was not altogether too kind to you. Since I know you had an early morning today and possibly more stress ahead of you, I decided to be a good little sister and make sure you were fed."

Bylur snickered at the thought of his sister, a formidable warrior and shieldmaiden, slaving over a stove for him.

"Who are you and what happened to my beloved Agda? My sister would never be so kind, and she certainly cannot *cook*."

"Shush, you...or else I'll be tempted to take it back. I can eat this breakfast all by myself, you know." Agda smacked him playfully on the arm as she handed him the already prepared plates of food.

Bylur snorted through his nose. "Oh, I know full well how much you can eat. You've always given us growing lads quite the competition. It has always been impressive. Perhaps even a little intimidating, " Bylur admitted. He gave a sigh as he dropped the humor from his voice, turning serious. "All jesting aside, sister, I appreciate you and this gift. It was intense yesterday, to say the least. I am quite glad that the villagers' testimonies are finished with, and we are nearing the end of this ordeal. Hopefully, the results will go in our favor, but no matter what, I have no regrets. Still, I have not been without stress. Your kindness is truly appreciated and has not gone unnoticed."

Agda gave her brother a sad smile as she patted him on the arm. "You are welcome, my dear brother. I hope you know you are not alone and we are right behind you."

A little while later, Bylur still considered this comment as he walked to the Mead Hall. His sister's words swirled around his mind like foam on a cold glass of mead. It was as it should be, a sister giving her brother wise words of comfort. Knowing that she and Frode, as well as others, were there to support him was a blessing he could put no proper words to express it adequately.

On the way to the Mead Hall, out of the corner of his eye, Bylur saw a figure running up to him. Initially, his body moved into that of a defensive stance, ready for whatever was currently flying at him. After the week he had, he was ready for anything and felt on edge as he waited for the other shoe to drop. However, relief coursed through his entire body and soul upon seeing Isis approaching, her full figure hugged by a Viking woman's dress, which Bylur identified as his sister's handiwork.

"Isis," Bylur breathed out like her name was a breath of fresh air.

She smiled brightly at him in return clutching his arms within her grasp as she looked into his eyes. "Bylur." Her return was as equally song-like as his had been. He still stood in awe at the loving reverence she held in her eyes when she looked at him, but he knew that his eyes held the same admiration when he was looking at her.

This was the love he had been encouraged to find by his mother for many years now.

As they embraced, wrapping their arms around one another, Bylur closed his eyes tightly, cherishing this moment for the beautiful treasure that it was. Hugging her felt like coming home, like walking in the fresh air of a forest after being locked up in your house for far too long. It felt like hearing music after too long in silence, like a cold drink of water after working hard in the fields for many hours.

As they pulled apart, Bylur felt his skin prickle with a chill, yearning to return to being close to her again already. She reached up and caressed his face, her eyes full of that deep adoration once more. Her gentle touch against his beard tickled, causing him to twitch his lips. Pulling her hand back, Isis laughed, the sound making his itching torment worth it.

Perhaps her knowing this particular weakness was a good thing. Maybe he could truly trust her with every part of him, even the soft spots.

Isis winked as she moved her hand further up his cheek in an effort not to tickle him again. The two grinned at each other like two lovers that were sharing a secret between them, which Bylur realized in awe that this was who they were. Even if that secret was as silly as the fact that he was ticklish under his beard, it still made that fact true. They *were* two lovers that shared a secret.

The realization nearly made Bylur giddy with the love he held for Isis.

Isis was soon called away by Bylur's sister, Agda, but not before she held him tightly once more and gave him a soft kiss on the lips. As he watched her walk away, he could not help but notice the gorgeous figure she had, and how her hips moved as she walked. His lips still tingled from her own lips' sweet caress, and his heart still ached for her despite the distance between them. With such a sweet and tender moment shared between them, Bylur felt like he could handle this day, no matter what came at him. Even if it had only been a few short minutes between them, it had been enough to spark life into his weary soul. If he had not had confidence before in his capabilities as a king, he knew resolutely now that he could fulfill his greatest potential as the leader of his people with Isis by his side as his queen.

When he arrived at the Mead Hall, most everyone had already arrived, much of the elder council looking like they obtained less sleep than he did. He frowned as he greeted his friends and allies, worried for their health and well-being.

He turned to the man on his left, who was named Jofir, and had been his father's advisor and ally on the elder council for many years before Bylur was even born. "I assume that you all have been concerned for the outcome of this meeting as much as I have been?"

"Yes, I believe we have been, King Bylur, concerned about this meeting, among other matters, such as giving over any of the relics to those in the future. I know that we had decided it was the best thing for our people at the time, but now that we have learned more of these people from the future, does that still hold true?" Jofir dropped his voice to a whisper, the dark bags under his eyes evident even in the low light of the Mead Hall.

Bylur pursed his lips, giving his elder a solemn shake of his head. "I understand your intention, Elder Jofir, and will dutifully consider your guidance with heavy consideration. For the time being, we need to focus on this meeting and the issues at hand."

Jofir furrowed his brows, giving a slow nod. "I understand your hesitation. But, to honor your request and return to the subject of the meeting, all of us on the elder council have been rather bothered by certain individuals in this village that have leveled their complaints like arrows towards us.

Their consistent pursuit of having an audience with every single member of this council has felt like harassment. I believe it is safe to say that we will all be extremely grateful when this is over and gone away. None of us are happy with the behavior that has gone on because of this. And trust me when I say it has little to do with you, King Bylur, despite what some of them would have us believe." Jofir coughed, his body racked with the assault on his lungs.

Bylur's eyes widened at the information, sitting back in his chair in horror. "I too was confronted by such individuals and their complaints a few days prior, but I shut it down as this was in the middle of my pursuit of Bodvar. I tried to tell them that there was a larger crisis, but they would not listen. I finally had to tell them enough was enough and that they could present their complaints here at the elder council if they had something to say. I was not about to risk my future Queen's life to hear all of their moaning and groaning. I had no idea that they were doing this to all of you as well. *This is unacceptable.* You are correct that this is harassment. I wish I would have known sooner, I would have put a stop to it at once. As the elder council, you all deserve far more respect than that."

Jofir rubbed his temple as he sighed. "I agree and appreciate your high esteem of us that you would wish to protect us in such a way. Just another mark of how great of a king you are. However, we all speculate that the complaints may not end once the meeting finishes. If they do not get what they want, they may continue to lodge their complaints against us. And that is part of the issue, we are not entirely sure what they want other than to simply complain and act victimized. If that is the case and we are continually bothered by their endless pestering, I am sure we will be calling upon you to handle them and put an end to the harassment."

"I would be happy to do so if that is the case. As I said before, you are all deserving of much more respect than that. And as the King, I will make sure that it is evident to all of my people that they understand you are to be respected, and that I will not allow for my council to be harassed and taken advantage of in such a way." Bylur looked out over his elder council, his companions and allies in taking care of his people. The thought that they could be treated in such a way angered him.

Jofir chuckled, grinning at Bylur. "As I said, a clear sign of just how great of a king you are. Don't go showing it off now, or I'll be tempted to take back my words. If you become too great of a king, you will make the rest of us look bad."

Before Bylur could give him a playful retort, one of the other men on the elder council cleared his throat, drawing their attention. His eyes were on King Bylur, his eyebrow raised in question. Bylur realized they had been ready for the meeting to start for a little while, but he and Jofir had been too distracted in their conversation to notice.

Bylur stood up, looking around the room. "My apologies for the delay. Let us get this meeting started."

Bylur sat back down in his seat, looking at the villagers that had congregated on the benches on the outer ring of the room. They waited for several long, silent minutes as they gave the final opportunity for anyone to step forward.

Finally, when no one else approached, King Bylur stood up once more and clasped his hands together in front of him. "It seems all evidence and testimony has been brought forth. So now we will conclude that time of the meeting and move on to the decision-making."

The discussion amongst the elder council was much more engaging and thought-provoking than the testimonies of the villagers had been the prior day. Bylur felt invigorated and thoughtful, whereas the day before he had felt accused, bored, and concerned.

He never felt slighted by his elder council, and it was clear they were not about to start now. They were careful to survey things from every possible angle, to be sure, but they made it clear that they did not believe Bylur was *entirely* at fault for this. Although the subject was discussed, it was soon dismissed without much conflict between the members of the elder council. Granted, it did cause a bit of a stir in the crowd of villagers that listened intently, but no one dared to disturb the meeting, besides some whispers filled with fervor.

Finally, after several hours, when a calm silence filled the Mead Hall, Bylur looked about the council with an eyebrow raised in interest. "So, does this mean we have come to a conclusion?"

Beside him, Jofir nodded. "I believe we have, our Great King. It seems we know what must be done. The evidence clearly points to Bodvar having guilt in the damage and assault of members of this village, as well as their properties. It is clear that he had malicious intent in creating some sort of rebellious uprising against the authority of yourself and this council, and one could argue even the gods themselves, and thus he must be dealt with swiftly and accordingly."

Bylur nodded, pressing his lips into a firm line, his brows furrowed with seriousness. "If that is what the elder council has decided, let it be so. If any on the elder council disagree, say so now."

Several moments passed without anyone on the council making a sound, besides one individual clearing his throat.

"We will now move on to discuss Bodvar's exact punishment for these deeds, as well as the punishment for any of those who are convicted of being in alliance with Bodvar, regarding this uprising. Speak your mind on what should be done about him, elder council."

The elder council was swift in their decisions regarding Bodvar and his followers. Bodvar would be banished from their society, allowed no longer to be among them. All of his belongings and properties would be removed from his possession, given to one of the families who received damage in his rebellion. As for his followers, they would be given a chance to renounce their allegiance with Bodvar, and then only fined for their behavior. If they did not renounce Bodvar and his behavior, they too would be shunned from this village or the great city, barred from ever returning.

The result seemed to come as a shock for several in the crowd, as gasps and even cries of alarm rose up among them. The noisiest belonged to Lady Agnes, the woman who had presented complaints against Bylur the day prior, who immediately became distraught. Upon hearing her outcry, one of the members of the elder council beckoned her forward. "I thank you for drawing attention to yourself, although I usually would never wish anyone to do so. In this case, I am thankful for it, as there is much to be done about you. It is clear that you have an allegiance to or with Bodvar, and that is an understatement, I believe it is safe to say. Although many of us have had compassion with you regarding your current marriage, that is no excuse when you are siding against your own people. What say you, Agnes Winterthaw, regarding your alliance with Bodvar Karsson? Do you renounce it, or shall you meet the same fate as he?"

The woman's lower lip trembled as she looked upon them with wide eyes filled with fear. She was as pale as a ghost, as her hands shook in front of her. In a moment she took a deep breath, crossing her arms and lifting her chin up in defiance. "I do not know what you speak of. I have no alliance with Bodvar or any of his men. I would never betray my King in such a way. Just because I brought evidence forth, does not mean that I have any sort of alliance with him. I hope that you would be wise enough to know that. Do not punish me for trying to speak the truth in the matter of justice. I do not think the gods would look kindly upon that, do you?"

The elder chuckled, seemingly unbothered by her religious threat. "I do not think that they look kindly upon injustice at all, no. This is why we are all for fairness and justice. These matters need to be handled correctly, as we are trying very hard to do. I also do not think that they look kindly upon liars, do you?"

Bylur did not think the woman could grow any paler, but alas, she proved him very wrong. Her eyes widened at the elder's retort, her mouth growing agape at his suggestion. She stuttered for a moment, seemingly taking aback by such an idea. "No, I do not believe they take kindly to liars at all. But..." She grew silent for a moment, her face one of contemplation and thought. "I do renounce my allegiance with Bodvar. I will have nothing to do with him or his ways any longer. This, I swear by the gods."

When the meeting finally came to a close, Bylur heaved a heavy sigh, and the rest of the meeting was concluded regarding Bodvar.

Before they were all dismissed, Jofir stood up, clearing his throat. "Before this meeting is adjourned, I have one last thing to discuss. In the madness that has ensued over the past week, we have forgotten that our beloved priestess has finished her pronouncements on all of the couples, and now this business is finished, which means the weddings can commence. I know we are all quite excited about this, and I think the weddings should be put forth as the highest of priorities in order to clear away the darkness of this week's past events. Let us move forward with celebration and light to honor the gods and the bright future of our people. What do you say, King Bylur?"

Bylur stood up, feeling light after the heavy material they had just gone over and discussed. "I think it is an absolutely wonderful idea, Jofir. I believe it is just what our people need after this week. The question is: shall we begin the weddings here? Or wait until we have returned to the city to do so?"

"A very fair question indeed, our Great King. I think the answer lies in the balance of the two ideas. Perhaps there are those who wish to wait no longer. If that is the case, they should be freely granted the opportunity to have their wedding here as soon as possible. However, if they wish to wait and return to the city, and perhaps their loved ones, in order to celebrate properly, they should be allowed to do so as well. As for you, our Great King, all of our people should be given the opportunity to celebrate the wondrous union of you and your queen. I would strongly recommend you wait until we return to the city for your wedding to be carried out."

Bylur's lungs felt a bit constrained at the notion of waiting so long to be joined in vows to Isis. But he knew that his advisor was correct. All of the people would want to celebrate their new queen and might feel cheated if they had their wedding without them. Isis' reputation and standing as a good queen might be threatened, if they felt the people were not given the chance to be a part of her entire journey in becoming their queen. It was good wisdom to wait, although he wished he did not have to. However, he knew that Isis was well worth the wait, and that he could muster the patience for her.

Bylur nodded, clearly displaying his agreement. "I absolutely agree with your recommendation, Jofir. In fact, that is what my exact pronouncement will be. All of those who wish to wed as soon as possible may freely do so under the Volva's care here in the village. However, if any wish to wait until we return to the city, they of course are more than welcome to do so as well. And just as Jofir has recommended, my own wedding will wait until all of our people are with us to celebrate. And with that, unless there is anything else to be said, the adjoining of the elder council has been finished."

A thrill of joy raced through Bylur at the thought of returning home and marrying his beloved Isis.

CHAPTER FIFTY-TWO

WEDDINGS COMMENCE

Isis darted around the Mead Hall like a busy bee working for her hive. There was yet *another* wedding taking place today, and Isis had volunteered to help with the preparations for the couple's big day, as she had for all of the weddings thus far.

There had been some squabbles over the final outcome of Bodvar's sentencing, and thus some of the villagers were upset. Frode had suggested that she help with the weddings as a way to connect with her future people, that they might become bonded with her as their queen.

She had barely seen Bylur in the past week or so, both of them handling a lot of matters separately. It was sad, but she knew nothing had changed between them. And Frode assured her that the time for their own love and union was drawing near. He had informed her that they would all be returning to the city in a week or so, where their wedding would become a large event and would take place soon after they arrived.

Which meant that in the next two weeks she could be married to the most tender and loving man she had ever met. Such a thought was blissful indeed. In fact, it was the only thing that truly kept her going as she helped assist with all of the numerous preparations and work that needed to be done for all the weddings that were seemingly continually taking place.

Another interesting thing she had learned was that several of the women that had joined her in coming to this time were previously employed in the wedding industry. There was one woman that was a baker and another that was a florist, both of the women happy to return to something familiar in their efforts to make the wedding as beautiful and joyful as they possibly could. Seeing as there were obviously no such bakers or florists amongst the Vikings, Isis was thankful for their help.

Isis reached up onto her tippy toes in order to properly place a flower arrangement they had gathered out of wildflowers onto the wall of the Mead Hall. "Well, hello there, friend. Keeping busy, are we?" Isis turned to see Violet striding in with a bright smile on her face.

"Violet! Yes, it feels like I'm always keeping busy these days. I did not realize I would ever be in the business of weddings, but here we are. Making do with what I've been given. What are you up today?" Isis finished perfecting the wreath and turned to her blonde friend.

"Oh, you know, this and that. Keeping busy just the same as you. Although, I know a lot more is being asked of you since you will be Queen and all that, which, by the way, is still crazy to think about. The fact that you will be the queen of everyone here someday soon. And speaking of making do with what you're given, I'm impressed you're able to do so, since your career was nothing like anything we're doing here or even *can do* here. Working with computers isn't something that's really useful here. But you seem to be making do just fine." Violet chuckled as she leaned against the wooden wall of the Mead Hall.

Isis nodded as she looked around the large room at everything she had accomplished in the past hour. "Yes, I wish that all my time, training, and experience was not worthless here, but it's not like I can invent computers or something like that. Kind of had to let that side of me go for now, possibly forever. We just don't know what's going to happen. I admit, I somewhat envy these women that can take their trades from our time and so easily do them in this time. Like Annabelle, who made this floral arrangement. She was a florist back in our time, and now she's able to take that skill and experience and use them for something needed here. My skills just aren't as easily convertible I guess. But what about you? Your skills are quite convertible. Being a teacher is always useful."

Violet nodded at Isis' assessment. "Yes, I agree that being a teacher is useful no matter what time or era you are in. Granted, I never imagined that I would need a skill to be useful in another time or era when I decided to go down that path for my career. And I do love children just the same as always. Even though, there aren't many children around right now since there haven't been many women. But with all these weddings, I imagine that will be changing here soon enough. Perhaps I could start a school someday?"

Isis immediately brightened up at the prospect of children running around the village and going to school where Violet was the teacher. "What a wonderful idea, Violet! I am sure you are a wonderful teacher and will do a marvelous job with teaching the children in this era. I can only imagine that you are not used to teaching kids in the same way you'll probably teach them here, but I think that your skills will still be extremely valuable and needed. All it will take is a small adjustment, and you will get on just fine, I'm sure. I know I'd be happy to send any children I have to your school."

Violet's entire face lifted with delight as she beamed at Isis. "You really think so? I never thought that I'd own my own school, but then again I never thought I'd meet a Viking. Yes, I agree. I don't think the kids would need to learn American History or English Literature. Thankfully, I taught younger students so I think a lot of my material is still applicable. Science is still always a good thing to know, as is writing and math.

"But, if I am to teach children here, I think I will have to learn some more useful skills for this time. I am afraid I have never been good at sewing or cooking or anything like that, but I am sure that that is what is most useful for the children to learn. School and education are all about proper preparation for their adult life, and their adult life will be very different from the children I used to teach back at home. Nonetheless, I think it'll be a very fun challenge for me to adjust my teaching material and style for this time. I am so glad you think it is a good idea, Isis. It really gives me hope for the future."

Isis looked out over the village through the open doorway, considering the era they were now in and the life that was before them. "I agree, I think we have more to offer to this time than we give ourselves credit for. We can do this, we can make a wonderful home here if we try. I think we all have something to offer that perhaps we aren't even thinking of yet. More than just being women and wives. But I can't help but wonder about your future beyond just the school. Do you think you will find a spouse here?"

Violet's eyes glanced away from Isis as she shrugged her shoulders. "Honestly, I'm not sure. There doesn't seem to be many men left, and after the whole ordeal with Bodvar, I am not rushing into anything. I don't want to make the wrong decision for a spouse. Is it wrong that I want love? I know that you and Bylur had an arranged marriage and then fell in love, but that is not something we are used to, is it? I really don't know what to make of it."

"I think you have the unique opportunity out of all of us to be able to choose who you want to marry. I understand your hesitancy after Bodvar. I'm just asking this because I noticed you and Frode seem to get along well and seem to have some chemistry. If I'm wrong, I'm sorry and I won't ask again. I thought maybe I noticed something, and my curiosity's pushing me to ask. But you know what they say, about curiosity and the cat." Isis chuckled and crossed her arms nervously, concerned she had overstepped with her friend.

Violet dipped her head as Isis noticed her cheeks growing a rosy color. "No, you're right. I do admit that he is a handsome and intelligent man, and his accent is just *wonderful*. I can't help but be a bit mesmerized by his intellect whenever I talk with him. And of course, he is a very attractive individual. I'm not sure what to do because maybe, he didn't choose a wife for a reason. Maybe, he isn't interested in romance at all. I don't want to push something and offend him when he might just want to be friends. I don't even know what the custom is for such a situation here. It all feels so nerve-wracking. As if dating wasn't hard enough in our time, right?"

Isis laughed, the sound echoing throughout the otherwise empty building. "No, I completely understand. I've been wondering why he didn't choose a wife either, like the rest of the men as well. But I noticed him looking at you, which could be just in my imagination, but from an outside source, it does seem he has some kind of interest in you. All you can do is remain open and continue getting to know him better until we figure out more of their culture."

Violet agreed with her before the two women parted in order to prepare for the wedding.

The days went by in a dizzying amount of activity that all blurred together until Isis could no longer remember which wedding was which. And, as soon as Frode informed her that all the weddings that were to be happening at the small village were now completed, her busyness shifted from wedding planning and preparations to packing and readying herself and others for the journey back to the Great City.

Isis kept so busy that when Frode greeted her one morning, informing her that Bodvar had been officially shunned from their society and released into the wild, she could not believe that she had missed such an occasion.

Could it be that he was truly gone? It felt relieving and exciting to have that chapter put behind them, and a new one was unfolding before her. A chapter filled with exciting new experiences of what a Viking city is like, learning what it is to be a Viking queen, and the great joy of marrying the man she had fallen in love with.

As busy and consuming those weddings were, each one brought their own flavor of joy to Isis' heart as she realized her own wedding lie soon before her. She could only imagine the bliss she would feel upon seeing her own special day being prepared for and arranged.

She would think about it often as she laid in Bylur's arms in the night, when his beard would tickling her cheek as his deep breathing soothed her soul. Isis knew peace;, she felt it bathe her very spirit until she was drenched in it, but still, she longed for the next step with Bylur. How could she not? She loved him very deeply, and felt his love for her in return. Their union would be bliss, and Isis felt overjoyed that it was coming soon.

It came as a sweet relief when the day finally arrived for them to journey to the Great City at long last. Bylur had his own wagon filled with his belongings, which she was invited to join him on. The morning was bright and cheerful, as the birds sang in celebration of their adventure to their home.

The night before, Isis had barely slept, trying not to toss and turn that much so she did not wake Bylur. She was far too busy thinking of all the exciting possibilities that could await her, including what the city looked like. She did not know all that was in store, but she was excited to find out. What would her new home look like? What would her daily life be like? What would it be like to be married to a king, much less one as wondrous as Bylur? Would she ever fully adjust to living in this era? Would she ever get a chance to return home? And if she did, would she take that opportunity and leave her new friends, as well as her handsome king behind?

The thoughts and questions stomped around in her mind all night, their loud voices keeping her awake. She had no answers for them at this time, but she knew she would have the answers to some here soon. As for the last one, that was something only she could answer with time and plenty of thought given to it.

But until such an opportunity arose, there was no point in dwelling on it. At least not from Isis' perspective. Instead, she longed to explore this exciting future that was spread out before her. Hopefully more of nights like Bylur and Isis had shared the past few nights, holding each other, whispering sweet nothings in each other's ears, kissing deeply, and making passionate love.

If there were more nights like that, then surely her future would be pure bliss.

CHAPTER FIFTY-THREE

FINAL JOURNEY HOME

The journey was long, but it did not feel as taxing as Isis might have imagined. The weather was mild and pleasant, with blue skies and a slight breeze to keep them cool. Isis chatted with Frode and Violet the entire way, sitting comfortably next to Bylur on his wagon. Laughter could be heard from a great distance behind them as all of the villagers that were traveling with them also enjoyed each other's company.

Isis tried not to smirk as Violet and Frode continued to talk and get along marvelously with one another. Turning to Bylur beside her, she arched a brow at him, and a sly smirk spread onto his face. Without even saying anything, the two acknowledged that they both recognized what was developing between Frode and Violet. Despite the language difference, it was clear that they both had the same idea regarding their loved ones. The mischievous excitement that was present upon Bylur's face nearly made Isis laugh out loud. Clearly, he was excited about such a prospect just as much as she was, if not more.

The only unpleasant thing that came of their journey to the Great City was how sore Isis' bottom was becoming sitting on the hard wooden wagon seat. The pain began to spread throughout her body at the continual rocking motion that came as the wagon dragged on, her body becoming stiff over the hours of travel that they were doing.

She grimaced as she reached behind to rub her lower back, feeling the hours of travel take a toll upon her. "You look like an old lady when you do that," Frode teased from his horse some several feet away.

"I *feel* like an old lady at the moment. I cannot imagine taking the trip longer than this on such a vehicle. Perhaps I am more spoiled from my modern conveniences than I thought. This was one adjustment I had not prepared for." Isis sat back in her seat, trying to relax.

Frode shrugged his shoulders. "I do not know what modern conveniences you could be possibly talking about since this is all I know, so I have nothing to compare it to in order to conclude if you are spoiled or not. I will say there is much that seems difficult for you future women, but if things are much easier there with inventions and whatnot, I suppose that makes sense. I am sorry you have to adjust so much, but there's not much we can do about that. Thankfully, there is not much further to go before we arrive at the Great City. And then a long hot bath awaits you there. I'm sure that will soothe your aching muscles greatly. We will all be a bit sore tonight, but I suspect if what you say is true, then you future women will have a worse time than the rest of us."

Isis locked on to his comment about a hot bath with fervor. That idea gave her the last bit of strength that she needed to finish out the journey.

It was late afternoon when something crested upon the horizon, a cluster of buildings rising into view over a hill. Isis leaned forward in her seat to try to get a better view, trying to gauge how big this place was and what it looked like from where they were. It was still too hard to see with a great distance in between them, but still, she craned her neck sitting as straight as she could to try to get a better view. Bylur chuckled beside her at her childlike behavior, but she simply could not contain her excitement and yearning to see her future home.

"Here we are, and the final stretch at last. Do not hurt yourself further, Lady Isis. You will get to see the Great City and all her glory soon enough, even up close and personal. In fact, there may come a time soon enough where you get sick of seeing her. King Bylur rarely leaves the city, since this is where most of his duties lie. We have established a good home here and there is little reason to leave. You might find yourself growing bored at staying in one place for so long." Frode grinned at Isis' antics, patting his horse when it let out a soft neigh.

Isis turned to Frode with a wide grin. "I am not so sure about that, Frode. I have always enjoyed staying at my home. In my time, they call that being a homebody. I have no shame in admitting that I have always been one. However, I do like an adventure every now and then. But I will also say that the past week or so has fulfilled my desire for adventure for a while at least. I think I will be very glad to stay in one place for a while, especially if it is as interesting as you all say. I am sure I will have much excitement in the form of learning your culture and ways as I adjust to being queen. It is strange enough to think I will be doing that as it is, without also realizing that I will be a Viking queen, which is very different from anything I have ever known. Suffice to say, I think I will have plenty enough excitement without ever even leaving the city."

"If you say so, Lady Isis, then I trust your instincts. I hope that is truly the case. I do think you will have your hands full with all of the people that want to meet you and get to know you. I know everyone is greatly looking forward to meeting their future queen and working with you as their new leader. In fact, I think that we will have quite a warm welcome waiting for us when we arrive." Frode looked out towards the city, giving a wistful sigh.

Isis arched a brow at her translator friend. "Oh? What makes you think that we would have a warm welcome such as that? They don't even know that we will be arriving. Though, I suppose they will be able to see us coming from quite the distance since we are a rather large group of people. Do you think that they will gather at the gates for us or something?"

Frode let out a large laugh. "Oh, they will surely know that we are coming, long before they even see us approaching in the distance. Our Great and Fair King sent a messenger ahead of us a day before we left to tell them to prepare for our arrival. It is custom to welcome your king when he is returning home anytime he departs from the city, but this time will be extra special since you will be also arriving. I have no doubt they will have a sort of celebration prepared for us to welcome you home. With the shortage of women, you are seen as nothing short of a miracle, trust me. I know they are all eager to see their new queen in all of her shining beauty and glorious wisdom."

Isis snorted through her nose at Frode's comment. "Oh, I am not sure about all of that, Frode. I think they will soon find out just how average and ordinary of a woman I truly am. My own people didn't really accept me before, I would not be surprised if I'm a bit of a disappointment for them. Other than the fact that I look quite different than anything they are used to. I am sure that would be a bit of a marvel for them. But other than that, you have never met such an ordinary of a woman as me."

Violet cut in, adding in her two cents. "I am not so sure about that, Isis. No other woman from our time who came here with us even bothered to think of the future or try to take care of herself. You were fully functional and capable of survival without any outside help. And you are just as beautiful as Frode said. Bylur's people would be stupid if they do not recognize your greatness as I have. The only reason why our fellow women didn't is because they were being led astray by that absolute imbecile Amanda. Being around that woman makes you lose brain cells, I swear."

Isis blushed at her friend's compliment. "Well, thank you, Violet. That is very kind of you to say. But the women that we arrived here with are not the first people to reject me. I have never been interesting enough for people, I suppose. But perhaps the fact that I look different and am from the future will be enough to make me interesting to these people. As for your comment about Amanda, I do agree on that account. I have never met anyone who was quite so determined to look like a fool before. She really is stubborn about getting her way and being right, no matter the cost."

Violet nodded, her brows scrunched in her own determined gaze. "But don't you see, Isis? The reason why she was so determined to invalidate you is because you were a threat to her. She saw the greatness in you the very same way that I did and still do. You have all the makings of a fine leader. There is a reason that King Bylur chose you. You need to have more faith in yourself. I know it is difficult when our society trained us for many years to feel insecure and doubt ourselves, but you are a beautiful woman with remarkable wisdom and a strong spirit. I know you will make a great queen and anyone with any sense will see it as well. Maybe Amanda wasn't so stupid after all, since she was able to see how fantastic of a leader you could be, which made her scared of you. She had to invalidate you so that you didn't become the leader of the women, and then they wouldn't see how stupid she was and make *her* the outcast. She probably felt like she had to make you the outcast before you became the leader and shunned her instead. Not that you would, but her own insecurity made her fear that you would. How sad is that?"

Isis let out a long exhale, furrowing her brows at the thought. "Very sad indeed. I had never thought of it like that. Do you really think that she felt threatened by me? I would not throw anyone out. Not unless they were threatening the safety and well-being of the rest of the village. But I do know that our own fears and insecurities easily lie to us. I have never seen myself as leadership material, but I can certainly do it if I have to. But that doesn't mean that I'm necessarily *good* at it."

Bylur placed his hand upon Isis' thigh, drawing her attention to him. "You are good."

Isis raised her brows in surprise at the simple phrase her future husband produced. Perhaps his language lessons with Frode were going more successfully than she had thought if he was able to understand exactly what they were talking about enough to form such a reply.

Frode barked out a voracious laugh at Bylur's comment. "Would you look at that, the stubborn King is learning something new. Good job, Bylur. That was good. I am quite proud. Look at how well your betrothed is doing, Lady Isis. This surely means I am one of the best teachers of them all, to be able to produce such fantastic results in such a short time with such a stubborn student."

Isis rolled her eyes at Frode. "It could also mean that Bylur is a wonderful student and a fast learner. Perhaps he's even able to learn in such a difficult learning environment as the one I am sure you have given him, with all your joking and teasing. I know you would not miss an opportunity to try to make a fool of himself if you can. I am impressed that he has been able to avoid such embarrassment as I am sure you have set him up for so far."

Frode placed a hand upon his chest, mocking offense. "I do not know what you could possibly mean, Lady Isis. I am the most gentle and caring of brothers, and the most patient and considerate of teachers. I would never do anything to purposely lead many of my students astray, especially one as close and important to me as my king."

"It is not the king part that I am doubting. It is the fact that he is your *brother* that makes me think you would do such a thing. I have noticed your relationship, as well as your sense of humor. Do not try to fool me into thinking that you would not do such a thing." Isis arched a brow at him, crossing her arms as she challenged the translator.

Frode let out a long, exasperated sigh as he continued on in his display of dramatics. "I suppose, if I had the perfect opportunity to do so, I may perhaps try to play a small prank upon my dearest brother. But that does not mean that I might enact self-control and refrain from doing so. I know what it is like to subject yourself to learning such a difficult thing as a new language, and how vulnerable it can be. I would not want to take advantage of my beloved brother in such a situation, where he is at a weak and tender place in learning a new language when you can feel like a bit of a fool enough as it is, to make him look like an even greater fool. I am not that much of a jerk, you know."

Isis raised both of her brows at Frode this time. "So you were telling me you have not led Bylur astray even once during your teaching? You have not told him that the word pickle means love or something of that sort?"

"No, I would never do such a thing. Even though that would probably be absolutely hilarious, I would never subject my king and my brother, not to mention one of my greatest friends, to such horrible embarrassment." At Isis and Violet's similarly incredulous looks, Frode feigned an offended gasp and continued. "*What?* Do you not believe me? Do you doubt my morality? Or do you perhaps think me a liar?" Frode peered at her with an intense look of sadness, giving her wide puppy dog eyes, which admittedly looked quite strange on the muscular bearded Viking man.

Isis narrowed her eyes at Frode, giving him a look of suspicion. "I do not know what to think about you and your mysterious ways, Frode. Just know that I am watching you and that I will try to soften any blow that comes Bylur's way. And I firmly believe in an eye for an eye and a tooth for a tooth."

Frode gave her wide eyes, letting out a low whistle. "Then I will have to keep my wits about me around you, to ensure I do not inadvertently offend you in some way. King Bylur is lucky to have such a strong and brave warrior as his future queen."

The journey continued in a similar fashion of joking and playful banter between the group of friends. Agda and Bylur also joined in at some points, speaking in their tongue and having Frode translate. There were even times where Isis and Violet spoke quietly amongst themselves as the Vikings shared in on their own playful conversation, with Frode chatting with his siblings instead of translating.

The closer they grew to the city, the more excited Isis became. As they journeyed nearer, Isis finally understood why they called it the Great City. It was a massive cluster of Viking longhouses, layered next to each other on hills and all fortified with a tall wall encircling it.

Sitting higher than the rest of the city stood a tall castle, made of a beautiful gray stone. Isis' jaw dropped at the sight. It looked like it belonged in some sort of fantasy theme park, and yet it was the place she was going to be living. With high towers on each side, it rose on top of the highest hill, making it seem even taller than it actually was. It looked strong, like it could battle any storm. It seemed mysterious, like many hidden secrets lay within.

Admittedly, it did look a bit intimidating, with its dark colors and sharp spikes on the outer wall, but Isis supposed that served an important purpose. It conveyed a sense of strength and might, that of which might be intimidating for any opposing forces that were coming to attack it. In truth, Isis had never been one for romantic fairy tales. Living in a strong and secure place seemed much more important. Besides, it was beautiful in its own way, and it renewed the sense of wonder she found herself feeling upon living in *history itself.*

A new sense of eager anticipation rose up within her to learn and explore the new world she found herself in. What would it be like to join herself in this society and culture, the likes of which she had never thought she'd ever have the opportunity to even visit, much less be a part of? What would it be like to learn to be a Viking?

As the massive double door gates of the wall opened for them, the happy cries and cheers of people reached Isis' ears. She saw at once that people lined the path into the city within the gates, waving colorful fabric around to welcome them.

Bylur hopped down from his wagon, sending out a command behind him, which was quickly obeyed by another Viking man who brought forth two white horses. Bylur turned to Isis, beckoning her forth with his outstretched hand. Isis climbed off of the wagon, joining Bylur on the ground.

Gesturing toward one of the horses, seemingly the smaller of the two, Bylur conveyed his desire for her to mount the horse. Quickly realizing what was happening, Isis rushed to please him, accepting his assistance in climbing atop the steed. Instead of joining her on the horse, Bylur instead climbed on the one next to her, making nervousness bloom inside of Isis' stomach at the thought of having to ride this horse on her own. She had never ridden a horse, except for the time she rode with Bylur out of her village. But she had not been in charge of directing and leading the horse, making this a very different experience.

Much to her delight, Bylur tapped his heels against his horse's side, sending the big stallion into motion, and her horse immediately began to follow without any prompting from her. The horses walked on, side by side into the gates of the city, where Isis and Bylur would soon be wed and would live for years to come.

Isis' future had finally unraveled before her. Her heart raced at the thought of all there was to come.

Chapter Fifty-Four

The Wonder of a Castle

Isis was so thankful that this horse could manage to follow Bylur's steed, as she was extremely distracted by all of the people that surrounded the city's streets, cheering for her and welcoming them home. Crowds of people pressed in from every side, making Isis wonder how the horse wasn't getting spooked. It must have been used to it as it seemed to be unbothered by all of the commotion. People waved around colorful flags of fabric, while others showered Isis and Bylur with the fragrant petals of flowers. The people were all over, they lined the streets and some even stood on top of the roofs of the houses, looking down upon them with wide smiling faces.

Isis had never seen such excitement from people. Not even in holiday parades had she experienced anything of this sort. And certainly, she had never been at the *center* of such an event. No one had ever been so excited for her in all of her life. Not even when she was born could she imagine people holding such enthusiasm about her appearance.

The people wore their finest clothing, either that or the people of the city wore much nicer everyday clothes than those of the outer village they had stayed in. But even Agda herself had shown her the finer garments she owned, which seemed to be similar to the outfits that the people on the streets wore. And Isis felt *sure* that the king's sister and shieldmaiden would have some of the nicest clothes in all of the city. She could not imagine that Agda would have lesser fineries than the rest.

The further into the city they went, the more the city seemed to grow. Longhouses rose on hills above the street level, beneath them sat other longhouses adjacent to the street. All of them seemed much more sophisticated than the ones in the village they had been in previously. None of them looked quite as weathered, which Isis supposed made sense since they had a large wall to protect them from the elements.

Small gardens were squeezed in here and there next to the longhouses, filled with growing vegetables and sometimes even flowers. Most of the flowers, she noted with interest, were devoid of any colorful petals, giving Isis her answer of where their celebratory confetti of flower petals had come from.

People continued to shower them with praise and happy cheering as they walked on. Bylur turned to her about halfway through their journey into the city with a small smile on his face. He pat her knee, and the twinkle in his eyes seemed to say *welcome home, Isis.*

It felt good to be home.

As they continued to trod on, Isis noticed that the people looked at her with wide eyes of awe. They pointed to her hair, caressing their own skins as they whispered to one another about her. She had been expecting this as these people most likely had never seen anyone that looked like her before. They did not seem to be making fun of her or saying anything negative. In fact, most of their whispered words seemed to hold smiles along with expressions that held a bit of awe and wonder. Was it possible for these people to meet someone that looked different and accept her freely without any prejudice against her?

The street ahead curved slightly, and as they rounded the corner, an arched gate stood in the middle of the street. Its doors were held open by two Viking guards. Beyond it, there seemed to be an open courtyard that held a large stable for the horses and other small buildings, before leading to the massive stone steps up into the castle.

Isis looked up as they entered the courtyard, looking at the high castle looming tall above them. She was not sure how many stories it was, but she had to guess there were quite a few. She could not even see where the castle ended on either side, as it stretched beyond past other buildings which blocked her line of view. Guards patrolled on balconies far up near the top of the castle, carrying crossbows. However, they all seemed to pause their duties to peer down at the new royal arrival.

Isis felt like itching, the weight of all of these people's gazes making her feel nervous. So much pressure came with their scrutinizing stares, even if they were already in approval of her. If they already liked her, then she felt she must have to work to maintain their approval and not disappoint them. However, on the other hand, if they were suspicious of her as it is, then she had to win them over, or so it felt. What would be her duties here as queen? What expectations come with her new role? This was not something she signed up for, so Isis could only hope that they would have mercy with her, although she felt people rarely did.

Perhaps she should have considered things more thoroughly than she had. But then again, refusing to be Queen would have been refusing Bylur's love, something she simply could not fathom now. Her grandmother—may she rest in peace—had always encouraged her to never forsake adventure because she wanted to cling to certainty. Yes, taking on this role of leadership as Queen was a risk. But to forego it because she was scared went against what her grandmother taught her. Marrying Bylur was an adventure, and that included everything that came with that marriage, for better or for worse. Is that not what marriage is all about? Loving each other no matter what, for better or for worse?

As they arrived at the castle steps, Bylur hopped off of his horse, a young man rushing forward from the stables to take hold of the horse's reins and lead the steed into the staples. Bylur turned his attention to Isis, reaching both hands towards her. She did her very best to be graceful as Bylur assisted her, dropping down off of the horse, a thrill of heat rushing through her at the sensation of both of his hands on her waist.

With both of her feet firmly planted on solid ground once more, she turned to continue her admiration of the castle. Bylur chuckled, the deep sound vibrating through her as she still stood very close to him. She looked to him once more, the two sharing a smile between them. There was a brightness in his eyes, one Isis could only attribute to him being excited to share his home with her. How *incredible* that was, that anyone would be so excited to marry her and share their prized home with her. It felt good to have anyone share anything with her especially something important to them. For Bylur to do this with her, with such love and adoration in his eyes, Isis somehow knew no matter what happened, Bylur was going to take care of her. She had nothing to fear as long as he was by her side.

Bylur reached out a hand towards her, which she gladly put her own hand in his. With intertwining fingers, they began to climb the steps as the same young man rushed from the stables to collect her horse.

The wide wooden doors into the castle opened as they began to climb the steps. Two servants bowed as they approached, each having opened one side of the massive double doors. Isis' eyes widened at the impressive large foyer that greeted her once she was inside. Wooden beams stretched high above her, forming pointed peaks of a triangular ceiling, looking like a longhouse but within the castle's architecture. Five massive braziers illuminated the massive room in a golden glow, the fires crackling in greeting as they entered.

Footsteps approached on the stone steps behind them. Isis turned around to see Frode and Violet joining them in the castle with grinning faces. "Wow, this place is incredible. I can't believe we're actually standing in a real-life Viking castle!" Violet said breathily as she stared around the front hall in wonder.

"I know, I was just thinking the same thing. It's so beautiful, isn't it " Isis agreed, walking up to one of the wooden pillars of the room and tracing her fingers along the edges of the artistic carvings that were whittled into it.

Bylur began to speak in the Viking tongue, and after a moment, Frode turned to them to translate. "Our Great King Bylur welcomes you to his home. He has much he would like to show you before you are shown to your rooms to settle in for the night. If you would please follow us, he is very excited to give you a tour of his home."

As Bylur led the way through his massive castle, Isis found herself smiling widely at him. It was clear during the tour that her soon-to-be husband was so excited and enthusiastic to show her every single little nook and cranny of his beloved home, raving about stories of his childhood growing up here, which Frode translated. She had never seen him so overjoyed in all the time she had known him thus far. Even Frode seemed to be enjoying his brother's excitement, laughing every now and then in amusement at his brother's joyful step, as the king nearly bounced on his feet, skipping along the hallways of the castle as they went along.

There were indeed many things to see here. There was a large dining hall, somewhat similar to that front hallway with its triangular ceiling and wooden beams, with a massive table even larger than the one that had been in the Mead Hall back at the village. Isis was sure that you could not hear someone unless they shouted loudly if one sat on one end of the table and another sat on the other end, and the rest of the room would have to be completely silent. Hundreds of people could feast here without any issue. She could only imagine the incredible woodworking that went into crafting such exquisite furniture this room contained.

There were also many sitting rooms and bedrooms, as well as a large training room to practice one's archery or sword fighting, or anything else you could think of. Isis also recalled seeing something similar in the courtyard in front of the castle. The Vikings were very serious about fighting skills, that much was sure.

Isis was very interested in seeing the massive kitchens that took up several large rooms worth in the castle. Many servants greeted them warmly at their presence. Many eyes darted to Isis as they all fidgeted excitedly from the visitation. She wondered what it would be like to be a servant working here. She imagined it was extremely hard and hot work as they labored near open flames.

Moving on with the tour, Bylur was extremely excited to show her a couple of rooms that were set aside for the teaching of children. Through Frode's translation, Bylur excitedly told her that he had been taught here, and had many fond—as well as not so fond—memories in these rooms. Apparently, he was always longing to be outdoors, so being stuck inside in a classroom was not always pleasant for him, even if he did enjoy learning.

Finally, they came to one of the largest rooms, which sat at the heart of the castle. Reaching all new heights for the ceiling, the throne room was bigger than Isis' entire old house back in the modern world. With exquisite carvings built into the entire back wall and painted, and a large wooden throne sitting just in front of the wall, the room was an intimidating and imposing feature. Anyone who had to be brought forth here with the King sitting on his throne certainly might feel like they were coming before god himself to be judged.

Beside her, Bylur sighed, and he spoke, Frode dutifully translated. "Sometimes I wish I did not have to show you this side of me. I wish I did not have to be this strong King. I wish wars did not have to be waged, or that bloody battles did not need to be fought. But it is unfortunately the reality we live in, so it is a role I have to take on as the leader of these people. While it is important to put on a strong front and be intimidating lest anyone get the impression that they can take advantage of us, I do not wish to always put on a cold and terrifying persona. It is not who I truly am.

"I think with you by my side, I will be able to put forth a much warmer and softer appearance, without losing any of my firmness and authority. That was how it was for my father and mother, the previous king and queen who sat on these thrones. Without her, my father had always been seen as a ruthless and sometimes harsh king. Although, that was not true. He was simply doing his best to protect his people as a whole and bring justice to the land. Still, people always perceived him in that way. However, all of that changed when he married my mother. People began to see them as a joint unit, with her bringing softness and a gentle authority that were not so easily dismissed. I know she would be very proud of the choice that I made with you as my wife. I think you two would enjoy each other's company very much if she were alive." Frode translated for Bylur, who stared at the throne with an intense thoughtfulness.

Isis could feel her heart beat with a fierce fondness towards Bylur's wondrous words. They exchanged a look of deep understanding. The steel-blue eyes shone so clearly in Bylur's utterly exquisite face. His eyes retold their stories: their secret meetings in the small village, their love-making in the forest and then his house, and all of the turmoil they overcame together before they arrived here.

With a tender smile, Isis nodded at Bylur and could only hope she showed just as much heart as he did.

Later that night, as Isis soaked in her hot bath, which had been drawn for her by a handful of servants, Isis considered Bylur's words heavily. While his words had sparked love within her heart, recognizing just how meaningful his message was added pressure to her, weighing heavily on her chest.

Being compared to someone's mother was an incredible compliment, but it was also a lot to live up to. Isis could only hope that she was not a disappointment for Bylur. She was starting to have a bit of doubt. Did he really see something within her that made her worthy of being queen? Isis did not know. What if he just chose at random and the rest was just wishful thinking?

Isis awoke the next morning feeling tired and weary. Her entire body was sore from yesterday's travel, and although Bylur's bed was probably one of the most comfortable beds she'd ever slept in before, the mattress filled with the softest feathers, and with heavy furs for blankets, she did not sleep much or well, despite it being a delightful experience to be snuggled into. Unfortunately, she was not in the best place to fully appreciate such a wonderful experience. She hoped in the next few nights that she would be able to relish it much more thoroughly.

The night prior, before they went to their separate houses, Isis and Violet had decided they would go adventuring through the castle together. There were many things that Bylur had only glanced over in their tour yesterday, including one of the towers which Bylur had given to Frode for his learning and research. Frode had explained that he used it to study and learn, as well as experiment with some things. He had told them there were many books to be found there and they were welcome to go explore it whenever they pleased. While Bylur had barely mentioned that tower, both women were very interested in seeing it for themselves today.

Isis prepared herself the best she could without Agda, trying to remember how to properly dress herself in the Viking garb from everything that Agda had taught her when they had shared the small house in the village. Feeling that strong sense of imposter syndrome rise up within her once more, Isis took in a deep breath and let it out slowly, before opening the door and setting out to find Violet.

CHAPTER FIFTY-FIVE

FRODE'S TOWER

I sis found Violet wandering the hallways near Isis' bedroom chamber. The blonde girl looked meek upon seeing Isis' arched brows. "Sorry, I was so tired last night that I didn't really pay attention to where your bedroom was. I couldn't remember where to go this morning."

Isis laughed, pointing towards her bedroom door. "You were pretty close. It's right over there. I was tired, too, last night. Wasn't that bed so comfortable? I was really impressed. Maybe the Vikings aren't behind in everything. I think that bed might have been one of the most comfortable beds I've ever slept in."

Violet nodded enthusiastically the entire time Isis spoke. "Yes! It felt like sleeping on a fluffy white cloud. I was shocked. I was nearly expecting to sleep on the floor with nothing but a thin mat for comfort. We got little cots in the village before, but they weren't too much more comfortable than sleeping on the ground. I guess those outer villages really are more rustic, huh? I didn't think that this era was capable of such luxuries. Perhaps if we ever go back in time, we can take what we've learned back home with us. I thought a feather bed would be itchy and pokey at the very least. But it wasn't that way at all."

"I know, I thought the very same thing. Maybe we're in for some surprises being in this new world. That's the problem with only knowing things from textbooks if you can even remember that much. There might be facts that are just plain wrong. But I am excited to learn, nonetheless. Speaking of which, where should we explore first in the castle?" Isis asked, looking around the hallway to see if anything interesting was going on. Her mind still had a hard time coming to terms with where she was. It was mind-blowing that she was in a real-life Viking castle and had stayed the night. Not to mention the fact that she'd be living here from now on.

Violet crossed her arms as she considered Isis' question. "Hmm, perhaps we should start where our stomachs might take us. I don't know about you but I'm feeling rather hungry. Those kitchens looked so cool. I didn't realize how elaborate everything needed to be. I guess that makes me appreciate both this time as well as modern technology that was able to replace so many things. Either way, I feel like my stomach wants to lead the way."

Isis felt her own stomach rumble in response to Violet's suggestion. "Yes, I think that's a wonderful idea. I'm feeling rather hungry myself. Besides, I am very curious to see what sort of food they'll provide here for us. I also found the kitchens and how they do things to be of interest, too. And the people were so nice! I suppose since we are going to be living here, and we should try to socialize in some form or another."

The two girls went off in the direction that they seemed to remember the kitchens being, when Bylur and Frode showed it to them the night before. It took a while of exploring and going down several hallways that all looked the same, making quite a few wrong turns and ending up in a storage room at one point before they finally heard the clinking of pots and pans as well as hushed voices talking in the Viking tongue.

Picking their heads in the open doorway, they found a kitchen full of people hard at work. While both women had been offered dinner the night before, they had both been so tired they didn't even feel like eating. All they had wanted to do was have a hot bath and jump into bed. Thus, they found themselves exceptionally hungry this morning as the smells of food being prepared rushed through their nostrils.

It did not take long before the two women were noticed and the entire kitchen stood at attention for them. Isis tried to communicate that this was unnecessary, but either they were insisting on it or they didn't understand due to the language barrier.

Through simple hand motions and pointing, Isis and Violet were able to communicate that they wanted something to eat. Within moments they were whisked off to a table, where plate after plate of delicious looking homemade food was set before them until the table was full. There was everything and yet *nothing* that Isis would have imagined for a Viking kitchen to produce. She'd expected heavy oatcakes, which she did have, but they were much more flavorful than she would have thought. There were also soups and potato dishes. All of them were much more flavorful than she thought capable of this time.

Isis had been very hungry as they had initially walked into the kitchens of the castle. But that was certainly not the case when they left them. In fact, she felt like she had almost eaten too much. They had put so many delicious foods in front of them, all of them with such interesting flavors that Isis was not sure she had ever really tasted before, that she had found it hard to refuse. And seeing as this was a new experience, she let herself indulge in everything they had to offer.

The people had been so excited to feed them, too, that she didn't want to be rude in one of her first interactions with people she would regularly see since she would now be living here. But even if she would never see them again, they were so eager and kind that she didn't want to be rude by refusing them. Hopefully, that excitement wore off as they grew used to her being there. She wasn't sure she could eat like that all the time, not without having a constant stomachache from eating so much.

"I can't believe that's what we'll be experiencing every meal time possibly from now on. That was *so* nice. I am so not used to being waited on like that. Just think of it, possibly never having to cook for yourself ever again? That sounds amazing." Violet sighed dreamily as they left the kitchens and returned to exploring the castle.

The two women decided together that they would be heading towards Frode's Tower, excited to see if his idea of a library was the same as theirs. The only thing cooler than being in a Viking castle was if that Viking castle had a gigantic amazing library of Viking literature. Isis wasn't sure how or if they even prioritized reading in this era.

A rather steep stone staircase was the entrance to Frode's tower. It spiraled up in a circular motion, the rounded walls decorated with colorful tapestries here and there. The one that greeted them first was a red and gold art piece displaying some sort of strange creature from mythology. Isis had no idea what it was or what it signified, her lack of knowledge regarding Viking folklore, history, or really anything about these people and their culture was coming back to bite her in the butt once again.

As they continued their climb up the spiral staircase, their steps echoing in the stone passageway, they were continually greeted with warm tapestries containing some sort of mythological image. Isis found them quite interesting and told herself she would return here to study each piece individually at a later time. There was so much to learn about this culture and their belief system that Isis realized she really hadn't even dipped her toe into it at all. It was both exciting and overwhelming since she knew there was so much going on in all of it.

It was one thing to experience a different culture and a different country, it was a whole nother thing to experience it not only in a different country but in a different era and time of the world altogether. When you visit other countries, there are some things you can rely on, such as some scientific truth being regarded as fact, or modern technologies such as cars, even if they aren't that common, or at least the people knowing something about where someone comes from, even if they have the wrong idea about your country.

But this was another level entirely. These Vikings had no idea what America would become, perhaps only possibly recognizing it as the landmass itself at best. These people from another time and place had no idea anything about the world Isis and Violet came from, since the government and culture where they originated from had not yet been even founded yet! It made relating to one another quite difficult, and adjusting to this world all the more severe. And yet, Isis saw it as a puzzle to be solved. A challenge to be overcome. A problem to be conquered. She'd always been quite stubborn when it came to things that challenged her, so she was quite excited for this new world. But that still didn't make it any less difficult or overwhelming.

When they arrived at the top of the spiral staircase, a large rectangular room sat before them. A large fireplace stood on one side, a crackling fire greeting them warmly. The room was indeed filled with something akin to bookshelves, although it was almost like the maker of them wasn't quite sure what bookshelves were and was doing their best to emulate it based on a description alone.

There was a large desk in the center of the room facing the fireplace, completely covered in old parchments and papers. The room was devoid of any human life, much to Isis' disappointment. She had hoped to see Frode here. And when she looked over at Violet, she noticed that her friend looked slightly crestfallen as well. Isis knew something would catch on there between them eventually, perhaps the two just needed a bit of time.

The two women explored the room slowly, enjoying the view from the large windows that displayed all of the city below. Isis could tell there were many interesting and exciting things to be found here, but unfortunately, many of them happened to be written in the Viking language, which consisted of runes that didn't even look like their alphabet even slightly.

Both her and Violet were a bit disappointed at the lack of things they could understand or study within Frode's lair. Granted, it made perfect sense that he would have it all in his own mother tongue, and Isis wasn't sure what else they were expecting, but it was slightly disappointing, nonetheless.

Isis and Violet nearly jumped out of their skin when a voice broke the silence behind them. "Ah, there you two are. I have been looking all over for you. I am honored to find you in my tower, but I did not think to look for you here first. I am pleasantly surprised. But never mind that, I need both of you right now. Something is going on that I think you should be there for." Frode still seemed to have his chipper attitude about him, which did not seem forced, making Isis not as anxious as she would have been with his words alone. However, there was a bit of seriousness about him, making her think that, he wasn't overly concerned about whatever was going on, but there was still a bit of worry within his demeanor.

"What's going on, Frode? You seem a little put off." Isis stepped closer to her friend, her brows furrowing as a slight prick of concern filled her.

Frode glanced off to the side, pressing his lips together into a thin line as he seemed to consider how to answer her question. "There is a visitor here to see King Bylur. He and I have discussed it, and Our Great King said that it is nothing to worry about and that he would handle it on his own. However, I think that you need to be part of it, Isis, at least to listen to the conversation. I feel this strongly enough that I am willing to go against Bylur's expressed wishes and bring you in on it secretly. I normally am strongly against disobeying orders, even though this was not quite an order, but I think that Bylur might be involving himself beyond his ability. As his brother, it is my job to make sure that he is taking care of even when he doesn't think he needs any help."

Isis raised her eyebrows in surprise. Biting her lip, she considered the implications of Frode going against what Bylur told him to do as his king. "I see. And who is this visitor that you would want me to listen to in this conversation? And why would it be any help? I will not be able to understand any of it. Or have you forgotten that I am not a Viking like you?" Isis teased with a wink.

Frode shook his head, taking in a big breath before exhaling it loudly. "But that is the thing, Lady Isis. Most of it will not be in the Viking tongue. Most of it will be in your language, as the visitor is from your time. The only parts that will be in the Viking tongue are what Bylur says in reply to them, and what I say while I am translating what they say to King Bylur. All of the rest of it will be in the English language."

Isis' jaw dropped at the information, as Violet audibly gassed next to her. "Who could be requesting an audience with Bylur from our time? It isn't that blasted Amanda is it?"

"No, no, no, it is nothing like that, have no fear, Lady Isis. I do not think that Bylur would have anything to do with that woman if he had any choice in the matter. He knows she is no good. The person that is meeting with King Bylur in just a few short minutes is not anyone you know. In fact, it is one of the leaders from your time that kidnapped you in the first place. They have come to collect on their side of the deal. I think that Bylur is quite concerned about the matter because he no longer knows what to feel about them. He does not trust them anymore and does not know if he wants anything to do with them, either.

"As much as I trust Bylur and his judgment, as well as me being part of the meeting as a translator, I am not sure that we know what we're doing with these people. We very well may be over our heads and are perhaps ignorant of their way of doing things simply because we do not know of their ways since we are not of that time. Thus, I think it is important that you are present so you can tell us of any inconsistencies or lies they might be producing. I think that we need you and your expertise of your own culture and time in this area. And thus I am going to smuggle you into the meeting, whether Bylur likes it or not."

Dread spread over Isis at the thought of someone from her government coming to collect whatever it was they deemed important enough that they would kidnap a bunch of women and trade them for it. Surely that was a bit of a risk for them, so whatever they were after must have been worth the risk. Curiosity stirred within her as well at what possibly these Vikings could offer the modern-day government that they did not already have.

Either way, Isis felt that Frode was absolutely correct. She needed to be present for that meeting. She needed to know what was going on and what the government had up its sleeves. It was possibly vital for not only her new Viking friends and the life she was trying to build here, but also for all of those from her present time. Many lives could be

387

at stake here as clearly the government did not care about throwing some people away to get what they want.

Whatever this government individual wanted, Isis didn't think they could have good intentions.

CHAPTER FIFTY-SIX

VISITOR FROM THE FUTURE

I sis shivered in the chilly air of the hallway. Their footsteps echoed throughout the passageway. Frode turned back around to face her and Violet, speaking over his shoulder. "There is a secret balcony above the throne room. It is very small, so both of you will have to squeeze in there. Bylur and I's father had it built when we were children, so we could listen in when he was having meetings. Looking back, I also think that he thought it was good for us to be introduced to what being in leadership was like. Bylur and I spent a lot of time up there together, and sometimes Agda, too, when she was old enough."

Violet and Isis shared a look between them as they followed Frode. It was hard to imagine Bylur and Frode as children, hiding up in the balcony of the throne room and listening to otherwise secretive conversations. It was intriguing to Isis that a king would allow his sons to do such a thing, lest they accidentally heard something beyond their young years. But then again, weren't Vikings known for being brutal and harsh?

Frode opened a small door directly off of a back hallway, the door squeaking open with his pull. Giving the two women an apologetic look, he grimaced. "We have not been up here in some time. But nothing else should be noisy, not unless you two make noise yourselves. The stairs used to creak, but our father fixed that so we never alerted any of his guests to our presence."

"Why did your father allow you to listen? What if you heard something you shouldn't?" Isis whispered her question, admiring the craftsmanship of the small wooden door.

"I think we were partially there in case we *did* hear something we should not. We were given explicit instructions on what to do if we heard certain things, such as a fight breaking out in the throne room. Who to go to, what to say, then where to hide, and so on. But we rarely had to follow through on those instructions, thankfully," Frode replied before raising a finger to his lips to request them to be quiet, before he led the way up the steps.

Frode barely fit in the narrow passageway of the staircase. His wide shoulders touched the walls of it on either side. Isis felt claustrophobic as she climbed, trying to focus on making her steps as silent as possible instead of how tight the space was. Although she wasn't the biggest of women, she also wasn't the smallest, and that was a fact she was always minutely aware of in tight spaces such as this.

Once they reached the top, Frode stepped to the side, gesturing to the tiny balcony that stretched both left and right of the tiny doorway. Isis had to crouch the whole way up, and Frode looked like he was folded in half. His story about it being built for children certainly made sense; this place barely fit Violet, who was rather petite.

Frode pointed to one side for Isis to take a seat. She did so, as silently as she possibly could. Violet followed soon after, with Isis scooting down the balcony to make room for her. Once the girls were properly in position, Frode kneeled on the ground. His voice was barely above a whisper. "Be careful how loud you two whisper. While it should be somewhat safe to do so, sometimes the voices can carry in the throne room. Try not to talk if you can help it." Frode gave them a reassuring smile before turning away and slowly leaving. "I have to go now, stay safe and I will see you later on after the meeting. I appreciate your help in doing this. I will return to you as soon as I can, but if I don't return after half an hour after the meeting, then feel free to climb back down yourself. I know you two can take care of yourselves just fine. See you soon." And with that, Frode crawled back down the narrow staircase, disappearing into the darkness.

Isis and Violet shared a look between them, arching their brows at one another at the interesting situation they were in. Isis could not help the strong curiosity that was pulling her towards listening to this meeting. Who was this figure from the future and what were their intentions with the Vikings? So many questions rolled around her mind and she was ready for them to be answered.

The two women waited for several more minutes before any sound entered the throne room. Isis did her best not to fidget while she waited, tapping her fingers against her thigh as she peered down the small cracks of the balcony into the large room below, looking for any sign of movement.

Finally, a door opened somewhere beneath them, and the sound of footsteps filled the throne room. Two masculine voices barked out throughout the room, and Isis instantly recognized them as belonging to Bylur and Frode. They were speaking in their Viking tongue, so obviously she did not understand what they were saying, but it seemed to be a serious discussion, presumably about the visitor and the meeting they were about to have.

After several minutes of them calmly conversing, their conversation dropped off and another door opened, a pair of footsteps echoing throughout the room. Isis straightened her back to be able to look down at a different angle towards the large room beneath her.

Within her line of sight through the cracks of the balcony railing, she spied a middle-aged man in an expensive three-piece suit. His skin was tan and almost leathery. His bleach-blond hair thinned at the top of his head. He wore a rather large grin as his eyes were trained on something directly beneath Isis. Considering what she had seen in the throne room the night prior, it made sense that his eyes were trained directly on the throne, which presumably Bylur was sitting on.

The man raised both arms in a little circle as he looked around the room. "Well, this makes quite the statement, doesn't it? This makes you look quite intimidating, King

Bylur. I can certainly see the appeal of this. Maybe I should look into building a throne room for myself."

The man only got one sentence out before Isis felt like smacking the smug look off of his face. She didn't like him, not one bit, especially with what he and his colleagues had done to her and other women, but even if she was not personally involved, she would have been disgusted by such a horrible man.

Isis could hear Frode quietly translating for King Bylur underneath her. Bylur gave a small scoff once the translator was finished. He responded flippantly in the Viking tongue, Frode pausing for a moment before translating. "Our Great King Bylur would like to know what you are doing here, in his castle, in his time, without an invitation."

The man chuckled as his shiny leather shoes clicked loudly on the wooden floor. "Why, that is a bit rude of a greeting, King Bylur. After all, we never needed an invitation before. We came freely as we wished and you never seemed to mind prior to this. Tell me, you are not thinking about going back on our deal now that you got what you wanted out of it, are you?"

Bylur grunted when she received the translation from Frode. "He says that was before he discovered that you had tricked him with women who did not volunteer to travel to this time and live here. Your choice of violence has resulted in a difficult situation. He was under the impression that you would be sending women who were willing and *desired* to visit this time, not ones kidnapped and dropped off without a choice, stolen in the night." Frode's voice was tighter and colder than Isis had ever heard before as he translated Bylur's words.

"Oh, do not try to act like you were desperate enough that you would take whatever you would get from us. We never promised you willing women. We just promised you women. And we followed through and fulfilled our end of the bargain. If you cannot handle what gifts you were given, that is not our fault or responsibility. So you should know exactly why I am here. We fulfilled our end of the bargain. Now, it's your turn. Do not try to use how we obtain the women as an excuse to back out now or else I am going to start to think that you are a swindler, King Bylur. And since I do not think that you want that, with how honorable you are, or perhaps how you *pretend* to be, then I suggest you do the honorable thing and deliver what you promised." The man crossed his arms, tilting his head as he analyzed the king on the throne before him.

Despite the fact the man did not look all that physically fit, looking like the only exercise he got was playing golf once a week, he looked confident and held no hint of fear in front of two men who were muscular warriors and could probably rip him in half. Either this man felt like he had no reason to fear King Bylur and Frode, or he was even dumber than he looked.

The room was silent for several moments as the man stared intently at King Bylur on his throne. Isis raised her eyebrows in exasperation. Were the two men really having a staring contest right now? Was this really how men exert dominance over one another? It seemed a bit foolish to her.

Finally, King Bylur's gruff voice broke the silence. Frode was quick to translate. "We will not be fulfilling our side of the deal on the basis that you lied and were misleading, not completely fulfilling your end of the bargain. You have proven yourself as untrustworthy and incapable of honor. For our people, that is an automatic reason to cut all ties with you, no matter what your petty excuses are. You try to bring up my honor as though I ought to give you what you want out of honor, but it is for honor's sake that I deny you. It would be considered foolish and dishonorable for me to work with someone who is of such low morals and is manipulative and making their deals. We do not appreciate tricksters in our culture."

The man from the future clenched his hands into fists at his side, and the smug smirk dropped from his face as his lips turned into a snarl. "You do not know whom you are dealing with, King Bylur. I have been respectful of your power and your position up until now. But I have to inform you that you were just a *little* king of a *little* city of a time gone by. Your most powerful falls far beneath our weakest. You have no idea of the weapons that we have.

"So I suggest that you reconsider your foolish actions before you are slaughtered in your sleep and you never even have a chance to regret it. Perhaps you will regret it in Valhalla or whatever afterlife you people believe in. But trust me when I say death will be the only option if you go against us. We are the most powerful people in our time when things are much more advanced and many more things are invented and known. Do not overestimate your power or capabilities. It is *nothing* compared to us. You are *fortunate* that we have acknowledged your mere existence in this time enough to strike a deal with you. You are *fortunate* that we have decided to play friendly instead of simply *taking* what we want from you. So I suggest you take a step back and lower yourself from this over-inflated pedestal you have created for yourself because that throne means *nothing* when it comes to us. Your muscles and silly honor will not get you through a war with us, because there will be no war with us. There will be only slaughter and death for you and your people.

"I will give you one day to rethink your idiotic statement and realize how fortunate you are that you are not dead already by our hands. And when I come back tomorrow, you better have the relics on the table polished and ready for me to take with me. No tricks, no arrogance, just giving me what I asked for. Do this and you just might escape your encounter with us without feeling our wrath. *This is your last warning*. If I come back here again and things are not precisely how I have just asked, I will not hesitate to decimate you all."

Without another word, the man turned around and stormed off. His face was red by the end of the encounter.

He did not wait for a servant to open the door. Instead, he yanked it open himself, slamming it behind him as he went.

The throne room was silent for a few moments before Frode finally turned and expressed the sum of what the man had said. Silence then reigned again for a few moments more before King Bylur sighed and quietly gave Frode a directive before walking off his throne and leaving the room.

Once the door was firmly shut behind Bylur, Frode waited for a few moments to make sure he had gone beyond earshot before he called up to Isis and Violet. "You two can come down now. He just requested a meeting with you, so we might as well come clean to him about you listening. I'm glad you were there for that. We need you more than ever, now that we are about to go into war, it would seem."

Isis' breath caught at the word *war*. Was adjusting to a new time not difficult enough without someone trying to fight them at every turn?

CHAPTER FIFTY-SEVEN

AS THE DAWN RISES

Isis clutched at her dress with her fists, grasping it like it would save all of them. She looked around the table that they were all sitting around, noting how weary Bylur looked. He ran his fingers through his beard, before running his hands over his face.

Bylur, Frode, Isis, and Violet had been discussing what the man from the future had threatened for hours now. They had discussed strategy on how to move forward and deal with it, but only one thing had truly been decided.

Bylur was firm on his stance on not giving a single thing to these people. The man's threat had only confirmed his suspicions that they were morally inept people with questionable morals who lacked all honor. Isis had felt numb ever since the end of that meeting. Her entire body felt nearly paralyzed with dread. She knew what the government from her time was capable of. Thoughts of tanks, guns, and other weapons filled her mind.

What were fierce Viking warriors with their axes and swords and muscles in comparison to the technology that those from the future possessed?

Violet sat deathly silent beside her. The blonde woman had barely spoken since the man from the future had stormed out from the throne room hours ago. Her behavior would have normally made Isis worry for her, but in this particular situation, she couldn't blame her.

Frode seemed to occupy himself with translating for King Bylur and Isis while inserting his own opinions here and there in both languages. The language barrier was bothering Isis more than ever, but there was nothing she could do about that now. That was a concern for another time, if she ever got another time beyond tomorrow to fix it.

Bylur pushed his chair out from the table, the seat behind him nearly clattering to the floor from the force of his shove. He began to pace back and forth throughout the room, with his hands clasped tightly behind his back. He began to speak, and after a moment, Frode translated. "Bylur says he does not know what to do moving forward. He knows what he is *not* going to do, but that does not provide an answer as to what he *is* going to do. And for that, I have no suggestions either. If things are as bad as you claim, Lady Isis, then is there even a point in trying to survive this? Is our only option not giving in and handing over the relics? Is our only option to fight this man until we are all dead and then he can take from us? All we can do is truly make him fight for it and stall him for as long as possible? Is that truly our only option?" Frode looked like he had aged five years just this afternoon, posing the question to Isis with desperation written in his eyes.

"I do not know, Frode. I cannot think of anything else to do. I can only guess at the level of technology and weapons they have at their disposal. If this is a secret organization of government spies or something, they very well may have inventions that Violet and I have never even *heard* of as members of the public. The government is known to keep secrets from us and harbor technology and weapons that they don't tell us about until years after. Not only is it possible that they have things more powerful than we even know, but even if they didn't, the weapons that they have that we *already know about* are more than enough to destroy all of us within minutes. These things that just explode and catch fire, or these advanced crossbow-like weapons. All of them could decimate us in mere seconds, just like that man said." Isis' voice was soft as she tried to find the words to explain bombs and guns to someone who had no concept of them prior.

Isis glanced up at Bylur who was still pacing. He had not seen all that upset when Frode informed him that she and Violet had already heard the entire meeting with the man from the future, but she did not know if he simply did not have the energy or actually did not mind their presence hidden up in the balcony. She truly hoped it was the latter, and she was glad Frode had made the decision to have her and Violet hear everything so they could have extra ears that were trained to understand the nuances of the language and culture. While Frode was extraordinary in his skill of speaking English, it was still a foreign language to him that he was still learning. He simply may not have been able to pick up on things that Isis and Violet easily could. But that did not mean that Bylur saw things that way.

She would hate more than anything for something to come between them now of all times.

As the hours ticked on, it was simply decided that they would battle with everything that they had, but there was nothing creative to be done about the situation. Bylur already had a plan in place with his warriors in case their city was attacked. All of their warriors were already trained to carry out this particular plan. It was decided that they would still follow this plan, putting up the strongest fight they were capable of and that would have to be good enough.

But they all knew it *wouldn't* be good enough. Not enough to survive.

About an hour later, Bylur and Isis sat by a fireplace in a sitting room near his quarters. Neither of them spoke as they stared into the flames, simply sitting in companionable silence close to one another.

Isis had never felt so helpless in all of her life. Not even when she had been kidnapped and taken to this foreign time had she felt so inept and incapable. When she first arrived in this time, she gathered her wits about her as quickly as possible and settled on a plan to ensure her survival and make do with this horrible situation. But listening and joining in on the conversation between Frode and Bylur, she felt like they had no real plan other than to prolong all of their deaths as long as possible.

It was no plan for survival. It was no plan for success or victory. It was simply a plan to *inconvenience* these people from the future.

And there was nothing she could do to make that plan into one of victory. There was nothing she could contribute. She had no choice but to accept that all of her new friends and family were doomed to a horrible demise.

Isis knew she had no fault in this, that she had not chosen to come to this time—none of the women did. She knew that if the Vikings had requested something else, perhaps like fortune, more horses, or something of that nature—something other than women—they would still possibly be in the same predicament if Bylur had caught onto the type of people that these government individuals were. His honor would not allow him to contribute to anything that went against his morals. And he would not allow himself to be blind to it, either.

And yet somehow Isis still felt to blame. If she had not exposed these people as having kidnapped her and the other women, they would not be in this predicament. If she had not allowed her anger and bitterness towards those that had stolen her away from her home to rise up and burst forth among Frode and Bylur, they would have never known and would not have felt so strongly about this.

Her mind knew it was illogical. She knew in her head that Bylur would have noticed who these people were. She also recognized that everything she told them was true. To dismiss her feelings would have been wrong; she deserved to feel this way. And they deserved to know the truth, that no woman had come there willingly. Lying would have been wrong. Suppressing her feelings would have been destructive.

And yet she still felt guilty about it all somehow.

If the Vikings were able to destroy these people from the future, she would have felt no guilt. She would have known that these government people were suffering the consequences of their own actions. They had chosen to kidnap them, they had chosen to rise up against the Vikings.

But knowing that the Vikings could not stand against guns, tanks, and bombs made her feel sick with guilt. She was caught in the middle of a tragedy and the only person she could blame and still actually make suffer was herself. If she pinned the blame on the government, then it would have been useless, as they would not have felt any remorse or consequences from her blaming them. She needed to feel like her feelings mattered, like she could have some effect in this world. Being snatched up and presented as an object to trade did something to her self-esteem. And so she blamed the only person who could feel the weight of the guilt and hurt from it. *Herself.* Perhaps everything she'd gone through since coming to this time was finally exhausting her. She claimed little sleep, and her mind was not at its best.

Long after the fire in Bylur's fireplace died down into glowing embers, fading until the room was bathed in darkness, Isis and Bylur still sat near one another. Isis' hands itched to hold his, but the tension in her chest kept her from reaching for him, paralyzed in place. As if Bylur read her mind, he seemed to shake out of the heavy thoughts that had a tight hold on him. Looking towards Isis, his gaze softened, and Bylur reached for her, intertwining his hand in hers. Isis squeezed his hand, smiling at her love. She was thankful for such a strong partner that was so determined to love her.

At some point in the night, Isis dozed off. Her sleep was light and restless, without any real depth or comfort. When she awoke, thin strands of light fluttered through the window of the room, announcing the coming arrival of dawn. Isis blinked, trying to get her bearings. The seat next to her was empty, Bylur gone from the room. A large, soft fur was draped over her, keeping her warm. Isis could not help the small smile that flickered under her face at the realization that Bylur had cared for her after she had fallen asleep in the middle of the night.

Isis pushed the fur off of her and looked around, finding Bylur's quarters to be completely devoid of him. Leaving his bedroom and entering the hall, she looked around to find the castle to be completely silent. Wandering to the room they had used as a sort of war room yesterday, she found it empty and lacking any trace of life since they had left it the night before.

The sound of her thin fabric shoes against the stone floor was the only thing that disrupted the silence as she continued on, searching for anyone to point her to where Bylur or Frode was. Finally, something caught the attention of her ears as the sound of clanking metal drew her attention. As she chased after the source of the sound, she found the training rooms completely full of warriors preparing for battle. The sight made her take in a sharp intake of breath as she scanned the room for a familiar face.

Finally, she found Bylur and Frode helping each other get their armor on.

Approaching the two Viking men, Isis almost felt meek in the presence of all of these fierce warriors. Frode embodied all of his usual cheer and charm as he greeted her as she approached. "Morning, Lady Isis. I hope you got more sleep than the rest of us."

Isis gave a small shake of her head. "I'm afraid not. I tried, but it wasn't very good sleep in the end." She watched as the many warriors trained. Their swords clashed in clanging noises that caught her attention. "So everyone is already preparing for battle?"

Frode gave a solemn nod of his head. "Yes, we want to be completely ready when they arrive, whenever that is. The sooner we are prepared, the better. And theoretically, the more time that we have, the more we can prepare. But we do not know when that man will consider a full day to be. So we will prepare for the worst while hoping for the best."

Bylur interrupted the conversation to point out of the door while still looking at her, saying something in the Viking tongue. Frode chuckled as he translated. "Our Great King Bylur is insisting that you go get some food to break your fast. He is very adamant about it and will not take no for an answer."

Isis rolled her eyes but could not help the smile that leaked onto her face at the concern he was still showing for her in the midst of all this horrific chaos. "Very well, I will try to go eat something. Are you satisfied now, Bylur?"

Frode did not even need to translate. By the time that Isis got the question out of her mouth, Bylur was already nodding his head enthusiastically. Isis laughed and moved towards the king, giving him a kiss on the cheek before she departed the room.

Despite many delicious plates of food placed before her once she arrived in the kitchens, Isis could only nibble on a little bit before she felt sick and resorted to simply appearing like she was eating in order to appease the servants who buzzed around her like mother hens concerned for their baby chick. They did not seem too satisfied when she told them she was finished and went to leave, but she was insistent as she felt like she could not take another bite of food, even though she had eaten very little.

When she returned to the training rooms, they were empty, only a smattering of leftover armor and weapons remaining behind. Listening to the sounds that echoed throughout the hallway once more, she followed the sounds until she came to the front of the castle, where the courtyard was filled with patrolling guards and commanders that were directing their warriors where to go and what to do. It was all very organized as Isis noticed with interest that they were all painted with the Viking war paint.

Around the courtyard, she found herself continually getting in the way of the men who were hustling to get into their positions. Going off to the side, she looked around to try to find any sign of where her king and his translator could have gone. Finally, she spotted two figures that walked along the upper wall of the castle, which she now saw connected to the outer wall that surrounded the city, their forms catching her attention. She recognized them as the two beloved men she was looking for.

Breathing in a deep breath, Isis decided she was going to be with him until the very end, no matter what. She felt love for Bylur well up within her chest. She was choosing him, just as he had chosen her all of those weeks back. And she wasn't about to give up on that decision. He'd proven to her time and time again that he loved her, and she would be sure to do the same.

Retracing her steps back into the castle, she tried to remember where she saw some sort of steps or staircase that led up to the balconies that Frode had told them about on that tour two nights prior. It took some time, but she finally found it, and she climbed the steps as quickly as she could. Maneuvering around the patrolling guards, Isis descended from the castle's wall onto the city's outer fortification wall where she had seen Bylur and Frode go.

Isis was out of breath by the time she finally found the two men. They were all the way on the wall that went over the front gate, where they had once entered through on their white horses. *How long ago that felt.*

Both men raised an eyebrow at her in surprise as she approached. "Lady Isis, have you really chased us all the way down here? You really *are* a good match for Bylur. Just as stubborn as he is. I highly doubt he's going to let you be here, you know. He's going to protect you as much as he possibly can until the very end."

"While that might be true, Frode, he is my future husband and King, but he is not someone who can control me. And I have chosen him as my future and my love. I will not give that up so easily. I will fight for it with everything I have and I will not cower in hiding while he is out here waging war. A queen's place is by her husband's side, is it not? In my time, when we wed, we vow to be there for each other for better or for worse, in sickness and in health, richer or poorer. And I think—no, *I know*—this is one of those situations where my vow to love him must be stronger than the circumstance itself," Isis said as she looked into Bylur's eyes, trying to convey all of her determined passion within their shared gaze.

Frode did not even get a chance to speak his translation before Bylur was nodding his head, speaking in English. "Okay."

Isis raised her eyebrows in surprise, as did Frode. "Well, that was easier than expected." Frode chuckled. "But I suppose that is love for you."

Isis opened her mouth to respond when a shout from one of the guards that stood on a watchtower let out a shout. Both Bylur and Frode turned in response to the man's call, looking out over the wall into the horizon. Isis followed their lead.

There were many men on horseback coming their way, all outfitted for war. Next to her, Bylur swore under his breath.

They had arrived.

And yet, it was nothing Isis had imagined it would be. There were no tanks, no modern weapons of warfare that she could see. Most of the group were Viking men. Isis tilted her head in confusion at that.

Leaning over the stone wall, she peered closer, squinting her eyes to get a better look. All of the oxygen left her lungs as she realized that Bodvar was leading the men, next to the man from the future who rode on a horse right beside Bodvar. The two were in cahoots, there was no question.

What was this fellow from her time planning? And why was he relying on disgruntled Viking men to fight his battle?

Isis wished she could freely hope this was everything the man from her time had planned. After all, she knew that with Bylur's warriors and fortifications, they could easily defeat Bodvar and his men, the few that he had left. But there was *no way* things were as simple as that.

Somehow, seeing Bodvar and his men there made her feel even less at ease. The man from her time was up to something, and the fact that he wasn't showing his cards was disturbing to Isis.

Dread washed over her in a new wave all over again.

CHAPTER FIFTY-EIGHT

NO BLOOD FOR THE WICKED

B ylur's entire body was tense as he stood on the fortified wall, looking down at the group of men that had gathered to attack him and his city.

The man from the future, who looked more like a sun-bleached hide than a man, strode forward on his horse, grinning up at Bylur before he began speaking with a sneer. "Here is your final opportunity to turn over the relics and have peace between us, King Bylur. Although by all appearances, it seems you are preparing for battle with us, despite it being futile and stupid, I will give you the benefit of the doubt and hope that you were just preparing for the worst and are still planning on handing over what is rightfully ours." Frode quickly translated for Bylur by his side.

Bylur grasped onto the side of the wall until his knuckles blanched white. "No." His voice barked out with the firmness he did not feel. He knew how to play the role of the authoritative leader even when he did not feel like he was capable enough. He spoke the refusal in the language of the foreign ones, skipping waiting for Frode to translate.

The grin dropped from the man's face for a moment before it flew back up into his face, growing wider as an evil glint sparkled in his eyes. "Very well. Then it is time for the destruction of your so-called *Great City* and the downfall of the *Mighty King Bylur*. I find it hard to believe that you, who is supposed to be this strong, fierce leader and warrior, would allow an emotional woman to sway him into sacrificing himself, his people, his throne, and his entire city for. You should know better, King Bylur. Listening to a woman is idiotic. They do not understand the necessities that one must do in order to gain power and do what is needed to be done. No, they only think of their feelings and stupid morals. They do not understand what it takes to lead anything."

Frode's teeth gritted tightly as he translated this for Bylur, whose fists clenched at his sides. Anger roared through Bylur like a mighty wildfire blazing through.

Without a second thought, Bylur sent a glance over at one of his commanding warriors that led his archers, making eye contact with a man as he gave a subtle nod towards him. Within the next moment, the warrior was quick to respond to Bylur's silent command, and he gave the order for his archers to shoot.

Arrows flew from the upper wall into the incoming men that crowded the locked gate into the city, only a few finding purchase as the men groaned and fell off their horses.

The man from the future snarled as he held up his hand, momentarily making Bodvar pause, who was quick to jump into shooting back at them in response. The man from the future nodded towards Bylur before speaking once more. "So be it, King Bylur. *It is time for slaughter.*"

Before Bodvar and his men could get reoriented into firing back, Bylur nodded once more to his commanding warrior, and more arrows fired down upon them.

They were not a large group. There was no way they would be able to subdue even the archers on Bylur's wall, not to mention all of the frontline warriors Bylur had waiting behind the gate. These fellows would not even be able to crash through the gate or conquer the wall with the limited amount of men that they had.

They had to have known this, Bodvar was a far better warrior than to waltz up to their gate like this and expect anything to happen. Yes, the man was prideful, but certainly nothing close to being *this* foolishly arrogant. There is more going on here than what Bylur could see, there had to be more warriors waiting to come and fight alongside them.

But where? Bylur could see no one else in the distance. He would be able to see any approaching armies in the horizon for possibly an hour before they actually arrived at the city. Even if they appeared in the next few minutes, the distance they would have to cover before they arrived at the gate from when they became visible would take far too long. This man from the future and Bodvar and their men would be demolished by then.

So then what was their plan?

The man from the future did nothing as arrows were shot back and forth. His eyes locked on Bylur as he grinned like a wild animal at him. So far, although arrows were flying back and forth, none of them had been able to hit one another as both parties seemed to be adept in dodging the other party's arrows as they were firing their own, making their aim weak.

The man from the future held up his hand once more making their archers pause their assault. Bylur considered doing likewise but then decided not to. Why would he? They were attacking *his* city and he wanted to finish this as soon as possible. Whatever they had hidden up their sleeve, Bylur did not want to give them a chance to even bring it out. And even if they did manage to reveal their secret weapon or whatever it might be, he did not want to give them a moment's peace while they pulled it forth.

The man from the future lifted a finger to his ear, pressing it in as he said something quietly, not loud enough to reach Bylur's ears. Another moment passed before something strange seemed to be appearing right behind Bodvar's warriors. Something that looked like silver sparks was erupting in the air, growing until they were wide squares, like a large door made of magic in the air.

As they finally stopped growing, people began to walk out of them, appearing out of nowhere through the spitting sparks. As they kept coming, all of them dressed in unfamiliar clothing, Bylur felt his stomach sink. This was the moment he was waiting for. He knew something like this was bound to happen, nothing else made sense. But seeing their arms filled with strange objects, Bylur assumed these were the weapons that Isis had talked about. *These* were the inventions that were to be feared, that his warriors could not stand against, according to his future queen.

Indeed, as they continued to arrive, Isis gasped, her face twisting in fear and horror. Moving to the other side of Frode, Bylur stood by his future queen, putting his hand on her arm and moving it down until his hand came in contact with hers. She turned to him with a look of aghast, breathing in a deep breath when her eyes met his. Realizing his hand was on hers, she opened her hand, and they intertwined their fingers tightly together.

They were standing together in this, *no matter what*, just as his brave queen said while they were waiting for their attackers to arrive.

It was such a difficult thing to do, allowing her to stand by him through all of this. All he wanted to do was protect her, but he knew she had other ideas. And he knew there was likely very little point in trying to protect her when they were all would most likely die this day. And so he would grant her wish. She asked to stand by him until the very end and do this together. Who was he to refuse her?

"You should have listened, King Bylur," the man from the future said with a smirk. They raised their weapons towards all of those who stood on top of the wall, including Bylur, Frode, and Isis. His hand was going numb from how hard Isis gripped it, but he could not blame her. He felt the very same way, wishing to grab onto anything for safety and cling to it. He was fortunate to be able to hold Isis' hand at this moment.

There was silence in the still moment that Bylur waited for them to shoot, holding his breath as he waited to see just what the weapons were capable of. And in that stillness, he felt a measure of peace. He was going down fighting, with his soulmate by his side. There were many worse ways to go, and Bylur felt strongly that he had done the right thing, that he had made the correct choice. And if you were going to die for any reason, it would be for honor, in protecting your people, and possibly even protecting the world. Bylur knew the relics were powerful. Many of them were capable of incredible things. What would these people do with them? What kind of terrible evils would they commit using the relics perverted with their technology as weapons, when they were so willing to hand over women whom they took against their will?

And in that silent moment, Bylur breathed deeply, allowing the peace to fill him. Bylur accepted his death, for better or for worse.

But as he took in that deep breath, something peculiar caught his eye. Something a short distance away from the group of people below was sparking, much like it had when those other modern people had arrived. Surely this was simply more modern people with their unstoppable weapons arriving, even though Bylur was not sure that was necessary. If these weapons were as powerful as Isis had made it seem, then only a handful could destroy them all in a matter of minutes. But what did he care if more of them showed up? At that moment, he might as well have been already dead. He wasn't even sure he would make it to see these newcomers fully arrive. But there was still a level of interest there for him. It didn't make much sense why more of them would come if their other compatriots already had everything well in hand.

The door sparked more enthusiastically with every beat of his heart, growing exponentially before his very eyes. The colorful sparks drew the attention of his attackers below, most of those that had their weapons raised towards them turned to look, becoming distracted from their original goal of wiping out all of those on top of the wall. *This was interesting.* Why would they get distracted from something they already knew was coming?

The magical doorway that opened was much larger than the one that his attackers had come through previously. Another one opened up behind his attackers, and then yet another on the other side of them. It seemed to be surrounding them on every single side except for the one closest to the gates of the city and all of the Vikings.

Modern people began to step through, surveying the scene they were walking into with an analytical coldness. Bylur's peace at that moment was not shaken, though he still did not understand why they insisted on bringing more of these people through.

But then his attackers began to fully notice these newcomers, and their reaction made his heartbeat race even more than it already was. They jumped upon noticing them, backing up in fear and cowering at the sight of them. The man from the future seemed especially frightened at their arrival. In fact, the only people that did not seem concerned or fearful were Bodvar and his men, who looked more confused than anything.

Could it be that there was a third party at play here? A group of people from the future that did not have the same goals and intentions as these people he had originally made the deal with? Could it be that there were people out there, possibly powerful people, that did not believe that the man from the future was doing an honorable task? What if they too disagreed with his methods and actions and decided to step in?

That would be a gift from the gods themselves.

A woman stepped to the forefront of the newcomers from the future, wearing a suit much like Bylur had seen the man he had dealt with prior wear every single time they had met him, except all of the pieces of her suit were black, where he had been wearing a white tunic of sorts.

With a cold authority that ran a chill of fear down Bylur's spine even though she was not directing her icy tone towards him, the woman began yelling as if to reprimand the man from the future. He jumped down from his horse, standing in front of her with an apologetic look upon his face, trying to interrupt her with what seemed like platitudes in their foreign tongue, but she would not allow him to interrupt, constantly silencing him with an angry look. The man quickly gave up trying to give her excuses and allowed her to finish her rightful verbal assault on him.

Looking beside him, Isis beamed with a broad smile. Her other hand that was not entwined with his raised to cover her mouth, her chest moving with relieved laughter. Whatever this woman was saying to the man, Isis clearly found it quite amusing.

The woman from the future flung her hand behind her, pointing towards the portal she had come through. Her entire body was tense with fury. The man that had attacked them bowed his head low in submission, walking towards the portal with his shoulders slumped in defeat.

She then directed several of her other men to round up Bodvar and the rest, pulling every bow and ax from their hands. Every single one of their attackers from the future was also disarmed and sent through the portals until there were no threats left to be seen.

Finally, the woman turned her attention toward the wall where Bylur still stood, moving her hands until they were clasped behind her back as she strode forward. "May I be presented with the opportunity to speak with the leader of this beautiful city?" Bylur raised his eyebrows as the woman spoke in their Viking tongue, not in the English language that most of the foreign individuals spoke.

Bylur nodded his head towards her, drawing her attention. "I am he. I am King Bylur, Lord and Leader of the Great City of Vikings, which you now stand before."

She dipped her head in respect for a moment before raising her eyes to meet his once again. "Greetings to you, King Bylur of the Great City. I am Laura Martin, an agent in a sect of the country that the women that have been staying with you are citizens of. I believe there has been a terrible tragedy that has occurred here. That man was a leader of a small but powerful secret organization of our government. We were not aware of his actions as of late, and he will be dealt with and punished to the fullest extent of our law for the crimes that he committed to both the women involved, and to you and your people. If I could be granted access into your city to speak with you privately, as well as the women that were involved in this terrible event, I would be extremely grateful. It is my duty here to try to clean up the mess that man created."

Bylur took a deep breath, considering the implications of her words. He agreed with everything she had said, for in his mind it was certainly a terrible tragedy, and he did want it resolved and redeemed as soon as possible. He eyed her for a second, trying to gauge whether he could trust her or not. After dealing with that horrid man, she seemed almost too good to be true. Was this a trick of some sort? Was this a ploy to get him to open his gates and allow them in, only to be attacked and taken over?

But if they had those terrible weapons from the future, where was the need in that? Isis had been so sure that they could overpower them easily. And the look of fear upon her seeing the weapons told him everything he needed to know. They had the power to wipe them out with those weapons. They did not need to pull a trick such as this. As he looked at the woman named Laura Martin, she seemed sincere and eager to put this behind her.

"Open the gates! Allow her in, and she alone." Bylur barked a command out to those guarding the gates below. At once, the men hurried to obey his order. The gate opened after being unlocked with the several bars removed from it. It creaked open and the woman stepped forward, swiftly entering inside.

Bylur took in a deep breath, preparing himself for whatever came next. He did not know what was ahead, but he surely felt it was better than the death he had expected just moments prior. His body felt weary from the adrenaline that had been coursing through his veins suddenly vanishing as he settled down with all threats removed.

Isis squeezed his hand beside him, her eyes wide with love and wonder. She was just as surprised as he was, but there seemed to be no rush to get away from him and flee to her own people as he might have thought. He feared losing her, but he was not a jealous man to hold his love hostage. She had her choice, she had her free will, and he would have to leave it up to Isis, their love, and the gods to decide what happened next.

A warrior ran up to Bylur, the young man huffing and puffing from the exertion of running up the steps and across the stone wall quickly. "My Great King Bylur, the newcomer requests you meet with her privately first and foremost. She is requesting to be brought into a place you find secure and feel safe in having some privacy as she converses with you."

Bylur dipped his head in a nod towards the warrior. "Very well. Bring her into the throne room and have her wait for me there. I will be there shortly. Thank you."

Frode raised an eyebrow up at him. "Do you want me to come with you?"

"No. This is something I wish to do myself. Be waiting in case I do need you, however. I do not know what this woman wants from us."

CHAPTER FIFTY-NINE

THE CHOICE

Isis paced the courtyard in front of the castle steps. Her arms were crossed as she waited for what felt like an eternity for this unknown woman, who had introduced herself as Laura Martin, and Bylur to finish privately speaking and return to the rest of them. She knew that Bylur could handle himself, so hopefully this woman wouldn't try anything like pulling a gun on him, but she still found herself concerned at the notion of them talking alone.

She knew nothing would probably happen, but it was more about what she thought *would* happen that was alarming to her. She felt like this woman would bring a choice for all of them. If she was a kind individual with power from their time, then the question that had bounced around Isis' mind might be brought before her, forcing her to come to a conclusion. *Will you go back to your original time, or will you stay here in this era?*

If that woman could simply make another portal back to the future appear, then it was all too simple for Isis and the rest of the women to return home if they wished. The question was *what did Isis want?*

Her stomach churned at the thought. She wished things could go back to simplicity, when she could simply go with the flow and focus on the here and now instead of making such a major decision about her future. Would this woman try to rush things? Or would Isis have time to think things over?

All of her life, Isis never considered this ever being a possibility. She never considered living among Vikings as an option. And then when it *did* happen, she was understandably shocked. But what could she do about it? She was stuck in this time and there had been no escape. All she could do was make do with what she had been given.

And so she did. She built a future with this incredible man that happened to be the king of the Vikings. She knew she had a pleasant future ahead of her, just like she knew back in modern times that she had a pleasant future before her there, too.

But never before did she have to make a decision between two futures, two worlds, two whole different lives. She knew that there was not a right or a wrong decision. Either one would be pleasant and lovely for her, because she had built both of them to be that way for her. She made tough decisions to make her life what she wanted. When life gave her lemons, she didn't just make lemonade—she made lemon meringue pie.

The question boiled down to this: *what did she actually want?* Not what could she make do with? Life had always just given her lemons. Yes, she had always made something delightful out of those lemons, but now she had multiple fruits to choose from. And while having choices felt brilliant and freeing, it also felt heavy with the weight of responsibility.

Isis was disrupted from her thoughts by the castle doors opening with a loud creak, and both Bylur and this Martin woman stepped through them and into the courtyard.

Frode stepped forward, giving a small bow as he addressed both of them in Viking tongue. He gestured back to the group of women he had gathered in the courtyard. Frode had already informed Isis that King Bylur had requested him to bring all of the foreign women to the castle's courtyard. Apparently, this Laura Martin wished to speak with all of them collectively, which only worked to further confirm Isis' suspicions, making her palms slick with sweat.

Both Bylur and Laura nodded, and Bylur put an arm out, gesturing towards the gathered women as he looked at Laura Martin, as if welcoming her to go ahead and do whatever she requested to do with them.

She stepped forward, clearing her throat. "Hello. I am Agent Laura Martin. I am a trusted member and agent of the United States of America's government.. I am here to offer all of you support through this difficult situation. I know you may not have much trust for people from our government, considering members of the government are the reason you are here in the first place. I understand it may be scary to even *see* me, considering that the last time an agent spoke to you or interacted with you was when you were being kidnapped and brought here. I am not discounting the trauma you have been through. *You were kidnapped*. It was not legal nor right, and we are not approving of it in the slightest. In fact, my only duty here is to fix the horrible wrongs that were done to you as much as I am able.

"If you wish to return back to your lives and homes in the future where you were born and lived, I am here to transport you back. If you wish to stay here, then my job is to set you up with a connection back to the future in case you change your mind. Either way, we will do our best to help you and right the wrongs that the rogue agents did to you."

In the courtyard, whispers erupted around all of the women at Agent Martin's words. Violet approached Isis, stepping up beside her and leaning in. "Do you think this woman is sincere?"

Isis looked up to peer closely at Agent Laura Martin. Isis' eyes narrowed as she tried to gain insight on her. After a minute she felt her intuition speak up. "I do. It doesn't make any sense that this would be a trick. Why would they kidnap us only to try to kill us or something? And that man that kidnapped us wanted something in exchange for us. Something he clearly didn't get. And they still *won't be getting* even if we go with them. Why would they want us back? What would they gain from having us in their possession? We are just ordinary women that lived in their country anyway, they could get just another group of ordinary women if that's what they really wanted. The only thing that really makes sense is that she's telling the truth and we can go back if we want."

Isis' field of view was blocked as Agent Laura Martin stepped into her range of sight. "Hello. You must be Isis Lozada. King Bylur told me a lot about you. You are the one that was set to be Queen, is that right?"

The entire courtyard fell silent as they waited for Isis' response. "Yes, that's correct. I'm Isis."

Agent Martin nodded, a stiff smile sliding into place. "I can imagine that this has been quite a difficult time for you. King Bylur told me about the difficulty with one of his men trying to cause an uprising all over being denied a woman.. I cannot imagine this has been a delightful experience for any of you."

Isis and Violet shared a look between them, before Isis turned back to Agent Martin and sighed. "Yes, it has been quite the roller coaster of emotions. But I have to admit, I never thought I would have such an opportunity to see historical longhouses in person, or meet actual Vikings. To be in another time. Hundreds of years before I was supposed to exist...it is just beyond my wildest dreams. I have had a lot of interesting experiences being here. And the people are kind and interesting, and the men aren't bad to look at, either."

Agent Martin and Isis shared a friendly laugh between them before the Agent nodded understandingly. "I can understand there having certain conflicting feelings in the matter, especially since the Vikings were not even aware that you were brought here forcibly. And they seem to be kind and respectful people. And yes, they are *quite pleasant* to look at. But that brings me to my next question. If there are mixed feelings going on here, then there's a decision that has to be made."

Isis felt her stomach squeeze in response to the woman's question. Isis raised an eyebrow up at her. The agent was right. Isis had a lot to think about. Was she leaning towards staying here? With the Vikings, along with the man who treated her with love and respect in a way she'd never experienced before, in a place where she was welcomed for who she was, and in fact, *celebrated* as the future queen.

Or was she leaning towards leaving this place? And returning home to her old life—one she had truly ever known—to modern technology, to luxuries, to the family she had left, to the skills relevant in her time, to her old job, and to a place of security and certainty.

Isis dropped her gaze to her feet and sighed. "It's a big decision and I'm not quite sure what to think."

"This is something that you need to figure out for yourself. I am sure you are already on the edge of a breakthrough. I can see it in your eyes. Nevertheless, you need to come to a conclusion rather quickly, I'm afraid. *All* of you do." The agent regarded all of the women now, speaking in a much louder voice that commanded the room. "While I am going to give you an avenue to contact us if you decide to stay, in case that you change your mind later on, we urge those of you who would like to return home to please gather closer around me, so we may help you prepare for the travel." Agent Martin looked past Isis to where it's the rest of the women as she spoke the last few sentences.

Isis looked towards the castle as Agent Martin continued to talk to the rest of the women. Isis was barely able to listen as her mind buzzed with thoughts. Her eyes landed on Bylur, who was looking at her with his shining steel-blue eyes. They were wide with fear, she realized—, fear that she was going to leave him. He knew full well the opportunity that Agent Martin had just presented her with, and if the look on his face was any indication, he wasn't happy about it. He seemed almost desperate, and yet, he still kept his space. Bylur smiled, but it did not reach his eyes. His gaze told her a story, one about being afraid to hope, to resigning himself to letting her go. And, no doubt, he could see the look of confusion and all of the mixed emotions she was sure were plainly written all over her face. Confusion on whether or not to leave him and return to her home. Which meant there was a possibility that she might.

His heart was on the verge of breaking.

His hands were clenching and unclenching at his sides, as if he wished to reach for her but was controlling himself for her sake. His body was stiff, tense with anxiety.

But still, Bylur nodded towards her. It was just one small single nod and yet, it spoke *volumes*. It told her everything she needed to know about that man. He was letting her know she could make her decision freely. He was telling her to go home if that was what she wished. That he wanted her to be happy. So much was evident within those big, round eyes. So much love and adoration for her. So much dedication and so much freedom. *Freedom for her.* Freedom for her to make her *own* choices, even if that meant leaving him behind.

He would rather have her happy than have her all to himself.

THE VIKING KING'S LOVE

Isis couldn't even think. It felt like everything stood still as she looked into those shimmering eyes. Her heart warmed at everything he was silently communicating to her. Everything felt meaningless, and yet, looking into those eyes, she felt like nothing was without meaning. Like the whole world consisted of the two of them and their love, and nothing else mattered. The passion between them held enough meaning all on its own.

She knew she was never going to be able to get rid of him from her mind. Those eyes would haunt her for the rest of her life, but it was now her choice whether she wanted to be reminded of them and smile with love in her heart, or have them haunt her in her dreams, only to wake up with regret and sorrow.

Maybe nothing else *did* matter. And maybe she really did know her answer already.

In a flash, she twisted around to look at Agent Martin, calling out to her and interrupting her speech to the other women. Frode, who had been standing near Bylur, stepped closer to the king, beginning to translate as if he sensed this moment would be important. Isis nodded towards the Translator before speaking, her voice filled with confidence. "You're right, Agent Martin. I already *do* know my answer.

Why would I miss this once in a lifetime opportunity to be a time traveler living in another whole time? Why would I give up this romantic adventure in exchange for security and certainty? Why would I choose the safe route when I have such excitement and love in store for me here? No, I will not be as idiotic as that. Who do I have waiting for me back at home? Barely anyone. What do I have waiting for me back in the modern world? Computers and technology and a job that I don't love?

"Is that really enough for a human to thrive on? No, it *isn't*. We need love, friends, and family for life to have any meaning at all. I don't really have that there in the future anymore. But here? Here, I feel *whole*. Here, I feel like I *matter* to these people. Here, I feel like I belong and I'm welcomed. Here, I feel safe in the arms of a man that cherishes me like no one ever has before.

"Yes, it had a rocky start, my time here in this land. But he *chose* me. He picked me out of all these women as someone he desired and admired and felt like he could live his entire life with. Yes, it could have started better. Yes, I would have much rather preferred if I chose to come here in the first place. But there's no point in whining and crying over that now. What matters now is that these people are kind and wonderful and make me feel like I can truly *be myself* with them, like I'm important and they would protect me at all costs simply because I have inherent value.

"What matters now is the future, not the past. What matters now is that I love a man and I cannot trade that love in for certainty. I cannot trade in such a valuable treasure for mere security because I'm too scared to step out of my comfort zone. No, I will not only step out of my comfort zone, I will leap out of it if that's what it takes. I've made my decision. I'm staying here. *End of story.*"

The entire courtyard rang out with silence at Isis' exclamation. Looking over her shoulder, her eyes connected with Bylur's, which were now filled with tears. The smile on his face clearly conveyed that he understood everything she had just said, loud and clear.

Maybe an expression of love simply didn't need to be translated. It went beyond language barriers. Maybe such vulnerability and love was part of the *human* language, not the English language.

There was a promise in his eyes. A promise of a future. Promise of love and life and hope. She had never seen him look as bright and full of life as he did now. She had chosen him, just as he had chosen her. They had chosen each other for love and for life.

Cheers and applause erupted in the courtyard and beyond. Isis herself was immediately tackled into a hug by Violet, and Frode was jumping up and down as he shouted out his happy cheers, waving his arms about like a wild man.

This was home. This was the world she belonged in, even if she hadn't realized it until now.

Isis didn't even realize she was nudging her dear friends aside while sprinting toward Bylur until she saw him charging towards her as well, and felt herself being lifted up into his arms as he picked her up and twirled her around. Placing kisses all over her head, face, and hair, Bylur was muttering sweet nothings to her in his Viking tongue. Isis held on to him with all of her might, wishing to never let go of him. She knew her grip had to be tight, but he didn't seem to mind.

This was home.

And Isis loved it. She was a homebody, after all. And she knew she wasn't leaving anytime soon. Her home had everything she needed. Love, adventure, romance, friendship, family, and a place where she belonged.

EPILOGUE

Isis looked in the long, wavy mirror at her reflection. While the Vikings did not have the best quality of mirrors, Isis wasn't complaining. In fact, the lack of proper reflection made her not as obsessive over her appearance as she once was. Amazingly, she found herself growing less insecure with every day that passed. Yes, it could be that all of Bylur's compliments and encouragement, as well as his lavishing of love and obvious appreciation of her looks and beauty, certainly helped matters. But Isis recognized that living in a world where mirrors weren't as prevalent nor as clear as the ones they had in the future were helping her more than she ever had considered before. Not being able to properly see herself often erased all of her anxiety about her appearance.

Except at the present moment.

Today was the big day she had been waiting for a long time now. As she stood in front of the somewhat fuzzy reflection of herself in the glass mirror, she tried to focus on calming her breath. She needed to look her best for today. And not being able to check to see if she was looking her best irritated her immensely. She could barely tell what she looked like in this mirror, not to mention if she had a hair out of place or if there was a big spot on her nose. What if her dress was wrinkled or had a stain on it and she didn't realize it?

Although, she doubted that was the case, as Agda had beautifully crafted this exquisite wedding dress with much love and care. She had help too, with many women of the Great City volunteering their time and skills to present Isis with a wedding day unlike any other.

But today wasn't *just* her and Bylur's wedding day, although *that* was the part that was most important to Isis.

No, this was the awesome day that Isis was to be crowned Queen of the Great City and all of her people. She wanted to be as presentable as possible for such an important event. It wasn't bad enough that it was her wedding day, or her crowning day for that matter, it was the fact that it was both simultaneously that made her especially anxious.

THE VIKING KING'S LOVE

A knock on her dressing chamber door distracted Isis from her wavering reflection. She bid her visitor to enter in Viking tongue, something she had been working hard on learning over the past months. Being immersed had helped her tremendously, having to hear and communicate with others only in Viking speech. She felt like she had a fairly good handle on the language, better than Bylur had on English, that was for certain.

Speaking of her beloved king, it was he who poked his head through the door, grinning like a fool. His smile only grew when his eyes landed on her, and he hastily entered the room, shutting the door behind him.

"You look so beautiful." Bylur said in his Viking tongue as he looked at Isis, almost like a swooning maiden would from those regency romance movies Isis had seen back in her time.

Isis laughed at him, swatting at him when he began kissing her neck tenderly from behind her. "Thank you. I am sure you tell that to all the women you are about to marry." Isis teasingly grinned back at Bylur, swept in his tender embrace, as their noses touched, lips dangerously close. "In my time, it is bad luck to see your bride before the wedding?"

Bylur smiled against her skin, chuckling into her neck. "My love, what is bad luck when you have the gods on your side?"

Isis raised a brow at him in the reflection of the mirror. "How do you know that the gods are on our side? Perhaps they are just up there laughing at us foolish little mortals and our sweet little love that we have."

Bylur scoffed, pushing her black curls out of the way to have better access to her neck. "Impossible. If they were not on our side, we would not be together. How else could it be that a Viking man such as I and an incredible woman from hundreds of years in the future should come together and fall in love? It was fate, it was *destiny*. Can't you tell we are meant to be? A love as beautiful and powerful as this is *impossible* for two little mortals such as us to forge all on their lonesome. It has to be anointed by the gods to occur. And no one will be able to tell me any different. I can recognize the gods' handiwork when I see it. I know that when something is as exquisite as this, it simply *has* to be divine. There is simply no other explanation for it."

Isis could not help the bubbling of joyful laughter that came forth straight from her chest. "You sound like you are drunk on love, my dear."

"Maybe I am. But even if I am, that doesn't change my opinion on anything." Bylur stood straight, standing quite a few inches taller than her.

Isis scratched at her neck where his long beard had been tickling her. She gave a sigh as their eyes met in the fuzzy mirror. "I know, my beloved Bylur. I'm not saying I disagree with you. In fact, I would like more than anything to think that someone out there, be it the gods or otherwise, would look upon me so favorably as to give me you."

Bylur wrapped his arms around Isis as he gave her a soft kiss on the cheek. "I am the most fortunate of men to have the honor of marrying you today, my Isis."

A blush began to rise upon Isis' cheeks, turning them rosy. She opened her mouth to speak, but was interrupted by another knock on the door. The person barely waited a beat before opening it, both Isis and Bylur turning to see who was invading their special moment.

Violet stood there with her mouth ajar. Her cheeks flamed red with embarrassment after a moment. "My apologies. I should have waited before coming in."

Isis waved her apology off. "No, you are supposed to be here. Bylur is *not*. I need your help to finish preparing anyway. He is only a distraction at the moment." She kissed him deeply on the lips before releasing him, which he obeyed with a hint of hesitance. "Go, Bylur. I will see you in just a short while. And then we will be united as one."

Bylur grinned as he leaned in for another kiss, his lips just whispering over hers in a soft embrace. "Yes, I will see you there, in the greatest moment of my life. I look forward to starting our forever together."

Isis chuckled as Bylur bounded from the room, nearly looking like an excited little boy on Christmas Day, waiting to open up presents.

Turning back to her best friend, Isis sighed, switching her language back to English. "How do I look?"

"You look so beautiful, Isis. I hope to look as gorgeous as you do on my wedding day." Violet approached, wrapping her arms around Isis' neck in a sisterly embrace.

Isis squeezed her friend back, smiling as she thought about Violet's future wedding day. "Well, we do not have long to wait to find out. I am so happy for you and Frode. It makes me so glad to know that you stayed and will be part of the family now, too. I don't know what I would do without you, Violet."

Violet laughed, the musical sound filling the room. "The feeling is mutual, Isis. I look forward to being part of the family with you, too. Keeping our husbands in line together, especially when they join forces and feel mischievous. I look forward to having children alongside you, and raising them together like sisters would. I look forward to watching you be queen, and having you visit my school and bring so much life to the children when you visit. I look forward to teaching your children as well as mine. I look forward to all of the many happy things we will do together in this life as friends and as sisters."

Isis choked back tears as her and Violet rested their foreheads together. "You are already doing so well with your school, Violet. Even though it started off as the most strange and stressful events of our lives, I am glad that this happened to us. I am glad to call you my best friend."

The two women took in a deep breath, feeling their sisterly love for each other warm one another's hearts. They smiled at each other before rushing to finish preparing for the big day.

After they worked together to finish Isis' preparations for the special event, Violet furrowed her brows with her eyes lost, as they stared out the window for several moments.

Isis chuckled quietly to herself and decided to get her friend's attention. "Violet?" Violet jumped to attention. "What pulled you away, Violet?"

Violet blushed in embarrassment, shaking her head as she joined Isis in quiet laughter. "Sorry. I was just thinking about this whole ordeal, specifically about the relics that our government came to steal. Has Bylur told you what they were or anything else like that?"

Isis exhaled, nodding her head affirmatively. "Yes, apparently he'll be giving me a tour of the kingdom's treasure room later tonight, including just why they had considered trading them at all, even though they are so important to them. Apparently, they are relics of the Order of the Supreme Goddess, though I'm not quite sure what that entails."

Violet snorted through her nose. "I *bet* he is going to give you a tour of his treasure room."

Isis rolled her eyes. "I didn't realize you could be that immature, Violet."

"Sorry, I couldn't help myself. Anyways, what's this about this...Order?" Violet tilted her head to the side in question.

Isis gave a small shrug on her shoulders. "I'm not totally sure. I guess I'll find out more tonight but...apparently she's

450

an important goddess. She looks over a lot of important things from what I understand. There are warriors further north who belong to a smaller tribe that serve her exclusively, and they often collect relics of hers. I don't know much more than that at the present moment, though."

Violet nodded in understanding. "Makes sense. It's all so interesting, isn't it? This in-depth religion that we've never even heard of before, or at least, not really. And yet, there must be some substantial power behind these relics, or else that horrible man wouldn't have been so desperate to get his grubby hands on them. Makes you wonder, doesn't it?"

"Yes, it does. It makes me wonder a lot..." Isis trailed off in thought, before jumping back into finishing off preparing herself for the day. "It makes me wonder enough to get distracted from what I *should* be focusing on right now, which I can't afford to do. Shall we put a pin in this conversation until a later time?"

Letting out a short sigh, Violet rushed to help Isis the best she could. "Of course. Sorry, I distracted you."

Isis patted her best friend's hand. "No need to apologize. I totally understand. I've been thinking about that a lot, too, lately. Something tells me we haven't seen the last of the importance of those relics..." The two women left it at that as they turned their focus on finishing Isis' hair.

An hour later of idle chatting about how Violet's school was splendidly going, another knock came at the door.

Frode peeked his head in, excitement evident on his face as well. "It is time, Lady Isis. The world is ready to accept you as their queen. And I'm pretty sure Bylur is *anxiously waiting* to accept you as his wife."

Isis took in a deep breath and let it out slowly. She closed her eyes, imagining being crowned next to Bylur, before embracing him tightly. Then the image shifted, seeing herself and Bylur looking over the city, hands intertwined as they made plans for the future together. Perhaps they could travel and see more of the Viking world together, perhaps they might have children. All that Isis knew was that, with Bylur by her side, and his lips pressing against hers, she would be happy. She would have hope for a bright future and a better life.

It was time to start the rest of her forever.

READ NEXT..

The Viking Warrior's Price

A lonely woman thrown back in time. A Viking warrior who may lose everything. They'll guard the only thing they have left: their hearts.

Nakisha Harold has always dreamed of traveling the world. But she gets more than she bargains for when she's sucked back in time, landing on an unfamiliar shore far from the safety of her home, business, and dreams. Kodran Arisson needs a wife, whether he likes it or not, in order to achieve his ambitions as an esteemed Viking warrior. When Kodran finds Nakisha stranded in the wilderness, he offers her a deal: pretend to be his soon-to-be bride and he'll care for her in these Viking times.

But as dangerous figures emerge from the shadows, Kodran and Nakisha must put aside their continuous conflicts to stop the threats upon the Viking people. Will they be able to accept one another as they are, in order to stop the looming darkness from taking over?

The Viking Warrior's Price is the second installment of the *To Love a Viking* series, but can be read as a standalone. This heartwarming yet sensual historical romance features a protective seasoned Viking warrior and a strong, ambitious modern-day woman. If you love Vikings and time-travel romances such as *Outlander,* this is for you.

Buy now to get swept away into the Viking times. Purchase your copy of *The Viking Warrior's Price* today! Free in Kindle Unlimited.

ALSO BY KENNEDY THOMAS

To Love a Viking series

The Viking King's Love

The Viking Warrior's Price
The Viking Spy's Prize

More coming soon!

KENNEDY THOMAS

About Author

Kennedy Thomas writes time travel and historical romance books. She loves exploring times and settings different from her own, inspiring adventure and swooning within her readers with every word. She enjoys writing flawed and interesting characters, each as unique and interesting as the last.

You can find her trying unique foods from across the world when she's not writing, or nose-deep in a non-fiction history book. She has enjoyed telling stories for as long as she has been able to speak. She loves the art of romance, beautiful poetry, fascinating history, thrilling adventure, and intriguing mysteries, all of which are reflected in her stories.

KENNEDY THOMAS

You can get more information at:

www.queenofcrowsbooks.com

ACKNOWLEDGMENTS

Have I said how much I love Vikings? Because I really like Vikings. I'm very thankful to be able to bring this world, characters, and story to life. I would love to thank my amazing editor, Maria, at Empowered Editing, for her incredible help and insight into polishing this story and making it so much better. I would also like to thank my partner, Rain, for supporting me in all of my writings.

And a special thanks to you, dear reader, for joining me on this journey with Isis and Bylur. You are greatly appreciated!

Made in the USA
Middletown, DE
19 May 2023

30982733R00258